T0287577

THE Immortal Twin

A Paranormal Romance

CamCat Publishing, LLC
Brentwood, Tennessee 37027
camcatpublishing.com

This is a work of fiction. Names, characters, places, and incidents are either products of the author's imagination or are used fictitiously.

Hardcover ISBN 9780744302028
Paperback ISBN 9780744303964
Large-Print Paperback ISBN 9780744300635
eBook ISBN 9780744322736
Audiobook ISBN 9780744302059

Library of Congress Control Number: 2020938163

Cover design by Maryann Appel

5 3 1 2 4

THE Immortal Twin

A Paranormal Romance

D. B. WOODLING

CamCat Books

In Memoriam

All my beloved departed friends awaiting me
on the Rainbow Bridge

CHAPTER 1

$\mathcal{I}$ don't remember the bomb blast that brought down the upper floors of the Kansas City Courthouse in 1997, but because of Bianca and one of her many special abilities, I now have a simulated memory of all the horror, chaos, and death that took place. Renegade vampires—or the Harvesters, as Bianca called them—perpetuated the savage carnage. They were amphibian-like creatures whose translucent membranes exposed throbbing black veins and glossy pock-marked bones while their demented crimson eyes pulsated like tacky neon signs—the pulsations possibly a form of herd communication. Capable of phenomenal speed, they soared through the air, their movements impossible to track with the human eye. Recalling how their knifelike fangs dripped a gooey bile substance while exsanguinating the mortals who had survived the blast sent a pronounced shiver down my spine.

"They will always be after you to snare your father," Bianca warned. Her usual flamboyant cheeriness was lost while accessing my private thoughts.

I returned my biological mother's photograph to the table, perhaps a bit too harshly. I had wanted nothing more than to recall the few memories I had of her, but now I decided this would be best accomplished once I was out of Bianca's clairvoyant radar. Today, after all, was the anniversary of the bombing.

"Tell me, darling, why is it you have those miserable traitors on your mind?" Her dark eyes turned darker, and she wagged a finger in my direction, her unfashionably long fingernail bringing to mind a miniature dagger. "It is best your thoughts never stray to such a formidable enemy."

"Why is that? Can the Harvesters read minds?" I asked as a chill once again wreaked havoc throughout my body.

"Yes, most undoubtedly." She threw frigid arms around me, afterwards lifting my chin and searching my eyes. "Know this, my darling: Those vile creatures desire Razvan's extinction above all else! Both you and Nicholas will forever be their pawns."

My twin brother Nick and I were only four years old when our parents died in the explosion. Memories of them too are a little fuzzy. Nick told me once he has never forgotten them, yet he didn't volunteer that information until *after* Razvan and Bianca Torok—commanders of the Realm's East Coast Coalition—told us they weren't our biological parents. So typical of charismatic Nick, the mysterious, secretive one.

The Toroks came clean the year my brother and I should have begun school. We'd become somewhat skeptical long before the physical disparities fed our suspicions. For starters, Razvan has thick black hair while Bianca flaunts vibrant auburn locks. Both Nick and I have blond hair, although to be fair, his calls to mind sunlight and wild daffodils while some have compared mine to dirty dishwater. Our eyes are blue, so different from the Toroks' distinct deep-set black orbs—their pupils surrounded by a golden halo, sporadically framed with a bloody blush when tempers flared—which should have been yet another aha moment. I followed Bianca into a kitchen the size of a school auditorium, yet mine were the *only* footsteps echoing throughout the eerily quiet manor, and it wasn't because she was barefoot.

I took a seat at the enormous marble island and watched as she struggled with the ritual of cooking, one of the few things at which she did not excel. Maybe she had at one time, centuries ago, when her daily sustenance and that of Razvan's included traditional food. I studied her eyes as she attempted a simple grilled cheese sandwich. Her heavy-handed application of eyeliner always brought Egyptian culture to mind; it's no surprise she insists she once taught Cleopatra a thing or two. *Everyone assumes Cleo was Egyptian, but she was the last of the Greek Dynasty to rule Egypt,* Bianca had offered more than once.

She set the blood-red, gold-rimmed china before me and slung her long hair behind her shoulders. Leaning across the wide counter between us, after displaying a dazzling smile, she said, "Cleo was quite homely without a little magic. Alas, the poor wretch."

I often wonder if she pities me in much the same way. Bianca possesses the level of beauty that stops traffic and turns heads. The only time I'd ever stopped traffic occurred while chasing a ball into the street. I cringe when asked if Nick and I are *really* twins because I know they're wondering how one can one be so perfect and the other such a dud. I looked away in my struggle to swallow a second mouthful, wondering how she could possibly burn the bread without melting the cheese.

She drifted toward the refrigerator, and I took the opportunity to hide the remainder of the sandwich in a monogrammed napkin. Across the room one nanosecond, and standing before me the next, she'd returned with a bottle of water. "Sorry, my darling, of course, you require something to quench your thirst. At times, I forget the mortal inconveniences. Has Nick decided who will accompany him to prom?"

I arched a brow and resisted narrowing my eyes. "As if you don't know."

"This may come as a surprise, Celestine, but I don't *always* know what Nick is thinking."

That was probably a good thing. Undoubtedly, Nick's private thoughts were comparable to an R-rated comedy. He was considered the hottest guy in Madison High School. Nick never had to ask anyone to prom. Five of the most popular girls, all cheerleaders, had already *begged* him. And I was confident, mostly because Drew Dandridge blushed and detoured around me, that Nick had persuaded the team's quarterback to ask me to prom. To my surprise, Warren Flaherty beat him to it.

"Do not waste your time on that lubberwort," Bianca said suddenly, her cobalt stare demanding my full attention.

I'd heard the bygone expression many times, usually when Bianca discussed my friends, and I immediately grew defensive. "Warren is not *lazy*, Mom. He's always working."

"My darling, Celeste! He is most certainly lazy, and the few thoughts in his head are not his, rather mere imitations of popular opinion. I suspect he was a mynah bird in another lifetime."

"Aubrey says he's not so bad," I said before thinking it through.

Bianca puffed her cheeks and blew out a Romanian insult. "What does Aubrey know?"

I felt my face flush. Heated words defending my only real friend gathered on the tip of my tongue.

"What do you have against Aubrey?"

"She's the albatross around your neck. Aside from that, darling, I have nothing against her."

My scalp was tingling now too, the way it always did when Bianca insulted Aubrey. I chewed the insides of both cheeks, knowing a verbal battle with Bianca was unwise.

"Just because she doesn't plan to go to some big university is no reason to hate her, Mom."

"Am I left to assume Aubrey has no collegiate plans?"

4

I kept quiet, realizing Bianca hadn't found this out yet.

Bianca's lips twisted into a smirk. "Aha, just as I presumed! Her expectations are limited to owning the latest fashion and bedding the football player possessing the most proficient anatomy." Her eyes flashed, and the oxygen temporarily left the room.

I attempted to shake off my growing resentment because I knew, deep down, most everything she'd said about Aubrey was the truth.

"Can we not talk about Aubrey or Warren?"

Whooshing around the kitchen island, before my eyes could even begin to follow, she wrapped an icy arm around my shoulders.

"You are a promising young woman. Why can't you see that? You mustn't settle for someone the likes of Warren Flaherty."

"I've already told him I'll go," I said just as Yesenia floated in from the expansive hallway. "Thanks for lunch, Mom." I hugged her and hurried past Yesenia—a fifteenth-century vampiress stuck in her thirties. To outsiders, she was Bianca's personal assistant. To those within the household and throughout the coalition, she was the Realm's trusted advisor. To me, she was a malicious, self-serving witch. Because her loathing for me had only increased over the years, I swept around her quickly toward the winding wrought-iron staircase that led to my room.

CHAPTER 2

$\mathcal{I}$ watched as Nick swaggered into the school lunchroom shadowed by his harem of five. He slung himself quickly into the seat beside mine as though afraid someone else might claim it. His vivid blue eyes squinted in my direction, and it was easy to understand why so many swore they could get lost in them.

I rolled my own blue eyes and scowled when Emily, Kaitlin, Amie, Brianna, and Olivia fought over the chair to his right.

Judging from the look in her eyes, Kaitlin contemplated removing me from Nick's left; I'd seen her pull that stunt on most of the other girls before. Nick ignored the chaos and faced me.

"I get the impression you haven't made your decision about prom yet," I said with a nod toward the power struggle in play to his right.

Nick grinned, and I wondered how on earth his teeth could be that white. He leaned close and whispered in my ear. "Actually, yeah, I have; I just like to watch them squirm."

I fisted his bicep but resisted a grin of my own. "You're such a jerk."

He cursed under his breath, pretending I'd caused him real pain, then suddenly furrowed his brows.

"You think Dadcula had anything to do with the timing of the graduation ceremony?"

I puffed my cheeks and glared. "Knock it off, Nick. You know how I hate it when you call him that."

As a young boy, shortly after the Toroks took us in, Nick openly idolized Razvan and accepted him as our father. Now he seemed to despise him.

I counted the number of times his jaw flinched before his expression softened; the combativeness left his eyes, swapped for the typical empathy he always reserved for me, his pathetic twin. "We don't owe them anything, Celeste." Nick glanced over his shoulder. Satisfied the girls were engaged in a new argument and oblivious to anything else, he added, "If it weren't for freaks like them, our real parents might have survived that day."

We'd had this conversation before, and I knew any response from me wouldn't change his mind. Maybe I'd made a mistake when I pleaded Bianca and Razvan to spare Nick the vision they'd revealed to me. They referred to it as going inside the Circle—a ridiculous label for something about as far removed from innocuous as a bolt of lightning. With their combined preternatural capabilities, Razvan and Bianca induced in their victim, willing or otherwise, a trance-like state, revealing anything they wished them to see. I'd always thought a better label for the Circle might have been the Time Machine, because that's essentially what they accomplished: transporting one either back in time or propelling them into the future. I blew out a fitful exhalation.

Maybe Nick witnessing the bombing firsthand as I had would have made all the difference. I didn't intend to tell Nick, but I was aware that the Toroks had everything to do with the commencement's time change. To express their gratitude for moving the ceremony from 5 p.m. to 8 p.m., the Toroks would fulfill their promise and contribute to Madison High School's renovations. This entailed an updated gymnasium to include new bleachers and sports equipment; a state-of-the-art computer lab; an auditorium twice the size of the current one, offering posh velvet seating, dressing rooms, an orchestra pit, and gilded balconies as well as a stage floor equipped with a trap door, ironically referred to as a Vampire Trap.

I touched Nick's arm softly and ritually traced the long five-year-old scar which extended from his bicep to his hand. He stopped me, as he usually did, but I knew from his expression that he understood how grateful I would always be to Razvan for saving his life one horrible night. I never mention his attacker—the werewolf, Vykoka—around Nick, not anymore. But we're both aware he's still out there and that he commands the majority of the werewolves on the east coast. After the injuries Nick sustained that night, he has never run away again.

"Nick! My man," shouted Brandon, a Neanderthal so feared he confidently and routinely strutted around school flashing disturbing spandex boxers and a tooth-barred, ominous smile with a full set of braces accentuated by tiny smiling skulls on nauseatingly full display. His voice reverberated throughout the cafeteria, causing a hush to settle over the entire room. To infer Brandon Closter was subdued was like insisting a candy bar belongs in the five food groups. "I knew if I found you, I'd find the hot babes," he told Nick. Then he snickered, more a growl really, as he picked up Emily *and* the chair she occupied, tilted it, and laughed as she spilled out.

"Asshole!" Emily snarled as she launched a knockoff Louboutin stiletto at his shin.

Nick unsuccessfully hid a grin. "You'll never get a date that way." He got to his feet and pulled Brandon aside. "You keep that shit up and the coach will kick your ass off the team."

Brandon puffed out his chest. "I'd like to see him try."

Nick's laughter rang insincere. "No, you wouldn't, asshole. Take it from me."

"I'm out of here," I told my brother and made a run for it. I collided with Aubrey as I rounded the corner.

"No friggin' way! Don't tell me you're leaving." She groaned and let her books slide to the ground, then dropped her arms to her sides. "Come on! I need some pizza."

"Sorry, but the caveman showed up and ruined my appetite."

"Brandon?"

"Who else? He's practically extinct, thank God."

"What have I told you about opening your mind to new adventures? I've heard when he shuts his mouth, he's not so bad."

"And I'd rather not know what it takes to achieve that miracle."

Aubrey laughed and twirled a hoop earring that she sometimes wore as a bangle.

"What's with the basketball hoops? Aren't you afraid you might catch those on something?"

She rammed her hip against mine. "Afraid? Good God, girl! I'm surprised you don't run screaming from your own shadow. Live a little, Celeste. Life is too short for what-friggin'-ifs."

She was right about that. I'm hopeful, but I often doubt Aubrey will live to thirty. "I'm only making an observation."

"Yeah? Well, it wouldn't hurt you to try a little harder. If I lived at that mansion with Tristan dropping in all the time, I'd sure as hell try to look like a runway model seven days a week."

My spine stiffened in response to her description of our house. Although the four-story monstrosity occupied one acre, swallowing up the majority of the land, the customary reference to the Torok home as a mansion never failed to make me uncomfortable. It was a difficult thing to deny. Aubrey's reference to Tristan only amplified my anxiety.

"Why's he always at your house anyway?"

"He does stuff for my dad," I said. "You know that, Aubrey."

"What does he do?"

I shrugged my shoulders. Whenever Razvan slid the pocket doors to his study closed, I'd always resisted the temptation to place my ear against the thick mahogany. Partially out of respect. Mostly out of consequence. I knew by Aubrey's intense stare that she expected some sort of response.

But how does one tell one's best friend that the class valedictorian, with the bizarre syntax who wears a hoodie regardless of the temperature, first walked the earth long before Jesus had?

Whatever he did for my father, he accomplished after dark, and it sure as hell didn't involve conventional assignments. I fought to refocus as Aubrey impatiently shifted her weight.

All I could come up with was: "How should I know?"

"Are you into him?"

"No," I lied, stammering unconvincingly.

"Bullshit! You are!"

Defiant, I locked both arms against my chest. "I told you, he works for my dad!"

"Okay, let's say that's true. And if it is, you shouldn't mind if I make a move."

"Knock yourself out!" I grabbed her by the arm, unconsciously digging in a fingernail or two. "Just not at the freaking house."

"Why not?"

"Seriously, Aubrey? Bianca will freak out."

"Why?"

I chewed my bottom lip and kept quiet.

"She doesn't like me, does she?"

"She thinks . . ." I took a deep breath and may have briefly squeezed both eyes shut. "She thinks you're a sex fiend."

Aubrey laughed, observing me out of the corner of one eye.

"You know what I think? I think she doesn't want any competition. Because *she's* interested in him. Maybe that's why Tristan's always at your house."

"Oh, my God! Do you know how disgusting that is? You're talking about my mom, Aubrey!" I thought about something I'd seen earlier in the day. Surprising them in the kitchen, I caught Tristan and Yesenia involved in some intense fondling. Thinking about it now, my pulse quickened, and I was convinced sweat now dotted my forehead. "Besides, I'm pretty sure there's something going on between him and Yesenia."

"Who's she? Your maid?"

I swallowed past the lie spilling from my lips. "She's my mom's personal assistant. Besides, what difference does it make?"

Aubrey stomped one foot and served me an impish smile. "Damn it, I knew I should have seduced him by now!"

"Oh, God," I muttered and rolled my eyes at the ceiling.

"So how old is this Yesenia?"

I shrugged my shoulders. "Older than the two of us, I guess." Yesenia was much older. According to Bianca, she'd courted both Julius Caesar and Marcus Antonius. Aubrey would need over two thousand years to perfect the kind of feminine wiles Yesenia held in her arsenal.

THAT NIGHT, Bianca took me shopping for my prom dress. It'd been some time since I'd made the trip from New Jersey to New York, and I assumed, mostly because of the way Bianca kept smiling, my excitement was palpable. Climbing from the limo, I took Bianca's cue and assumed the lead. Bianca was lagging far enough behind that the store associates greeted me with a disinterested once-over, changing their attitudes drastically once they recognized Bianca Torok, *the* socialite.

"Let me guess," Bianca teased me, "the gown one might choose to wear on an expedition."

"Why? Because it's green?"

Bianca tapped a fingernail against her cheek, examining the gown I had chosen. "Is it? I thought it brown, although come to think of it, it does bring a swamp to mind." She grabbed both my hands and pulled me toward her, then away, as if we'd found ourselves in a senior citizens' ballroom rather than a posh department store. "Oh, darling, the red taffeta is much more becoming! Why would you want to cover your body in that insufferable fabric?" she asked, nodding toward my selection. "Never mind the absolute lack of style! It looks as if something a toad might wear."

"Mom, you promised," I managed through clenched teeth.

"Yes, yes, I know I did. But darling, I merely want you to find yourself the belle of the ball."

I blurted out laughter. In my defense, it erupted involuntarily, like a fart in church. "And you honestly think a dress is going to make all the difference?"

Bianca pulled me close and whispered, "It will certainly shine a light on my brilliant star."

"Fine, I'll reconsider, but it's not going to be the red taffeta."

"But darling, why not?"

"Because I don't intend to look like a hooker."

"What, pray tell, is a hooker?"

I had to think about it for a moment and take into consideration Bianca's limited grasp of current slang.

"A courtesan. A Mata Hari."

Bianca's hand flew over one breast.

Soon after, she shared explosive laughter. I scanned the store, aware that all eyes were now upon us.

"Exactly my point. Maybe now you can understand that is not the response I want when I walk into prom."

"Oh my good God, Celeste! In my time, you would have positively starved. Men ruled the world, and with an iron fist, I might add. A young maid's only salvation was the hope of attracting a well-to-do mate."

"Mom, attracting a mate is the farthest thing from my mind. Right now, the only thing I want to find is a dress we can both agree on."

"Of course! How I do rattle on. Consider my point moot. How fortunate you were to be born into a time of grand possibilities, Celeste!" She drew me close and studied my eyes for what seemed like a long time. "You can have whatever pleases you. I just can't believe how much time has passed."

"Me either." I squeezed her hand as I thought how much I loved her.

"And I adore you, Celestine," she whispered in my ear as she handed me her credit card. "You were truly a gift."

Upon leaving Bloomingdale's department store, located in the heart of Manhattan, we planned to celebrate our compromise over dinner. Instead of the red taffeta gown, we agreed on a sapphire-colored one, embellished with far too many sequins. Slinging the bag over my shoulder, I lugged it through the revolving doors toward the limousine and a chauffeur, who was compensated handsomely for his patience.

"I so enjoy the energy here," Bianca said as the limousine, per Bianca's instruction, detoured past Central Park, Times Square, Carnegie Hall, and Rockefeller Center. "It's positively electric!"

~

Once seated comfortably inside the *Ocean Prime* restaurant, off 52nd Street, I placed my order. Bianca, as usual, convinced the waiter she was dieting.

I wrinkled my nose as the overwhelming flavors of grapefruit, lime, and elderflower from my nonalcoholic margarita assaulted my taste buds.

"You react like this every time," Bianca said behind a grin. "Why don't you order something else?"

I shivered involuntarily. "It's usually perfect. But, for some reason, this one is just so bitter," I said, scrunching my face and sticking out my tongue.

Bianca waved her napkin through the air, and the waiter came running. "Please bring my daughter something else," she said, nodding at the glass between us.

He cocked an eyebrow my way. "Of course, Miss. What will it be?"

"I'll have a sweet tea," I said, ignoring the glint of contempt I saw in his eyes.

"As you wish," he said and hurried off.

"Your friend Aubrey has been paying a lot of attention to Tristan," Bianca said with a sniff.

It sounded more like a warning than casual conversation.

"Oh?" I said, deciding ignorance was the best possible defense.

"Yes, indeed. It's pathetic, the way she looks at him! Her eyes seem to devour every inch!"

I assumed a half-shrug and looked away.

"Have I told you the story of Tristan and Servilia Caepionis?"

I shook my head. She twisted the rings on her fingers and appeared to be having second thoughts; she would probably offer little more or a censored version.

A wicked smile trespassed her lips, and the gleam in her eyes suggested a delicious revelation.

"Ah, Servilia! Her eye wandered more often than did an

unwelcome leper. Those she fancied, she invited to her private chambers. One night, crawling from a terribly crowded bed, Tristan—the sole male occupant, by the way—discovered his untamed ways could very well be the end of him."

"Mom, everyone will hear you!"

"I hardly think so, my darling."

My eyes followed hers as she glanced about the restaurant. Everyone, aside from Bianca and me, appeared frozen in time. Customers sat rigid like works of stone, most of them with forks perched near their mouths. Not an eye blinked in our direction, nor did a lip move to allow a scream to escape or even a mortified gasp. My mouth hung open, forming a perfect "O."

"Alas, poor Tristan," she continued as if nothing had happened.

"My God! Mom, what did you do to them?" I bolted upright, unsure how to react.

Bianca flicked her wrist. "Not to worry. Merely a little deception we either refer to as In Mora Temporis or In Silentium. Now, may I continue?"

I chewed my lip while attempting to recall the little Latin I knew. "What does it mean?"

Bianca sighed. "To translate would be to say the Pause of Time or the Silence. Time as we know it stands still—is altered if you will."

"Will they be all right?" I said, still unable to take my eyes off the statue-like people around me.

"Of course, darling! Have you ever known me to cause harm to the undeserved? Now, where was I? Oh, yes, Tristan was ordered to be beheaded the next morning."

"By who? Servilia?" I asked, suddenly drawn back into the conversation.

"Most definitely not Servilia! I'm quite certain Tristan had enthralled her by that point. It was Julius Caesar who demanded Tristan's capture and his head on a platter. Understandably, he did not appreciate Tristan seducing his mistress. And that was the last day Tristan occupied this earth as a mortal." Her words trailed off, and her smile disappeared.

"So, who saved him? Was it you?"

Bianca shook her head. "Perhaps we should have told you this long ago."

I gulped, the sound becoming amplified in the eerily quiet restaurant. "Oh God. What?"

"His father saved him."

"His father?"

She was looking at me now, as if picking my brain, deciding whether or not I could survive what she was about to reveal.

"Yes . . . Razvan."

My hand flew to my mouth. I thought I might vomit.

"I can't believe you've never told me this! So, this means you're his mother?"

She shook her head. "I would have told you some time ago, but the story was not mine to tell. Although your father and I have recently agreed, it is time you were made aware. All things considered."

I had a feeling that by *all things considered* she meant my infatuation with Tristan. Of course, she had to know; I rarely thought of anything but him.

She graced me with a sly grin.

"It is quite the day for you, my darling. A new dress and a new brother to boot."

I narrowed my eyes, then just as quickly attempted to disguise my feelings.

"Well, it's not as if we're genetically related."

"A discussion for another time, my pet," she said, patting my hand. "Let us not spoil such a wonderful evening."

I relented and changed the subject. "Did I see Dad leave with Nick earlier?"

Bianca nodded and hid sad eyes behind a full wine glass.

"That sounds promising! I'm so glad they're spending time together." Now, she seemed angry rather than sad and I realized my choice of conversation was suboptimal.

"We have done all we can for your brother, Celestine. I'm certain you're all too aware of the sacrifices we've made!"

"I know," I managed to murmur past the lump in my throat.

"It's not as if we could take him to a therapist," she suddenly blurted.

I choked on a laugh and spewed my first bite of lobster mac and cheese all over the pristine tablecloth.

She threw her head back and laughed.

"Can you imagine, Celestine: the entire family snatched up by a panic-stricken regime, then delivered to scientists for archaic experimentation?" Her expression quickly turned serious again, the crease between her brows deeper than I'd ever seen it. "We don't expect Nick to accept us or even love us, but we do expect respect and a decent disposition."

"I know." Feeling some allegiance toward my brother, I resisted telling her I would never understand why the only sentiment Nick felt toward them was a fierce loathing.

Bianca left her side of the booth and joined me on mine.

"Particularly when your father disregarded the oath he took, nearly two hundred years ago, upon our arrival in New Jersey."

"What oath?" This was the first time she'd shared this information. Salivating over the possibilities, I tossed my fork aside and gave her my full attention.

"To simplify it, Vykoka had agreed to keep his pack outside a one-hundred-mile radius of Fremont, henceforth considered Torok Territory. In turn, your father agreed to the safety of the pack inside the township of Wilshire, an approximate one-hundred-fifty-mile circumference."

I thought about my own experience years ago. "But that night I lost my way at summer camp, what about that?"

"The attack on you, Celeste, was due to anarchy within Vykoka's pack. Not only did Simeon fail to become the pack's leader, but Vykoka ordered his destruction for disregarding the oath."

"So, the night Nick ran away and ended up in Wilshire, the pack considered him fair game?"

"Yes. And because of your brother's insubordination, we lost a few of our own that night; your father was nearly destroyed too. The oath dissolved, this placed both the were-wolves and the Realm in great jeopardy."

I remembered the night when members of the Realm rescued Nick; I was standing outside his room waiting for the coalition's physician to finish suturing the long laceration on his arm. My father retreated to his bedroom for nearly two weeks. Sometimes, I could hear him through the double doors, instructing various people on who knows what. Bianca had been distracted—almost in a fog, worried, and she avoided Nick altogether for a long time after. Ever since, every time she looked at him, her expression changed; mostly the look in her eyes. She never appeared mad or disappointed, just indifferent.

I thought back to the events that led up to the attack, more specifically, the reason Nick ran away, threatening he'd never return. Angry with Razvan at the time for forbidding me to attend a sleepover, I wanted an ally. I told Nick about my experience with Simeon, the werewolf. But it was the revela-tion involving the Circle that ultimately destroyed the relation-ship between Nick and the Toroks; the description of my firsthand account of the horrific bombing and what came after.

"I'm so sorry, Mom," I said now, although I assumed she'd known all along. "I shouldn't have—"

"You were a child, Celeste. I'm sure had you realized the implications of your actions, you would have made another decision."

"But Nick was a child, too," I whispered.

She didn't respond. I watched her eyes glaze over, and everything came to life in the restaurant: the sounds of silverware clattering against plates, servers bustling about, and the buzz of robust conversations. I exhaled enormous relief and settled comfortably in my chair.

 ~

ONCE WE WERE SEATED in the limousine, I said, "Can all of you perform In Silentium . . . ? If I'm even pronouncing it right."

She patted my hand, then shook her head.

"Not all of us, for it depends on the Maker. Only those given the Adaptation by one of the ancients inherit this power."

"And Razvan?"

"Of course, darling. One of the many reasons I was attracted to him from the onset. Aside from his fetching physical appearance, I found your father's abilities irresistible," she said followed by a coquettish giggle.

CHAPTER 3

*W*hile sitting in Social Studies and debating the legitimacy of an ancient Indian curse placed on our country's future presidents, I noticed Nick signal me from the hallway.

Because of his urgent expression, I vaulted from my seat and asked permission to leave the room.

"What's wrong?" I sputtered and searched his eyes for a clue as I stepped into the hallway.

Nick handed me a hall pass, no doubt it was one he'd forged from the stolen stack in his locker. He jerked his head toward my fourth-period teacher, Mrs. Lynch, who appeared nearly as anxious for an explanation.

"What's wrong?" I insisted a second time, ignoring his instruction.

"We've got to go. Give her the pass!"

A few minutes later, with my backpack and a few books in hand, I sprinted past him toward the nearest exit.

"Hold on!" Nick called from behind. "Drop that shit in your locker."

When I turned back, he'd already successfully opened it.

"Wait, how do you know my combination?"

His cocky expression convinced me he considered me intellectually inferior. He jerked my belongings from my hands and tossed them inside, their harsh landing echoing down the long hallway.

"Come on!" He barked, tugging me along.

When we reached the car, I folded my arms across my chest, refusing to get inside.

"I'm not going unless you tell me what's going on!"

Nick marched around the car, opened my door, and pushed me inside. "Trust me, Celeste, for once in your friggin' life."

Steering the car successfully around a few students who were absorbed in thoughts of grand illusion, no doubt, he exited the parking lot.

I leaned across the console and grabbed his elbow.

"Why won't you tell me what's wrong?"

He grinned sideways, and I suddenly realized I'd enabled a truant.

"So, you *forged* the hall pass? And there's no emergency?"

He winked in my direction. "There's hope for you yet."

"You're such an asshole, Nick!"

"What's the matter, Celeste? Your life just gonna fall apart without that *Perfect Attendance Award?*"

I jammed my arms across my chest and stomped my feet a few times.

"Poor Celeste," he taunted, imitating a pronounced pout. "She isn't going to get her shiny, wittle, gold star."

"Shut up, Nick! And for your information, it's not little, and it's a trophy!"

"Oh, a *trophy*! Were they going to engrave your wittle name on it too?" he asked, still laughing.

"Where are we going? And why do you need me?"

Brushing a clump of hair from his face, his eyes quickly searched mine. "Okay look, it's our senior year. I just thought we could spend the afternoon together."

"That's what weekends are for!"

"Maybe yours. I've always got plans."

"You mean, things more important than spending time with your sister."

He didn't respond. Instead, he detoured onto Garden State Parkway, and even though I knew he planned to keep the destination one big fat secret, I gave it another shot.

He turned toward me, his blue eyes gleaming.

"I'll give you a hint: What's big, wet, gray all over, and spouts off more than you do?"

I only hoped he didn't realize my excitement! Whale watching was something I'd enjoyed for as long as I could remember. I'd always thought the creatures an enigma: enormous yet graceful.

Nick leaned over the console and flicked my hand. "So, you figure it out yet?"

"I'm not stupid," I said without so much as a smile. I wasn't ready to let Nick off the hook.

"Or, apparently, grateful. Just don't get your hopes up."

"What do you mean?"

Nick arched a brow and swept his attention from the road.

"How many times have we been to Cape May?"

I shrugged my shoulders. "Five, maybe."

He shook his head. "Double that. And how many times have you seen a whale?"

"Once," I said, smiling at my reflection in the side mirror as a vivid memory struck me.

"So, like I said: Don't get your hopes up."

I felt his astute stare and kept quiet, still unwilling to confess my happiness.

"Bet that shiny trophy's pretty lame now."

"We had better see a whale, Nick."

He whipped into the parking lot. My lunch ricocheted off the walls of my stomach as he brought the car to an abrupt stop. Five minutes later, once he'd produced a credit card

Razvan told him to use only in case of emergencies, he impatiently ushered me aboard the Cape May-Lewes Ferry.

~

AN HOUR into our three-hour excursion of the bay and the Atlantic, Nick dug into his back pocket, pulled out a tube, and slathered my face with a malodourous lotion, the container touting an insultingly high SPF.

"Borrowed it from your boyfriend," he teased.

Convinced he meant Tristan, I wrinkled my nose in protest.

"Shit, Celeste. You look like a dead chicken. You ever see the sun?" Before I could answer, he whispered in my ear, "You're not one of *them*, are you?"

I jerked away and rubbed the pasty mess in myself.

He rolled his eyes, clearly disproving of my technique.

"Seriously, you *already* look like a freaking lobster. Remember when every time you'd get near the ocean, you'd puke?" he asked, laughing as a misty breeze off the Atlantic ruffled his perfect hair.

"I never did that."

His blue eyes were dancing now; his smile attracting the attention of every female under the age of ninety. "The hell, you didn't! Just the sight of fish made you gag."

"Un-uh," I uttered like I was five years old.

Without warning, he slipped an arm around my shoulders. "We've had some good times."

"And some not-so-good."

He jerked his arm free. "Let's not go there."

Because Nick actually wanted to spend time with me, something that didn't happen very often anymore, I rerouted the conversation immediately.

"Remember the time you stole the yacht?"

Nick thumped my shoulder and laughed along with me.

"I didn't exactly steal it, just kinda borrowed it for an extended length of time."

"All day, Nick."

"What are you griping about? That little exploit boosted your popularity for a day or two."

I shook my head. "Guilt by association only goes so far. And besides, you kidnapped me, basically, kind of like today."

He chuckled and then grew serious. "Do you ever think about them?"

"Mom and Dad?"

Nick nodded and turned away, gazing out at the ocean.

"Sometimes," I offered, the word hanging in the air. Then I laughed softly. "I remember the times they'd read us a bedtime story: Dad impersonating all of the characters while Mom . . ."

". . . just sat there smiling at him like . . ."

". . . he was the most important thing in the world," we both said in unison.

The craft suddenly shifted viciously to the left, nearly capsizing. Uprooted from my seat, Nick caught me as I tumbled headfirst toward the port side. He locked one arm around my waist, the other onto the handrail as screams filled the air. The sky turned dark as the other passengers fought the pull of gravity.

CHAPTER 4

*O*f course, Nick and I were the only ones aware of the supernatural phenomenon surrounding us.

"She knows we ditched class!" Nick yelled over the crashing waves.

I shook my drenched head and spat water.

"Bianca wouldn't do this. Think about it, Nick!" I shouted, spitting up brine.

Dark shadows passed overhead and obscured the sun in its entirety. Nick and I turned our attention to the sky, while the rest of the passengers aboard the *Cape May-Lewes* either hugged one another or their life preservers. Malevolent forms skyrocketed into the atmosphere, diving in and out of clouds, representing something far more malignant than meteorological changes or a newly discovered seabird. I clutched Nick's hand as the creatures multiplied and swarmed the horizon.

Over the passengers' screams and the Captain shouting words of encouragement, I barely heard the shrill, chilling screeches of the Harvesters. A deadly battle was in progress miles overhead, and Nick and I had little choice but to cling to each another and trust the Torok Realm to keep us safe. The craft rocked sharply to the opposite side and began taking on more water. A few passengers failed to maintain a tight enough grip, and the angry waves tossed them toward the starboard side of the ferry. Thrashing about and screaming, a woman sailed overhead, then disappeared within a turbulent sea.

Nick guided both of my hands onto the handrail, snugged my life preserver tight, and turned his attention to the woman bobbing sporadically above the water while struggling against the waves. Realizing his intention to go in after her, I latched onto him.

"Let go, Celeste!" he yelled, the waves drowning out most of the syllables. Nick pried himself free despite my determination to never let go of him. With one foot on the deck and the other on the rail, he prepared to vault overboard just as a dark specter plucked the drowning woman from the water and soared overhead. Nick turned to face me, eyes wide, his mouth agape. He and I seemed to be the only ones who had witnessed another paranormal event. Returning to his seat, he pulled me close but avoided my eyes. I sensed he was afraid; a phenomenon in and of itself. He would never admit fear, and I would never ask him to verify my suspicion.

"Janet," a man cried out from the portside. I recognized the gut-wrenching panic reflected in his eyes and easily identified the absolute terror in his voice. Losing his balance as he attempted to cross the boat, he slid toward us, feet first.

Nick managed to grab him before he skimmed through the guardrail. When neither of us could restrain him, Nick pleaded for anyone's assistance, but the other passengers either ignored him or were perhaps too afraid to move.

"She's gone! There's nothing you can do!" Nick told the old man again. Inconsolable, he stopped resisting. His body went limp, and he slumped onto the deck, defeated.

Once slivers of sunlight began to reach the deck, I assumed the skirmish overhead was nearing an end. I squinted into a choking fog and caught sight of the sky. Only a few dozen phantoms remained engaged in battle, and swirling ever higher, their piercing cries hinted at vicious collisions. Either the other passengers misinterpreted the noise, or the unworldly sounds fell on deaf ears.

The captain continued his battle with the waves, his broad, muscular forearms heaving the wheel to keep the ferry moving against the swell. Huge surges were no longer breaking against the hull, and with one more violent rock, the vessel shifted upright maintaining the center of buoyancy. While the captain assured his passengers that the ferry remained seaworthy, Nick and I exchanged a look, and I knew he too was confident that the Realm had claimed another victory. Those passengers no longer in a state of shock scrambled to their seats and stared blankly at the ocean, as if grasping for a logical explanation. If only Nick and I could possess such glorious naivety.

Within minutes, members of the crew wrestled themselves into diving suits before plunging into the inky waters of the Atlantic, in search of the woman swept overboard. Before all the men had submerged, the Coast Guard arrived, and the ship's crew happily relinquished their search. The waves slapping the sides of the craft and the low drone of the motor were the only sounds heard as the captain steered the ferry toward the harbor.

When we arrived, Nick and I assisted the still-unsteady passengers onto the boardwalk before starting toward the empty parking lot. I trudged behind him a good ten paces, catching up once he'd stopped to light a cigarette.

"Nick, do you think . . ."

". . . the Harvesters got to that guy's wife?" He shook his head. "No, they would have taken more."

"So, you think the Realm saved her?"

He delivered a curt nod, his jaw tightly set.

It's true what they say about twins; Nick must have sensed that my anxiety level had increased. "Relax, Celeste. It's over."

"It's not that. I don't want to go back."

He flashed his infamous grin.

"Afraid Dadcula's gonna spank your ass?"

"Stop calling him that, Nick! Think about it. If not for them, who knows what would have happened today!"

Nick threw both arms in the air. "Are you being freaking serious, right now? If not for *them*, we wouldn't have found ourselves in this situation in the first place! We'd be in Kansas City with—"

"With who, Nick? Some shitty foster parents? And we'd probably be split-up. At least this way, we've always been together."

With his face red and both nostrils winged, he turned to me. "Sometimes you really piss me off! Do you *ever* think about Mom and Dad at all?" When I didn't answer, mostly because I found this a stupid and insulting question, he stormed off and headed for the car.

BEFORE EITHER OF us could settle inside, a powerful and bitter-cold breeze blew me off balance.

Nick and I looked at one another and, in unison, we said, "Bianca."

Nick suddenly tumbled north, and I knew Bianca hadn't come alone. The sudden appearance of both our parents, given the truancy situation, was frightening. I braced myself as Bianca towered over me, her expression an imposing mix of contempt and relief. The ends of her waist-length auburn hair began to writhe like disturbed snakes in every direction, even-tually ensnaring my waist. Though she'd successfully conveyed a threatening reprimand without uttering a single word, I knew a verbal exchange was coming, and I prepared my lungs for Bianca's arctic exhalations. Overhearing a lot of commo-tion, including a stream of Nick's profanity, I whipped my head in that direction. Without laying a hand on him, Razvan had effectively restrained Nick. Pinned flat on his back against the car hood, Nick struggled to break free.

When he cursed Razvan a second time, I closed my eyes, held my breath, and felt my pulse throb my eardrums. I swallowed hard and heard nothing but eerie silence. The air was heavy with an electrical charge. I opened one eye and then the other one. Razvan's eyes glowed yellow before they turned a brilliant red, interspersed with flecks of silver within a starburst pattern. I begged Bianca to intervene.

CHAPTER 5

*I*n the parking lot one minute, within the Torok Mansion the next, my stomach churned, and I envisioned my intestines were a maze of jumbled cords. I was aware teleportation was one of my parents' preternatural capabilities, but I'd never before experienced it firsthand. A glance in Nick's direction convinced me he hadn't fared much better. His skin was pale and clammy, and his pupils were fixed and dilated. Without coming into contact with a single stair, Razvan and Bianca waited on the landing of the second floor.

"Come!" My father was the first to utter a word. "And you shall see the result of your impudence!"

I heard Nick take a deep breath. He clasped my hand, pulling me along behind him until we reached the top stair. We followed them, Bianca keeping in step with Razvan, though her feet never touched the floor. The two stopped outside a large suite at the end of the hallway. They turned to face us in a unified manner so dramatic and atypical, we took a step back.

"Is it too much to ask that you obey a few simple requests?" Razvan asked, his long sinewy arms locked across his chest.

Bianca caressed his shoulder.

"Iubirea mea. My love," she whispered, "perhaps we should have told them."

"Why do you persist in coddling them?" I heard him mutter. "They should obey with or without explanation!" Bianca stroked his cheek then kissed it. "As you wish," he relented a moment later past a tortured smile.

Bianca clasped her hands and pressed them against the hooded purple velvet cape she often wore during daylight hours. Her dark eyes flashed a warning, and we knew to pay attention. "Quite recently, members of the coalition have witnessed the Harvesters drawn to the ocean in the midst of a feeding frenzy. One might say that their behavior is similar to a wake of vultures or a shiver of sharks, should you prefer."

"Because of the blood aboard the fishing boats?" Nick interrupted.

Bianca nodded. "Most are new in the blood and have little restraint. While they possess heightened senses, their intellect does not extend beyond a meal."

"So, they're basically dining on fast food?" Nick said with blatant sarcasm.

Razvan stepped forward, looming over Nick. "Did you not intuit the danger to which you exposed your sister! Imagine their surprise, Nicholas, when they anticipated a nibble and encountered a feast." He thrust open the door to the suite. "Inside with the two of you! Cast your eyes on the fruit of your insolence."

I covered a gasp when I saw Tristan lying on a table motionless and swept away the tears tracking my cheeks. Puncture wounds covered the majority of his body, even the parts of it once shrouded in clothing now tattered and shredded as if raked by razor-sharp talons. The flesh surrounding his cheeks lay open. That which remained intact resembled Swiss cheese. One eye dangled from its socket, the area around it swollen and black and blue.

"You have Tristan to thank for your survival!" our father boomed, his words echoing despite the stucco walls, dense carpeting, and draped windows.

"If not for him . . . well, I shudder to think of the possibilities," Bianca murmured.

"Possibilities? Possibilities!" Razvan exclaimed, and the floor and windows shook. His expression communicated a level of rage I had never seen. His pupils elongated horizontally, like those of a goat, as his body emitted pulsating sparks. "Without the Realm's intervention, your time on this earth as you know it would have come to a halt!"

Bianca nodded in agreement and moved to the head of the table where she laid a hand on Tristan's chest. "Have the decency to look at him, Nicholas! Then you will see what it is you have done!" She waited for Nick to comply. "By the time we'd arrived, the battle was nearly over. Tristan bravely carried on despite his injuries. And all due to your incredible selfishness. I so hope you two enjoyed your little escapade!"

I took a deep breath before asking the question: "Will he be all right?"

Bianca didn't answer. Instead, she and Razvan shared a telepathic exchange. She vaporized, for lack of a better word, returning seconds later with something that resembled two feet of narrow plastic tubing.

After collecting a dagger from a desk drawer at the opposite end of the room, Razvan reappeared in an instant at the head of the table. Nick and I had an unobstructed view, which I assumed was our father's intention.

Digging a cavernous hole in his arm, Razvan threaded one end of the tube inside, then stuck the opposite end in Tristan's mouth. Dry heaving, I sank to my knees. Nick, pale and terrified, tugged me to my feet and tilted his head toward the exit.

Bianca must have interpreted his intention and blocked our path. "You shall bear witness to what unfolds!"

Blood flowed from Razvan through the tube to Tristan at such a volume, a stream seeped from his lips. A protracted heartbeat later, Tristan blinked to awareness and uttered an apology of sorts; I thought I'd heard, *Dearest Master, can you not bequeath my extinction?*

Bianca knelt beside him and whispered words I couldn't hear. Based upon Nick's expression, he couldn't either. Soon after, Tristan began to thrash about, his crimson-rimmed eyes wide, the irises kaleidoscoping from black orbs to gold starbursts, occasionally arcing sparks, some bouncing off Nick and me.

"The Harvesters have ignored our warning," Razvan told Bianca only minutes later, his blood still flowing into Tristan.

"Innocents have become their targets," Bianca reinforced. "It's only a matter of time before the resistance follows suit."

Razvan dropped his head. I'd never associated my father with anything other than bravery and decisiveness, yet for a fleeting moment, he seemed to possess neither.

"I have requested all factions of the Realm assemble," he eventually said. "A war, unlike either of you have yet to witness, is at our door."

My thoughts ran to the courthouse, to the terror my parents suffered on the day they died, and my knees buckled.

"Because of our efforts today, further attacks have been discouraged," Razvan boasted, his lips testing a grin.

"This is, undoubtedly, short-term," Bianca corrected, addressing Nick primarily. "Your father remains convinced that once this reckless horde increases in number, they will strike again. For this reason, you must obey our *every* command, Nicholas!"

"Never violate the directives again!" Razvan said, his demand rattling the many curtained windows.

Unexpectedly, Yesenia emerged from within a smoky shroud, exchanged a soundless clash with Bianca, and ushered both Nick and me from the room.

She escorted us to the landing, where—at breakneck speed—her feet left the ground without warning, and she flew in Nick's direction, kicking him and propelling him down the stairs. Swooping toward the first level, she hovered over him, an eerie smile stretching her lips.

"How fares the imposter prince now? Oh, the times I have recommended you both be hanged in the basement like any meat worth its salt, only to have my suggestion disavowed!" She leaned over him, and Nick turned his head when her lethal incisors dripped a sickening slime onto his forehead. "A mortal serves only one purpose," she began, sucking her teeth, "and it is not to drain our master of precious time and resources!"

"Go, Celeste. Run!" Nick cried as he scrambled to his feet.

Yesenia's eyes whipped in my direction, and she took flight, returning to the second floor before my brain could register her movement. Grabbing me by my hair, she flung me first against one wall, then another. A moment or two after, I could only recall the sensation of falling.

Briefly losing consciousness, I woke in a heap near the foyer. I searched for Nick. I remembered he was halfway up the stairs before my blackout, but now I didn't see him anywhere. A loud crash drew my attention to the second floor, and I cried out Nick's name, just as an inconceivable shriek shredded the silence, and Yesenia soared in Nick's direction. He hit her squarely in the nose when she reached him, which provoked only a guttural laugh, and she grunted her promised vengeance. Both she and Nick squared off, assuming a stance one might expect from two warriors preparing to engage. Before Nick could make a move, Yesenia gripped him by his shirt collar and launched him toward the ceiling, where he remained, as though cemented in place. Yesenia once again proved herself the more experienced opponent.

Seconds later, she returned her attention to me. She suddenly levitated me to the second floor, and I watched helplessly as she telekinetically sprung open a window. I braced myself, reasonably assessing her intent. Just as the clock struck 6 p.m., Nick and I sailed through the sprawling window—arms flailing, feet kicking—and landed with a consecutive *whoosh* in our Olympic-size swimming pool.

Scissoring my legs, I cut through the water and easily surfaced. Nick was already sitting poolside. Yesenia hovered above the pool, laughing and taunting us. "You pathetic mortals!"

A crackle sounded, like a sparkler on the Fourth of July, and Trandafira materialized suddenly, her dominant stance opposite Yesenia imposing.

"Did you think me not aware?"

Yesenia smirked, firing a few fiery arcs from icy fingertips.

"It matters none to me."

"I always know your actions, despite our tangible division, dear *sister*, or have you forgotten?"

Yesenia's maniacal laughter was far more grating than fingernails against a chalkboard, and her expression guaranteed more violence.

"You are no more my sister than that wretched brat cowering in the pool," she howled and jabbed a finger in my direction.

"If you think I shan't alert Bianca, think again. A severe penance you will pay."

"She surely knew my intentions when we said our last farewell," Yesenia responded. "Perhaps she thought it time these revolting mortals learned a lesson most valuable."

"In the event she did not, I shall make alerting her to your misdeed my foremost mission."

Yesenia cocked her head and grinned, exposing her daunting fangs.

"That would be a grave mistake. Perhaps you've forgotten our last little skirmish during the Battle of Bannockburn.

More importantly, you seem to have forgotten which of us prevailed."

"Ha! It would seem *your* memory of these events some seven hundred years ago is less than adequate, Yesenia, dear."

"Quite the contrary: It was a midsummer day—the feast of St. John the Baptist, to be more precise. And you, quite the spectacle, gorging yourself on the blood of so many fallen Englishmen!"

A sly smile blazed across Trandafira's lips as she remembered the event vividly. "Ah, yes, what a grand festival!" She laughed suddenly. "King Edward II scarcely escaped to Dunbar Castle, as I recall. And all due to your insatiable desire for that fopdoodle, Robert-the-Bruce! Not only did you fail to snare Robert as your immortal slave, but you allowed the King of England to escape." Trandafira cocked her head sideways and tapped a finger to her chin. "Which of us is the bigger fool? I do believe most would agree that you, dear sister, deserve that title."

"I cry your mercy! Undoubtedly, you must admit the blood of the Scots is the more delectable; delightfully irresistible," Yesenia said through protruding, blunt incisors.

"Indeed," Trandafira agreed, her fangs also overhanging slightly. "Although, there is most certainly a bit of a Haggis aftertaste. And don't think I haven't noticed your proclivity to abandon the discussion surrounding Robert."

"Ah, Robert, of the family Bruce," Yesenia said, licking her bottom lip. "Such a willful young brute. I bestowed upon him the gift of immortality, and how did he thank me? He spat out that precious offering!"

"A gift," Trandafira mocked. "Call it what you will, but you drained the unfortunate fellow, and quite ruthlessly if I know you. I'm also certain that you didn't bother to explain the ceremony in all its glorious detail."

Glaring, Yesenia drifted closer still, but Trandafira held her ground.

"I slit my wrist and told him to either drink from it or die. What more do you want?"

"Humph! Imagine his confusion; he was already dead."

"I have often wondered how Edward managed to escape you," Yesenia taunted. "Such a small, meek little man. Child's play as I see it. After all, as you've since admonished, my attention was elsewhere."

"How?" Trandafira scoffed. "A pox on you, Yesenia! The King's sorceress's spell: that's how! The cunning witch! What I perceived a dark horse galloping toward Dunbar was, in point of fact, Edward's spineless escape. Imagine, all that distance on all fours?"

They both giggled, causing ripples to course throughout the pool.

"I presume you retaliated?" Yesenia asked.

Trandafira managed a sarcastic smirk. "I'm told, to this day, her skeleton reflects her angst and discomfort at the point of death. Let us go now and reminisce. Leave these children to our master's wrath."

Nick waited until they were out of sight, and then assisted me out of the pool, wrapping his arms around me.

"Stay away from that psycho bitch, Celeste, because, I shit you not, she wants you dead."

CHAPTER 6

A chill nipped my spine as I successfully entered Tristan's room unnoticed. I approached the walnut coffin pinched between the massive entryway of a closet that was more like a cave. With the draperies completely pulled together and the exterior shutters secured over the windows, not a single sliver of sunlight invaded the bedroom. The room was eerily quiet, save the occasional tap-tap-tapping of the shutters in response to intermittent wind gusts. Fearing discovery, I retraced my steps, then locked the door.

Wrapped in total darkness, I was attempting my return to Tristan when Bianca sprung up beside me.

"Perhaps our definitions of disobedience are somewhat divergent!"

"I . . . I just wanted to see how he's doing."

"Trandafira thinks it may be to your advantage to keep your distance."

I wondered if she knew Yesenia assaulted Nick and me. I considered broaching the subject, then decided it was best left alone. Yesenia could get to me anytime she wanted as she'd proven on several occasions, and pitting Bianca against her was a scary proposition.

"I came to apologize. Why isn't he awake?"

"His slumber is a blessing, Celeste, as he suffers excruciating pain. I doubt the easing of your conscience will lessen that pain, so off with you!"

"I am so sorry, Mom," I mumbled and started for the door.

"According to Trandafira, Yesenia considers you a threat," she called after me, her words flowing through gelid condensation. "I counsel you to keep your distance. Torok obligations only go so far."

"Wait! She thinks of me as a threat?"

"A fierce competitor likely is a more accurate description. I see by your stupefied expression that this is news to you. Do close your mouth won't you, Celeste; it's most unbecoming."

"Now, it all makes sense . . ." I spoke the thought aloud.

Taking one look in Bianca's direction made me wish I'd kept it to myself. She clasped her hands together, and a smoldering fog closed the gap between us.

I will never become accustomed to this odd phenomenon my mother possesses, but it nearly always occurs when she becomes either enraged, overly excited, or sad. I've even witnessed its occurrence when my father envelopes her in a passionate embrace.

I assume this strange event has something to do with her core temperature, which probably hovers around the freezing mark, affected dramatically when her blood pressure skyrockets.

Over the years, I've asked a lot of questions, and I was surprised to learn that the undead function much the same as mortals: They all bleed. They all cry.

"You have become a beautiful woman, Celestine, despite what you may think. Regardless of the impact this may or may not make on Tristan, Yesenia is a fool to even consider he might act on such a desire, for it is forbidden." She unclasped her hands and drifted closer. "Regardless, I counsel you must avoid our gallant warrior as opportunity permits."

I nodded, wondering to whom she referred—Tristan or Yesenia.

"Both," she said with an arched brow and led me from the room. Her arm in mine, she guided me down the hall, stopping briefly before the long staircase. Remembering the events of the night before, I found the need to steady myself against her.

"Let that be a lesson to you both," she whispered.

"Can we stop a minute?" I said, my mind reeling from her latest revelation. I crossed the hall and studied a portrait I'd always admired.

"That, as you know, was my mother," she said and wrapped an arm around my waist, looking up at the same portrait with a sad smile. "Turning a deaf ear to *her* mother's counsel, she befriended Queen Catherine of Aragon upon the Queen's banishment to Kimbolton Castle. King Henry saw this as heresy and ordered my mother's execution a short time thereafter. To this day, I can still smell her burning flesh."

I blinked back tears as my mind drew a vivid visual.

"You've never told me that."

"A ghastly event; of that you can be sure. I avoid the topic at every opportunity. I mention it now, only in the hope my painful disclosure might be of benefit to you, Celeste. For you see, at times, a mother truly knows best."

I wanted to ask her mother's age at the time of her execution, but I wouldn't risk causing Bianca more pain.

"She was but forty-one years old when she died, the portrait painted some years before," Bianca said, hiccoughing a tormented sigh. "I have often wondered how the ravages of time would have affected me had I not received immortality."

"She was so beautiful," I managed and didn't know what more there was to say. Most wouldn't consider remaining twenty-nine forever, as Bianca had, such a horrible fate.

"Come, your father wishes to discuss your sanctions."

Nick was already in our father's office, poised combatively, and as far from Razvan as humanly possible. I noticed Bianca wince as Nick scraped a sliver of mud from his shoe onto an ancient, intricately woven Persian carpet. I forced eye contact with my brother and silently pleaded he not further enrage Razvan. He ignored me and instead plopped down and sprawled across an ivory sofa that was rumored to have been in Bianca's family for centuries, his muddy shoes leaving damaging imprints. Razvan charged toward him, and Nick suddenly inverted, his feet facing the ceiling and his *Imagine Dragons* T-shirt obscuring his face.

"I plan to make this brief," Razvan boomed. "Considering your current position, Nicholas, one would assume that much to your advantage. It is *only* because your mother has pleaded the importance of your high school prom—such a ridiculous mortal affair—that I will allow you and Celestine to leave the grounds. Tristan shall accompany you, depositing you back here the instant the celebration concludes. Preceding and following the event, you will remain within these walls until stated otherwise. Are we in agreement?"

A FEW NIGHTS LATER, I intentionally waited outside my father's office, though a considerable distance away, in the hopes of seeing Tristan. He stepped out a short time later. Startled, I ducked behind a column. He was speaking from the doorway, his attention on whoever spoke from inside. I stole another glance and felt my heart swell and my pulse quicken. His hair shone like a raven's wings: dark, glossy, and nearly iridescent.

Classically long, it flirted with his shirt collar. Many of my classmates often compared him to Thor—as played by Chris Hemsworth, and it was not surprising: Casually dressed in a dark T-shirt and darker jeans, both fit him snugly and left little to the imagination. His powerful biceps and chiseled oblique muscles were on full display.

Finished with his conversation, he started down the hall. My hands were shaking, my heart racing, but I took a deep breath and followed. Tiptoeing behind him, I zig-zagged between the columns spanning across the long hallway, separating one room from another. Heading in the direction of the courtyard, he suddenly vanished.

"To where are you off, Celestine?" he asked from behind me.

Taken by surprise, I screamed, a pathetic yelp really, and he laughed.

"Why do you seek me out?"

"I . . . I just wanted to make sure you're okay," I stammered without turning around. Looking directly at Tristan always made me break into a sweat and tremble like a wet dog left out on a cold day.

"Don't I look okay to you?" he asked playfully, his words stinging the nape of my neck.

I opened my mouth, inhaling a burst of air, stalling. Always aware that it was a possibility he might hypnotize me with his wise, salacious eyes, I reluctantly turned to face him. "Don't tease me," I managed, riveting my eyes to my Converse All Star sneakers, still somewhat soggy from the ferry adventure.

"The blame is not yours," he said softly. "Nicholas on the other hand . . ."

"You could have been . . . I mean, you might have been—"

He lifted my chin and placed a cold finger against my lips.

"Why is it I only suffer what I have become in your presence, Celestine?" he asked with such a degree of seriousness, I dared look him in the eye.

Without thinking, I threw my arms around him.

"I'm so glad you're okay," I whispered before running back to my room.

Later that evening, as I was dressing for the prom, Bianca softly knocked on my door, then opened it a crack.

"Do you need some help with your makeup?"

Wanting to tell her I didn't plan to wear any makeup, I instead invited her in.

She waltzed into my room—her feet never once contacting the floor, clutching a jeweled bag that undoubtedly contained the same type of concoctions she'd once used on Cleo. Before I could object, she began slathering my eyelids with something green that smelled medicinal.

I squeezed both nostrils shut. "That smells awful!"

She muttered something foreign and shot me a universal look.

Committed to allowing Bianca some mother-daughter time, I sat perfectly still, avoiding my reflection in the mirror, despite the temptation to monitor her every move. Fifteen minutes later, I smothered a groan when she produced a curling iron.

Following a few superficial burns to my forehead, with a grand flourish, she announced, "Huzzah!"

Normally, I loved every one of her Renaissance expressions, but today was an exception. I worked up the courage and furtively glanced at the mirror. Although she stood directly beside me, I saw only my reflection. When I was younger, this phenomenon always made me cry. I would question whether Bianca was real or just a figment of my imagination. Losing one mother wasn't easy; questioning the existence of her replacement proved too much. And although I was certainly never destined to become a Rhode's scholar by any stretch of the imagination, Bianca's lame explanation did little to ease my anxiety.

"Well, what do you think?" Bianca said, wielding the curling iron like a samurai warrior's sword.

Critically examining the only woman that stared back at me, I gasped. "What did you do to my hair?"

Bianca's arms dropped to her sides; her lips pinched in a pitiful pout. "I suppose you don't like it."

I barely recognized myself, and I considered that beneficial by anyone's standards. "No, I do! It looks amazing."

She pinched both my cheeks. "I have only just begun."

Bianca began to sing, which made anyone fortunate enough to hear her, smile. Her tone, though soft and sedative, encompassed a range so diverse, she put any modern-day songstress to shame. "There!" she announced a few minutes later, waving a blush brush through the air like Michelangelo upon the completion of a masterpiece.

I looked up from the Vogue magazine she'd dropped in my lap and hid utter surprise behind both palms. I was gorgeous; me, Celeste Torok! "But how did you—"

"You are beautiful, my darling. Absolutely beautiful."

"Oh, my God! I can't believe it's me!"

"I suppose, to be fair, it's Van Gogh who deserves the accolades. He taught me everything I know of artistry. I always found his use of color superior."

I cringed. I'd already heard plenty about Vincent.

Bianca took the gown from the closet and slipped it over my head. Then she twirled me around so I could see the back of the gown in the oblong antique mirror. The color was perfect and, because it was strapless, it accented my biceps; they were my best feature, in my opinion.

I tugged at the neckline, remembering that the gown I'd tried on had not been nearly as revealing, and I heard Bianca giggle.

"*What* happened to my gown?"

"A slight alteration, darling. It is flattering, no?"

I was second-guessing the response on the tip of my tongue when someone rapped lightly on the door.

"Come in!" Bianca twittered happily.

Razvan opened the door a crack and peered through the small gap. "Off to the ball?"

"Iubirea mea," Bianca said, still giggling as she crossed the room, her lips tenderly brushing his cheek. "They have not labeled them such for centuries!"

He pulled her close, and I shut my eyes. Over the years, I'd witnessed things I honestly felt might blind a kid. The term *sparks fly*—in their case, and nearly every time the two of them met, is not applied metaphorically. The first time I happened upon the two of them involved in what I was left to assume vigorous foreplay, I thought they'd kill one another; I've witnessed less frenzy on an episode of *Animal Planet.* I kept my eyes closed tight until I heard Razvan say, "You look beautiful, Celestine."

"Thank you, Father," I said as he walked my direction. For whatever reason, Razvan never drifted nor whooshed, popped-up, glided, nor floated in either my presence or Nick's.

His expression was unusually warm. He kissed my cheek, then took Bianca by the hand and escorted her to the door.

"We shall see you again before you leave for your celebration," Bianca told me before they left the room.

"Is the coast clear?" Nick asked as he entered my room, uninvited, and vaulted on top of my bed. Following a long dramatic whistle, he said, "You don't look too bad."

I felt my face flush. "But not as good as you?"

Nick puffed his chest, reached for a hand mirror, and studied his reflection. "Yeah, sometimes, it's hard to believe we're related."

"Tell me about it."

He dropped the mirror and nearly bounced himself from the bed. His satin tuxedo jacket tickled my bare skin as he wrapped an arm around me.

"I'm only teasing, Celeste. You look beautiful. Warren's a lucky guy. Or is all that really for Tristan?"

I winged both nostrils while clenching my fists. "Stop it, Nick!" If only he knew I'd give just about anything to spend the evening in Tristan's arms. But Nick knew nothing of disappointment. He had it all—looks, charm, and intellect. While my GPA was much higher than his, I'd spent grueling hours earning every single point. Nick had somehow managed a 3.0 and studied nothing, well, unless you count female anatomy. My brother could have anything or anyone he wanted. Me, on the other hand . . . my lack of self-confidence allocated whatever I might achieve, whomever I wanted to love me more than a fool's daydream. "You look so handsome, Nick . . . like Dad on his wedding day."

Nick looked away suddenly. "They should be here. For the both of us."

"Maybe they are," I whispered, attempting to salvage the mood.

Nick's eyes cut to mine, and I thought he'd either laugh or wound me with some off-the-cuff remark. "I wish I could be more like you, Celeste. Ever the optimist."

I didn't recognize my sarcastic laugh. "Me? You're kidding, right?"

Nick shook his head. "Not everything, or everyone, is how it appears. The difference between us; I quit taking life seriously because it's here one minute, gone the next. So, take my advice, Celeste. Live your life and screw anything that gets in the way." He lowered his head. Gracing me with an angelic grin, he lifted only his eyes and added, "Just to be sure we're clear, I didn't mean that literally. One hell-raiser in the family is enough."

CHAPTER 7

*O*nly half-awake, I lunged for the lamp on my bedside table and clumsily switched it on. Fumbling for the remote, which opened the shutters, I closed my eyes to the bands of sunlight falling across my pillow covered in mascara, blush, and foundation residue. Ironically, the vivid pink *rouge*— as Bianca called it—looked much better on a white pillowcase than it did on my cheeks.

Although it was nearly 10 a.m., I had only been in bed for five hours and asleep for four, and I was certain the majority of the Realm lay asleep within tufted velvet and satin uphol- stered coffins several floors below. As usual, my mind had refused to shut off, replaying all my awkward moments and hoping the school paper's videographer hadn't captured them all. I took comfort in knowing at least one of those moments wouldn't include me on the dance floor. Rather than by my side, Warren spent most of the evening alongside the refresh- ment table, stuffing his face with pizza rolls and assorted pastries. Hopefully, the videographer hadn't captured the multiple globs of food splattered across Warren's tuxedo.

The prom had ended at midnight, but Nick had enticed Emily away immediately following the crowning of Prom

King and Queen. As if that wasn't somewhat scandalous in itself, he'd arrived with Amie but abandoned her side once they'd performed the traditional King and Queen dance. Laughter rocked the auditorium when Amie called him everything *but* Nick and hurled her crown in Emily's direction as the couple left the building hand in hand. It came as little surprise that neither Kaitlin nor Olivia attempted to comfort Amie when she fled the auditorium with tears streaming down her face. Nick had that effect on women. Bianca had once jokingly suggested he invest in Kimberly-Clark stock, the makers of *Kleenex*.

I'd arrived home by 1 a.m. I'd planned to wait up for Nick but abandoned that idea around five in the morning. For my brother's sake, I hoped Razvan and Bianca had found better things to do. I shivered at the possibilities that lay in wait for Nick had they not, which is why I chose to hide out in my room, rather than sit there and fixate on the what-ifs.

I wasn't surprised that Yesenia had eagerly suggested she serve as Prom Chaperone. It seemed as though I had become her primary focus; her intent to make my life as miserable as possible. Considering Nick's escape, I wondered if she thought it such a good idea now. Nor was I surprised Razvan thought it a good idea, while Bianca was understandably troubled that he would appoint Yesenia the task of protecting me. But was it possible my father was unaware of Yesenia's underlying resentment toward me? Most, if they knew my close association with vampires, would assume I was an expert on their behavior. Nothing could be further from the truth because about the time I'm confident I know all there is to know, something new and terrifying emerges. Maybe they're not much different from humans, I decided. Maybe Bianca possesses a woman's intuition while, of course, Razvan does not.

Much of the time before finally dozing off, I worried about Tristan's blame in Nick's absenteeism. Although the

Realm resembled a close-knit family, Razvan was their leader, and those who failed to comply with his order could expect severe ramifications. Despite my parents' secrecy when it came to the Realm's business, I'd witnessed the consequence of Razvan's fury, the inconceivable aftermath awarded to those who blatantly, or inadvertently, disobeyed my father. Following one occasion in particular, Razvan frightened me to the extent I avoided him for weeks. The subject of his wrath, a young warrior probably no more than seventeen—at the time someone gifted him immortality, anyway—was banished to the lowest level in the mansion, the dungeon as Nick called it, from where my father generated implausible shrieks and cries, which permeated every inch of the house until daybreak.

When the earsplitting noise finally ended, and the Realm had retired to their respective coffins, I stealthily invaded the basement. Huddled in a dark corner, behind a reinforced storage area, lay something neither human nor vampire, relegated to an otherworldly state. Its outer shell was neither healthy nor pale flesh but rather a cocoon-like substance resembling that of a caterpillar. Trapped within its sticky swaddle, its eyes noticeably aware of my presence, its mouth opened suddenly, knife-like incisors failing to penetrate the jellied enclosure. Repulsed yet somehow drawn to it, I approached uncharacteristically fearless. Following a brief interaction—and I have no specific memory of this, the information merely offered to me secondhand—I retraced my steps to a workbench nearby and from it selected a large box cutter.

I've since come to realize my approaching the cage didn't arise from a morbid curiosity or even an inherent empathy, but rather a summoning I hadn't the ability to disregard. Since that occasion, the first of many, I remain grateful for Bianca's clairvoyant ability and have lost many a night's sleep wondering what would have been had she not intervened.

Tristan was once again at the forefront of my mind. As a distraction, I took the gold ring Warren had given me with the

tiniest diamond imaginable from my nightstand drawer—
hidden intentionally beneath a stack of college brochures that
interested Bianca a lot more than they interested me—and
then berated myself for ever having accepted it. Having spent
an entire evening with Warren, I was beginning to think
Bianca was right; Warren wasn't the person with whom I
wanted to spend the rest of my life, or possibly another
minute, which brought my thoughts back to Tristan.

I closed my eyes, hugging my body as if it were Tristan
holding me in his arms, my head nestled against his chest. I
shivered and pulled the blankets up to my chin, knowing that
alone wouldn't put an end to the goosebumps I always experienced anytime Tristan was near.

I blew out a long sigh and wondered what I could ever
have found the least bit attractive about Warren. The only
time he had given me goosebumps occurred after he'd pushed
me into the pool last summer.

I heard Bianca's signature *knockity-knock-knock* on my
bedroom door and dove completely under the covers. No
more than a ten-count later, she called my name, her lyrical
lilt not something easily ignored. Outside the door one
minute, sitting on the edge of my bed the next, she said,
"Clearly, Nicholas enjoyed your little prom. Can the same be
said of you, Celeste?"

Exposing my face inch by inch, I exhaled an agonizing
breath.

"It was okay; the best part was when they crowned
Nick—"

"Yes, *King*; I am most aware. Such a preposterous tourna-
ment! What I can't understand is why those ill-bred fools
would not find *you* worthy of a crown, cheap imitation, or
otherwise."

"Pfft," I muttered under my breath. Hesitant to make the
inquiry, I eventually asked, "Have you talked to Nick?"

Bianca cocked an eyebrow, and her eyes darkened.

"Fortunately for Nicholas, your father was needed elsewhere. It appears the Harvesters are delighted with the recent unrest in Nicaragua, the opportunistic cowards!"

That would explain Tristan's disappearance after the dance. "So, Tristan——"

"But of course Tristan battles alongside! How else do you suppose Nicholas managed escape from prom? Yesenia has received quite the tongue-lashing for—how do the contemporaries put it?—dropping the ball."

I smiled inwardly and wished I'd been witness to that.

"Such an infantile reaction, Celeste," she admonished. "Ah, the resentment but the one thing you and Yesenia have in common . . . Tristan being the exception. Are not either of my children mindful of my guidance? You and your determination toward a man you cannot have and Nicholas with his apparent desire to break free from a life he deems wretched. Nothing can come of a liaison between you and Tristan. How many times and in how many ways must I speak of it?"

"Mom, for God's sake! You've got to give me some space. Besides, I don't want to talk about it," I said, blinking past a tear.

"Very well, a matter for another time. As for that pathetic trinket tucked away beneath your pillow, you are correct, you should not have accepted it." She bent down, and I prepared myself for her icy lips against my forehead, soon after experiencing the equivalent of brain freeze. "Perhaps you do, on rare occasion, listen to my advice." She stood, nearly on the floor, and whipped off my covers. "Now you must get dressed! Trandafira has prepared your breakfast and—much to my dismay—Aubrey awaits your arrival downstairs. I think it best you expedite her exodus, Celestine. After all, this is not the time for outsiders."

~

"Hey, girl," Aubrey called to me as I came downstairs, her obnoxiously loud voice reverberating down the long entry hall.

I pressed an index finger to my lips and rolled my eyes.

"Shush! You are so freakishly loud!"

Aubrey threw her head back and laughed. "What, you afraid I'm going to wake the dead?" If only she knew that was exactly what I was afraid of, given several members of the Realm lay sleeping a floor below us. "So, did you see Brandon making out with Kaitlin?" she asked around a ridiculously large mouthful of some sort of strawberry pastry, droplets of red goo escaping her lips and bringing to mind unpleasant images.

"You know how much I hate gossip."

Aubrey allowed the pastry to freefall from ringed fingers, then wiped the remaining residue on her jeans. "How are we even friends?"

I sighed in response. It was way too early to get into any type of confrontation with Aubrey.

"God, you are such a goody two-shoes! I don't know how you can even sit there with that big stick up your ass." She snarled, snagged a muffin from Trandafira's breakfast display, and devoured it in one mouthful. "And let's not forget," she began, showering me with shrapnel, "you're the one that said, just last week, Kaitlin despised him. Who's the gossipmonger, now?"

I pitched my arms in surrender. "Okay, okay, you're right. Sometimes, I get dragged into all the drama."

Aubrey smirked. "Oh yeah, right. You get *dragged* in."

"Let's just agree to disagree."

Aubrey mocked me, then said, "You'd have more friends if you didn't act like you were born in another friggin' century."

"Oh come on, Aubrey! If this is your idea of being a friend, I'm glad I don't have any more *friends*!"

"Chill, Celeste. I'm just messin' with you! About Kaitlin, that's her game you know, playing hard to get."

"Yeah, definitely not the way you operate."

She fisted my shoulder and nearly knocked me out of the chair. "Funny, real funny. Did you hear Brianna accused Coach Werner of sexual harassment?"

I must have missed a lot when Warren took me outside to give me his ring. "No way! Why?"

"I'd tell you, but you hate gossip."

I rolled my eyes and growled a sigh. "Just tell me."

Her eyes sparkling, she said, "If you insist, here goes. He told her she looked lovely. After that, she made a beeline and ratted him out to the chaperones."

I considered telling Aubrey that her predilection for movies like *Goodfellas* was having an untoward effect. Instead, I said, "So telling someone that they look pretty is considered sexual harassment?"

"Yup, I guess so . . . if it comes out of an old geezer's mouth."

While I pinched off a bite from a strawberry torte, Aubrey gulped down the rest of her orange juice. "And Brianna wonders why she was voted the Girl Most Likely to Never Get Laid."

After nearly choking on the pastry, I unconsciously scrunched my nose. "There is no such category!"

"There is . . . now," Aubrey said with a wink, her words trailing as she glanced toward my father's office. "So, where is Tristan, anyway?"

CHAPTER 8

*N*ick had been unusually quiet during the entire
drive to Madison High School. Sitting shoulder to
shoulder in the backseat of the limo, I sensed his rare anxiety.
Once we reached the circular drive in front of the school,
Nick flung the door open and jumped out, without saying a
word to Bianca, Razvan, even me.

"Don't forget your cap," Bianca said, as I stepped out of
the car, intent on catching up with Nick.

By the time I arrived on the football field, my hair
dripped sweat from running after him, and a valley of it
ran down my back, a steady stream flowing from my
armpits. I finally caught sight of Nick's blond hair, as a
good majority of our senior class surrounded him, laughing
and talking excitedly. I thought to join them but always felt
like a fifth wheel, regardless of the large entourage he
always seemed to attract. He waved, then gestured I join
him. I pretended not to notice and instead took a seat in
the back row.

He was frowning as he walked toward me, a quizzical
expression marring an otherwise beautiful face. Several of his
friends trailed close behind, undoubtedly harboring hope that

they'd find themselves the lucky ones who would sit alongside Nick Torok during the ceremony.

Although students in every row he passed asked that he join them, Nick chose a seat next to mine.

With the moon rising near the twenty-yard line, I was feeling more than a little grateful, perhaps a little nostalgic, and I covered Nick's hand with mine.

"We finally made it," I squealed and squeezed his hand.

Nick suddenly grew tense and looked away.

"What's wrong?"

"NYU didn't accept me."

I heard myself swallow. "You're joking. Please tell me you're joking, Nick!"

"No, I wish I were." He wrapped his arm around my shoulders and rested his head against mine.

"How long have you known?" I asked, disappointment pinching my vocal cords.

"For a couple of months." Nick took off his cap and wiggled his sunglasses from his shirt pocket, and as I watched him put them on, I realized he was crying. I hadn't seen him cry since that awful night five years ago. I tried to muster a shred of compassion but instead felt only mounting irritation.

Rage coursing through every part of me, I demanded, "Why didn't you tell me?"

"Because I thought the ole man could fix it!"

"That's your solution to every problem," I said under my breath. "So, you're telling me he couldn't fix it?" I found it impossible, considering Razvan's important connections, not to mention his extreme wealth, that anyone would deny his every request.

Nick ripped off his sunglasses and glared. "Okay, couldn't isn't the right word; he wouldn't even try!"

Suddenly, the past no longer mattered, the present was too surreal, and the future seemed too painful. I sat there, numb.

"Why are you just now telling me this, Nick?"

"Because I only found out this morning when I came home. He said he didn't want to——"

I was sitting on my hands to stop them from trembling. "Didn't want to . . . what?"

"Just forget it. What difference does it make!"

"Tell me, Nick. For once in your life, spare me the bullshit!"

"He didn't want to ruin your prom."

I covered my face, angry tears threatening to spill over. Out of the corner of my eye, I saw Tristan taking the stage, getting in position for his valedictorian speech. "Maybe it's not too late. I'll talk to Bianca. Maybe——"

"Screw that! The ole man found out I wanted to study forensics and criminal law instead of biology, mathematics, and chemistry, so he doesn't give a damn if I go on to college or not."

"When did you decide to change your major?"

"What are you looking at?" Nick said combatively to two students in the row ahead of ours, who'd made the mistake of turning around. He waited until the eavesdroppers turned to face the stage once again. "I've always wanted to be a cop, Celeste. But Razvan has always had my future plotted out. You know that!"

I nodded. I had forgotten Nick talked of little else but becoming a police officer, like our biological father, from the time he learned to speak until he discovered hanging with boys his age a lot more fun than spending time with me.

"He only wants to see you succeed, Nick."

"Yeah, as long as that involves a career at Torok Laboratories."

"What are you going to do?" I asked, pushing out the words.

Nick took a deep breath, stretching his spine its entire length, and shrugged. "Enroll in the Police Academy, I guess. I figured I'd have a better shot with a degree, but what choice do I have now?" I was surprised when Nick suddenly threw an arm around me and buried his face in my neck. "It'll all work out," he whispered. "The only reason I wanted to go to NYU was to be with you."

Then you should have studied harder, I wanted to scream. When was he going to stop blaming Razvan and Bianca for his own mistakes?

An enormous fireworks display began. Nick turned toward me, his face masked with a scowl, and mouthed, "Damn Bianca! I bet she did this!"

After the last Roman candle exploded above the field, the crowd's frenzied adulation slowly subsided. When Tristan clutched the microphone and cut loose a primitive howl, everyone turned their attention to the stage. Rather than raise the microphone to accommodate his six-foot stature, Tristan propped one elbow on the podium, arrogantly resting the opposite hand against his hip.

"Okay, this is where I'm supposed to tell you what majestic roads lie ahead, blah-blah-blah," he began, "unless you're one of those dumbasses who barely squeaked through high school, like Brandon over there." His painstakingly rehearsed teen-speak garnered thunderous applause.

Tristan paused while Brandon, the accurately appointed dumbass, stood and exaggerated a bow.

"Instead, my only advice is—to paraphrase Steven Tyler of Aerosmith—You Don't Want to Miss a Thing." Strumming an air guitar, Tristan ended his speech with, "Live. Love. Exist," groped the microphone and gave it a defiant lick. "That's a wrap," he told a captivated audience and dove off the stage, crowd-surfing across every row.

The class continued to roar, long after Principal Henderson demanded everyone quiet. "When I call your name, come up on the stage and receive your diploma."

I bumped Nick's arm, wondering if he'd heard Principal Henderson squawk his name over the loudspeaker.

"Nick . . . Nicholas Torok," Henderson repeated.

With the veins in his forehead noticeably throbbing, Nick eventually got to his feet. Rather than take the stairs, he hopped up and onto the stage in typical melodramatic fashion. Taking possession of the microphone, he said: "My name is Crenshaw, Nick Crenshaw. Not Torok."

A confused gasp fell over the crowd. The principal—probably assuming this just another one of Nick's pranks—flared his nostrils in response, then tossed Nick his diploma. After my name was called, I accepted my diploma and noticed my brother waiting on the sidelines. He took my hand, once I reached the bottom step, intending he escort me back to our seats.

I pulled my hand away. "Why did you have to do that?" I managed through clenched teeth.

Nick grabbed my arm and stopped walking. "Because that's our name, Celeste, whether you like it or not!"

I bit my lip, determined not to cry, as we passed rows of our fellow classmates, all appearing shell-shocked by Nick's revelation.

"They have always tried to make everything perfect, Nick!"

"How? By embarrassing us with some tacky-ass fireworks display? They probably could have paid for a couple of scholarships for the less-fortunate kids instead of blowing all that money on this freaking sideshow! But I guess they can't help it, Celeste. Because that's what they are; a couple of circus freaks."

I took my seat, not knowing how to respond. Nick did have a point when it came to the Toroks' grand gestures; having the wealthiest parents in the entire state had its drawbacks. Their over-the-top attempts at kindness often proved much more embarrassing than they were endearing. It was no secret that Torok Laboratories was international and held the second-highest corporate ranking by Forbes Magazine three years running. Razvan had repeatedly declined the offer to grace the cover of *Time Magazine* for more years than I can remember. My parents' corporation guaranteed not only an eternity of wealth and social advantage but, more importantly, the source of their sole sustenance; blood.

As I silently fumed, Nick broke the silence.

"You riding back with me?"

I wagged my head. The ride home with Bianca and Razvan promised gut-wrenching tension at best, but I preferred their company to Nick's right now. I also thought it important they know they had one child on their side.

Nick must have mistaken my anger for sorrow.

"Hey, don't be sad, Celeste. Maybe I'll apply at the New York academy."

The words on the tip of my tongue seemed implausible. But rather than tell Nick that I no longer cared what he did, I decided it might be a better idea to give that revelation more thought first. Nick suddenly popped upright and told me he'd see me at the party.

I hitched a thumb toward the stage where our classmates waited in a long procession in the process of receiving their diplomas. "But aren't you going to wait—" I managed, the rest of my sentence moot as Nick cantered off the field.

THE LIMOUSINE SAT IDLING at the curb, the air-conditioning fogging the windows, obscuring anyone inside. I approached slowly, wringing my hands and counting each step, a throwback to those days when I was little more than a petrified mess. My hand fluttered on, then off, the door handle. I inhaled—to the point I became lightheaded—and wrenched the heavy door ajar. Inside the limousine, Bianca snuggled against Razvan while I huddled as near the door as possible. We rode in silence for what seemed an eternity.

"It doesn't involve you, Celestine," Bianca said, finally breaking the silence.

Seated at the opposite end of a rich leather seat, Razvan shifted uneasily.

"But it *does* involve me," I stammered.

Bianca threw her head back and sighed. "Why must you always feel the need to watch over Nick?"

"Someone has to," I said without thinking.

"Which brings me to a point aptly suited. Nick is a grown man, whether we wish to acknowledge it or not. And being so, your father felt it necessary, and high time mind you, Nicholas accept responsibility."

"Why start now?" I muttered, unknowingly fisting both hands.

"Speak up, Celestine! Whispering is but a coward's shield!"

"I'm sorry, but I've dreamt about the day Nick and I would attend college together. And now—"

"It was my duty, Celestine," Razvan interrupted in his intimidating, authoritative tone, "as his father, whether he accepts me as one or not. I have warned him for nearly two years, and he chose to ignore me."

I didn't have to glance in his direction to get a sense of his mood.

His intensity was palpable.

"Do you not think it difficult for your father to deny Nicholas assistance?" Bianca chimed in. "It was one of his most grueling decisions, I can assure you."

I looked past her and addressed my father. "So, you could have helped?"

"Of course, but a generous contribution to buy Nicholas' admission would have only helped NYU. Can you not see that, Celestine? After much deliberation, convinced Nicholas would continue his reckless, insouciant ways, I thought denying him my assistance would be a most valuable lesson."

The only thing I understood was my brother would no longer be a part of my everyday life.

"The fact that he came to me for help meant a great deal to me, Celestine. And had he conducted himself in a manner most proper throughout our conversation, my decision may have been different."

I didn't need the details. I knew how Nick could be. I also knew Razvan considered their conversation personal, and I doubted he would share any more information. I wasn't sure I cared enough to hear it, anyway. Long before the driver stopped the car, I was anxious to make my escape, my hand hovering over the door handle.

Razvan reached across Bianca and grabbed my hand before I could vault from the car. "You must know how we adore both you and your brother, Celestine, and I'm sorry if my decision has upset you. Your brother's blatant disregard for his future left me little recourse."

I bit my lip and squinted past tears. "I'm sorry Nick doesn't see things the way I do." Why he didn't, is something I'd never understand. Razvan had saved both our lives and more often than once.

I was in my room packing my duffle bag for the party when I heard footsteps on the stairs and Nick talking on his cell phone. I knew from his seductive tone that he was speaking with either Amie or Olivia.

I opened my door before he knocked. "Finally ready?" he asked, taking my overnight bag and grimacing dramatically at its weight. "No wonder it has taken forever." He stopped at the door, then whirled to face me. "Well, are you coming or not?"

When I didn't answer, he dropped the bag.

"Still mad at me?"

I puffed my cheeks. "I wouldn't call it *mad.*"

Nick stared at the floor, wagging his head. "Look, Celeste, if I could change the stuff I've done, I would, but I can't. So, can we just have a good time tonight? The rest of it will work out, you'll see."

Before I could respond, Bianca trilled from downstairs.

"Nicholas, Celeste, come! We have something you must see!"

Nick picked up the bag and shifted his weight. An expression of annoyance swallowed the air between us.

I tugged on his sleeve and laid my head on his shoulder.

"Please, Nick, give them a break."

Downstairs, Razvan eyed Nick like a hawk might a field mouse.

"Your mother has gone to great lengths," he said, the warning directed at Nick, his underlying threat left to simmer in the electrified air.

"You'll never guess!" Bianca squealed excitedly.

Razvan swept an arm around her waist, cocked his head sideways and kissed her. "Don't make them suffer, iubirea mea. It's been a long day."

"As you wish, my darling. Follow us!" Bianca announced, then danced outdoors. "Close your eyes, the both of you!" She took Nick's hand, and I felt Razvan's hand close around mine. I shut my eyes as he guided me along the paved path leading to the driveway.

I heard Nick groan, then Razvan barked, "Nicholas! Allow your mother this simple request!"

"Prepare for a surprise most . . . well," Bianca laughed, "surprising!" My eyes blinked open to two gleaming Ford Mustangs, one red, the other black, the price stickers still attached. With Nick lumbering over to appraise the black one, I happily staked claim to the red one, opening the door and pawing the leather interior.

"Sweet," Nick said flatly, but a tiny gleam washed over his

eyes when they fell on chrome wheels. "What are we supposed to do with them?" he asked sarcastically, not a beat later. "We're grounded, remember?"

Bianca pinched his ear mercilessly. "Your father has agreed to a brief postponement of your punishment. Nevertheless, you can expect Tristan to escort you this evening, and you must observe an incontestable observation of a midnight curfew."

About that time, I heard a car engine race and saw Tristan's black Porsche, idling partway down the drive.

Although I would have much preferred to drive myself— or better yet, ride with Tristan—at my father's insistence, I obediently threw myself into Nick's car. Not long after we turned onto the road, Nick's Mustang held its course through several hairpin curves as we traversed the coastal drive. Tristan roared past and took the lead, apparently an attempt to slow Nick down. A half-mile further, Nick whipped into a convenience store parking lot. The Porsche spun an impressive donut, caught up, and shuddered to an abrupt stop alongside. Tristan flashed a threatening glare and clambered from the sports car.

"Are you lost, Nicholas? Because your destination is that way," Tristan said, jerking a thumb over his shoulder.

Nick puffed out his chest, reminding me of a Sylvester Stallone movie. Slipping from the Mustang, he told Tristan, "I don't take orders, unlike you."

I watched, somewhat frightened, mostly fascinated, as Tristan swaggered around the Mustang and approached the driver's side. He gripped Nick's bicep and shoved him back inside the car. "This night, my friend, you shall make an exception."

CHAPTER 9

*A*s the Mustang rumbled onto the Country Club's property, I gaped at the enormous stone structure, dumbstruck. It wasn't my first time seeing it or the gorgeous grounds, and it wasn't as if the lone building rivaled the size of the Torok Mansion. But, unlike home, the portico wasn't masked with vines of trailing English Ivy; flowers of every variety spilled from massive pots, cascading from window boxes, while still more rested snugly within the English gardens.

Dogwood, cherry blossom, and rosebud trees lined the winding drive, providing visitors a breathtaking canopy bursting with color. A large lattice trellis, supporting the impressive weight of gigantic climbing rosebushes, served as a welcome mat just outside the entrance.

The Club had steep membership fees not within most of the community's reach. Only a sprinkling of my classmates had ever ventured onto the grounds. I felt certain my parents had plunked down an exorbitant sum to ensure that our class party was unforgettable for both the privileged and disadvantaged.

Pondering again what my life might have been like had I

been raised on the salaries of a county clerk and a police officer, I was very aware of the many advantages the Toroks' wealth provided me. Would I have rather grown up surrounded by my biological parents, even if that meant giving up countless and tremendous benefits? Yes, without a doubt.

As I wrenched myself out of the Mustang, it seemed every one of my classmates had arrived, and were now gathering within a courtyard hosting a myriad of vendors and entertainers as well as some well-known celebs. The lights surrounding the pool were red and blue—Madison High School's colors—which twinkled, dappling the water with intermittent patches of vibrant hues.

Custom-made signs at every caterer's station identified the cuisine, and—not surprisingly—John's Brat and Dog Stand, a famous Manhattan vendor, boasted the longest line. Heavy Hearts, the hottest band on the entire East Coast, was setting up, and I assumed my parents shelled out at least twenty grand to seal the deal.

Nick offered a lame apology before abandoning me altogether. My insecure gaze hovered over the crowd, and, despite the large turnout, I had never felt more alone. Tristan's eyes met mine from across the lawn, and I couldn't draw a breath. *Please, please, please don't come over here!* I watched him approach, quickly realizing I wasn't the only one that couldn't tear my eyes away. Luna McCormick's tongue was nearly on the ground. She glared in my direction when Tristan landed at my side.

"Celestine, I'm so glad you survived your brother's lunacy," he said, in a tone that exuded all things testosterone. My thighs quivered, and I prayed he didn't possess Bianca's mindreading capability.

I responded, the words coming in shudders so that most of what I'd said was undecipherable. I tried again. "Well, you know Nick. He always has to push the boundaries."

Tristan motioned toward the far end of the courtyard where I caught a glimpse of Nick's back disappearing through the crowd.

"Speak of the devil. It would seem Nicholas is attempting another escape. I shall return posthaste," he said, the crowd pressing his body against mine, causing my every muscle to twitch. "Save a dance for me!" he called over his shoulder, and I considered making an escape of my own.

Left to fend off a barrage of jealous glares from nearly every female within range, I acknowledged Warren waving from Cortez's Tamale and Taco food line. I waited until he took a seat at an empty table beside the pool, then joined him. I sat patiently beside him and watched as he inhaled a second taco.

Warren shoved in the last bite and parked it inside a cheek.

"I need to talk to you about something," he said, pausing long enough to pick a glob of shredded cheese from his bottom lip. "I told my dad about us. You know, about the ring and everything."

I shrugged my shoulders, creating a little distance between me and his cilantro and cumin-scented breath.

"So?"

"I need the ring back," he stammered, never once taking his eyes from his plate. "I mean, you can keep the ring, but it can't mean anything."

"Oh . . . so now we're officially unpromised?"

Forking a whole tamale, Warren managed only a quick nod as he crammed nearly the entire corn delicacy into his mouth.

"Why?" I asked, but only because I felt he owed me an explanation.

Warren's eyes darted to everyone within earshot. "I don't think we should talk about it here."

I took off the ring and set it beside his plate, then I popped to a standing position and considered calling Bianca for a ride home.

"It's because my dad thinks your parents are atheists, okay?" he whispered, pulling me back down and pressing the ring into my palm.

"And because your dad's a minister . . ."

"Yeah, it's a really big deal."

"For your information, my parents are not atheists!"

"That's not what my dad says."

I tossed the ring on top of his other tamale.

"You know, it's probably for the best, Warren. I mean, who wants to spend a lifetime competing with food!" I pulled Bianca up on my speed dial as I walked away, then reconsidered. I wasn't in the mood for a conversation consisting of *I told you so*, whether communicated in Romanian, English, or any of the other numerous languages she'd had centuries to learn. Instead, I decided to search for Nick, even though he was most likely christening the backseat of his new car with who-knows-who.

The wind unexpectedly came up. Dark menacing clouds replaced puffy pristine ones. Needle-like raindrops pelted the crowd, and everyone scampered for cover.

"No one seems capable of forecasting the weather," I heard Tristan say behind me as we filed inside. He clucked his tongue playfully and added, "In this day and age—what with all the meteorological instruments available—that is dreadfully inexcusable. I must say Aristotle's probably turning in his grave this instant; that conceited Greek could predict fair weather by simply observing a red moon!"

I indulged him with a smile. Aristotle was another of whom I'd heard my fill. "Did you find Nick?"

Tristan whispered in my ear, "I know exactly where he is. I doubt you wish to hear the details."

He was right. Thanks to Tristan, my ears were tingling enough as it was.

"Allow me, m'lady," he said, pulling a chair from a table dressed in fine linen. "I shall return with a feast intended for a . . ."

His eyes swept over the various food vendors, who'd since moved their carts indoors, and he produced a dramatic sigh. "I shall do the best I can."

I shouted after him. "That's okay, I'm really not . . ." In truth, I was famished. But I knew with Tristan seated beside me, I'd be lucky if anything other than drool made its way to my stomach.

When he returned, I hid my trembling hands under the tablecloth. "Perhaps, I should have solicited your input," he said, setting a plate consisting of various raw vegetables and fruits before me.

"No, no, this is fine. Thank you," I said and took a mouse-sized bite from a carrot stick, pretending anyone and anything else within the room held my interest.

I heard him laugh—a shameful tactic meant to gain my attention—and I felt I had no choice but to acknowledge him.

"Celestine, why are you always so skittish around me? I am, after all, your father's son."

I failed to disguise a shiver as I fought a wave of nausea. I suddenly wished myself invisible. If only I had Bianca's capabilities.

"Why is it you cannot think of *me* as a brother . . . think of me as Nick?"

I laughed. Actually, it was more a pathetic chortle.

"Well, you and Nick *are* a lot alike."

He threw his head back and laughed, his eyes crinkling at the corners and bursting with amusement. "Why do I get the impression you did not intend a compliment?"

I arched both eyebrows and wagged my head. "Most every guy in here would consider that a compliment. *Every* one of them wishes they were Nick."

With one eyebrow wiggling mischievously, he said, "Yes, I

imagine this is true." He cocked his head in the direction of the parking lot. "Particularly, at this very moment."

I puffed my cheeks and mumbled. "Like I said, you and Nick are a lot alike."

"Perhaps, you should announce yourself before entering a room."

I knew he was referring to his and Yesenia's hookup session I'd witnessed in the kitchen. When I didn't answer, he ducked his head so he could see my eyes. My cheeks flushed, and a wave of nausea struck. "Can we change the subject?"

"Ah, now I've gone and embarrassed you."

"It's not me who should be embarrassed."

"You know, Celeste, every once in a blue moon, you might consider giving into an urge of your own."

Jutting my chin toward the ceiling, I said, "I don't know what's wrong with a little self-control. It's what separates us from the animals."

He bumped my shoulder playfully with his. "Oh, so now you think me an animal?"

"Go ahead; make fun! Life is so easy for people like you and Nick. All you two have to do is smile your wicked little smiles, and anyone with a pulse falls at your feet!"

He propped a cold finger under my chin and forced me to look at him.

"I don't think your issue lies with self-control, or a lack thereof, but rather the fact you have yet to master the art of persuasion. I must say, envy is a most unattractive and futile emotion, particularly as it involves you, Celeste."

I turned away. "Yeah? Well, thanks for the advice, but I doubt my thinking differently is going to change how people see me."

"And how do they see you, Celeste?"

I shrugged my shoulders and focused on the band setting up.

"Shall I tell you how I see you?"

I slapped a hand on the table and whirled to face him. "This isn't about me! It's about Nick. And I was wrong when I said you're just like him because you're not! You'll always have your great looks and all that," I paused and ran my eyes over every inch of him, "swagger and charm. But Nick won't.

Someday, he'll just be another pathetic old man, who awakened one day to find life had passed him by. Some pathetic old man offering women money in exchange for a little attention."

"Celeste," he whispered, his tone calm and reassuring, "Nick is merely going through a phase, sowing his oats, if you will. You mustn't take life so seriously."

I turned my back on him and dug through my purse in search of my cell phone.

"Celestine, please. I'm sorry if I have upset you. Can we begin again?"

When I faced him again, I saw a glimmer of sincerity in his eyes, something I'd never before seen. "It's not just you."

Tristan put his hand on my shoulder. "Please, enlighten me."

I rolled my eyes and sighed. "Warren asked for his ring back. He said his father thinks Razvan and Bianca are atheists."

His posture stiffened, and every muscle in his face flexed.

"Ah, the timeworn squabble. Men waste precious time on the judgment of others."

"Are they . . . atheists?"

A few minutes passed before he said anything.

"It is not that they have abandoned God, Celestine." He shook his head. "No, quite the contrary. They fear it is God who may have abandoned them. I cannot say for certain."

I nodded my head and swiped a tear from one eye. My parents were immortal, so of course, I just assumed *eternal life,* in a spiritual sense, wasn't something they would concern themselves with. It had never occurred to me that once I died, we would never see one another again.

Tristan misread my sudden and overwhelming sadness.

"I am sorry this boy has ruined your evening."

I wanted to explain, wanted to discuss the finality of death, as it applied to me and the only parents I had ever known. Instead, I said, "Honestly, I was relieved. I guess I feel a little guilty about that."

He laughed and took my hand in his. "Celestine, this is what makes you special. You put the feelings of those you care about above your own. Believe it or not, I was once the same way."

Over the next half-hour, he told me about many of his failed relationships; all the women he had loved and lost and how he would have given his life for one in particular.

"You were married?" I interrupted at one point.

The sparkle in his eyes ebbed to dark lifeless orbs. "Yes, a long, long time ago."

"But why . . .?"

"Isn't she with me?" Following my nod, he offered only, "She died."

The question I wanted to ask was infinitely more difficult than the traditional *what happened?* I was relieved when he asked it for me.

"You want to know why she wasn't immortal, like me."

I nodded and heard myself swallow.

"Many years have passed, centuries to be factual. You see, I could not bring myself to interfere with her mortality nor our son's, even when presented the opportunity, and even though that meant losing them, forever. I miss them terribly," he added, long lashes hiding what I assumed were haunting memories.

"I'm so sorry."

"Now, perhaps you can understand why I do everything

and anything to distract myself." Before I could protest, he dragged me toward the dance floor.

"Uh, I don't dance," I said as he wrapped his arms around me.

"We shall see."

We danced one dance, then two, and by the third dance, I'd become numb to just about everything, including Aubrey's malicious glances. I felt a sensation of floating within Tristan's arms. With each revolution we made, I scanned the dance floor, and I got the sense that for the first time in my life, I was the envy of every girl in the room—for something other than being Nick Torok's sister.

CHAPTER 10

$\mathcal{T}$he building shook following another clap of thunder. The lightning illuminated the grounds beyond the windows. The power blipped off, then on consistently, giving the dance floor a Disco vibe. The musicians abandoned their instruments and rushed offstage, when suddenly a scream sounded from outside.

Tristan was already halfway to the exit when another bolt of lightning lit up the swimming pool beyond the glass enclosure. I strained to see through a curtain of brutal rain and caught a glimpse of Nick floating lifelessly.

I ran madly toward the exit, and once there, I managed to fling the door open despite the competing wind. Tristan was already in the pool. Nick's companion looked as if she'd seen a ghost, and I suspected she'd witnessed Tristan defy the laws of gravity.

"Inside, Celestine!" Tristan shouted. I refused but ushered the stunned girl to safety.

When I returned, I watched Tristan drape Nick across the pool deck, my brother's lifeless body still smoking; the apparent result of a direct lightning strike. Tristan slanted eyes my way, and his solemn expression told me everything I needed to know: my brother was dead.

I screamed again, Nick's name ringing in my ears. I rushed to the pool, but Tristan blocked my path. Somehow, I bulldozed my way past him and crumpled beside my brother. His eyes were open, locked in a dead stare. I attempted CPR, despite Tristan insisting it hopeless.

"Do something!" He ignored me and merely stood there, shaking his head and scrubbing his face. "Bring him back, Tristan! Please bring him back!" When Tristan didn't respond, I lunged for him, my fingernails lancing his thin tee shirt.

He grabbed my hands and held me at arm's length.

"Nicholas is gone, Celeste! We must accept it."

I broke free, hammering fists against his chest. "Do it! Even if it means he's to become one of you! I'm begging you, Tristan!"

"Celestine, I cannot! You know it is forbidden!"

I couldn't look at Nick. Sobbing uncontrollably, my body melding with the pavement, I raised my head an anguished heartbeat later, only to discover Nick and Tristan both gone.

I HEARD Bianca yelling somewhere off in the distance. Slipping and sliding, I darted across the slick pool deck, running past the anxious and awestruck expressions of several classmates huddled beyond the windows. I followed Bianca's voice into several acres of dense timber. With branches tearing at my arms and face, I kept going, the deep woods eventually yielding to a lush meadow. There I discovered her involved in a heated standoff with Tristan.

"What have you done?" she shrieked in a decibel so shrill, I instinctively covered my ears. Immediately aware of my presence, she instructed me to return to the clubhouse.

"No! Not until I see Nick!"

"I'm here," I heard Nick say from somewhere beyond Bianca. "Come here, little sister," he said, his voice unfamiliar, eerie, almost singsong.

"Nick," I cried as I once again attempted to fight my way past both Bianca and Tristan.

"No, Celestine!" Bianca shouted, her index fingers spraying sparks like downed electrical lines.

Suddenly freefalling through the air, I landed on my butt the opposite side of the meadow. Jumping upright, I bolted once again in Nick's direction. Halfway across the wide expanse, I encountered an invisible but sticky shield, preventing me from going any farther.

"Please, Mom, I have to see him!"

"She must not see him like this," Tristan said, towering over Bianca despite both her feet hovering a foot or more above the ground. His chameleon eyes transitioned to red with sporadic emerald green fissures slithering across his retinae.

"Perhaps she should! Then maybe she will understand why certain measures must be taken."

"I forbid it!"

Bianca laughed and levitated until she stood eye to eye with Tristan, the ends of her long hair morphing into tiny blades and slicing through the air. "*You* forbid it! Ha! You shall rue the day you challenge me!"

"I only beg that you reconsider."

Bianca threw her head back and screamed something Romanian into the dark clouds racing overhead. "Very well! Off with you before I change my mind. Return Celestine home posthaste. The Counsel shall decide your fate!"

Within the meadow one minute, my feet were planted on the courtyard at Torok Mansion the next. I staggered, and Tristan gently seated me on a bench.

I hardly recognized him. His skin glowed, and his pointed incisors were still visible. Blood dripped from his chin, which I assumed had come from Nick. Shivering, I summoned the courage and finally asked.

"So Nick—"

"Yes, Nick is immortal." Tristan interrupted before he turned away, refusing to look me in the eye. "Just remember, Celeste, this is what you wanted."

I wanted my brother in my life, even if it meant he'd become one of them. "What's going to happen now?"

"If he survives, Nick will require constant monitoring."

"*If* he survives?"

Tristan whirled to face me, and I fell back. His skin was totally transparent, a phenomenon I knew occurred when vampires surpass the equivalent of an emotional breakdown, extreme rage, or the result of a pack mentality during battle. Pointed fangs, now much more pronounced, poked through flaccid gums.

"As I said, Celeste!"

"I . . . I don't understand. If he's immortal, he can't die. Isn't that true?"

Tristan ignored me and suddenly sank to his knees. "Dear God, what have I done?"

I ran to him, cradling his head in my hands, his bloody tears smoldering before they contacted his cheeks. "I'm so, so sorry, but I couldn't lose Nick."

Tristan pushed me away.

"You must prepare yourself, Celeste. Because Nick is reckless and disobedient, his survival is doubtful. To die a mortal death is a Godsend by comparison."

"What do you mean?" When Tristan didn't respond, I sprang to my feet, fisting both hands. "Tell me!"

"If he refuses instruction, he will be destroyed."

"Destroyed? By who, my father?"

Tristan sighed. "What does it matter, Celeste?"

Fisting strands of hair at the roots, I shook my head hard, like a child in the midst of a tantrum.

"Why weren't you with him? This is your fault! You were supposed to be looking out for him!"

"And I shall pay the price," Tristan said softly. "Get away from this place, Celestine. Go, live your life."

I pushed him away. "I'll never leave Nick."

"There is nothing you can do for him," Tristan whispered, taking me in his arms. A moment after, he was gone.

I remained standing in the courtyard, looking wistfully in the direction of the Country Club. Eventually giving up my intent to wait outside, I sagged through the front door, where I collided with Yesenia.

"Do you not possess the slightest bit of intuition? As I've said before, you are pathetic."

Sweeping hurriedly past her, I asked, "Where's my father?"

"Undoubtedly, he is preparing to clean up your mess. That's what Nicholas is, you know. A mortal mess if ever I have seen one." She laughed suddenly. The discordant sound coerced a flock of reluctant eastern goldfinch, feeding at an old ornate metal birdfeeder—crafted by Leonardo Da Vinci and gifted to Bianca—into flight. "Perhaps the more recent chain of events warrants a correction. Nicholas is an *immortal* mess if ever I have seen one." She flicked her hand, and I landed with a thud against a marble column. "I have always known you would be Tristan's end," she pushed past pointed incisors. After that, she vanished, the house enveloping me in an eerie calm.

~

FROM MY BEDROOM WINDOW, I witnessed Nick return home shortly after midnight. Thrashing about and wailing as if someone had set him on fire, Tristan, Bianca, Razvan, and Yesenia all struggled to bring him indoors. Despite the distance between us, I hardly recognized my brother or his agonizing cries.

Yesenia looked up, her menacing stare trained on my window, and I immediately shrank back. Wringing my hands, I left footprints on the dense lavender carpet I hadn't thought attractive long before my twelfth birthday and pressed an ear to the door. When my legs began to cramp and the outer edge of my ear grew numb, I gave up and went to bed. I was just surrendering to deep sleep when Yesenia's ominous shadow fell across my bed, her breath falling across my face, the scent reminiscent of a biology experiment gone wrong.

"I have come to share your precious brother's suffering." I mustered a glare, which seemed to effect little discouragement. "Imagine, if you will, your body pulled apart bone by bone, muscle by muscle, cell by cell, all the while both heaven and hell vying for your soul! Do you honestly think your dear brother will thank you for bewitching Tristan into *saving* him?" Her mouth frothed, ice crystals spattering on my forehead. "He'll hate you for it! But not nearly as much as Tristan shall. Once Razvan orders annihilation, your name will be on his tongue as the sun ravages his core. You have destroyed them both, you selfish little wench!"

She flicked her wrist—her irises now a piss yellow, the pupils a steely gray and pulsating like a strobe light on steroids —and I sailed across the room. Disoriented, my ears began to ring. I shook my head and resisted an urge to blackout. A cloud of smoke wafted through the air, and Yesenia appeared directly in front of me. She bent over me, then morphed into something grotesque. Now, resembling an octopus with a dragon's head, her mouth flew open, and fire erupted from it, scorching the wall at my back. I sprang onto my feet and nearly made it to the door when giant slimy tentacles encircled me. My ribs ached. I considered she may have broken or cracked, at the very least, more than one. A scream lodged in my throat as I gasped for breath.

CHAPTER 11

*Y*esenia must have sensed Bianca nearby because she released me and disappeared within a heavy veil of smoke, a sulfuric smell lingering in the air long after. My head throbbed, a consequence of blocking my thoughts from Bianca. I was fearful of what might happen to her should she and Yesenia ever engage in battle. I knew my mother was a formidable warrior, but I had never met anyone, immortal or otherwise, who embodied evil quite like Yesenia did.

Though they'd secured Nick in the basement, two flights below my room, I could still hear his incessant, mournful cries. Similar to what I'd heard inside the Circle, Nick interspersed his cries with demonic laughter and insincere promises. Bianca suddenly appeared beside my bed.

"You are forbidden to see him. This is not open to discussion!"

I knew this was something her clairvoyant ability would alert her to, but I had thought her wrath was a small price to pay for even a miniscule chance of laying eyes on Nick.

I nodded in agreement. "What will happen to him?"

She arched an eyebrow and looked away.

"Why won't you tell me?"

Her expression softened and she knelt beside the bed. "This is not something that can be forecasted, Celestine."

"And Tristan, what about him?"

"That is none of your concern. Tristan made his choice."

"But I—"

"Unlike Tristan, you will have years to reflect on your mistake."

"He did his job," I shouted. "He made sure Nick came home."

"We both know that is absurd, Celestine! As you yourself told Tristan, if he'd done his job, this would not have happened."

I grabbed her arm, pleading. "Doesn't he deserve another chance?"

I saw a glimmer of sadness wash over her eyes. "It is for your father to decide, though a vote is customary in an instance such as this. Be advised, Celeste, Yesenia and a few others have already called for extinction."

I bit my lip but considered telling Bianca all Yesenia had done. All six windows in my room suddenly flew open, and I yanked the covers over my head. Several panes shattered, littering the floor with daunting shards of glass.

Bianca's eyes locked on mine, and I felt a familiar tickle like a feather stroking my brain. I attempted to block her.

Scowling, Bianca loomed over me. "What are you hiding, Celestine?"

"I'm not hiding anything." Admitting Yesenia's behavior would only make matters worse. "Won't you talk to Razvan?"

"What could possibly make you think I do not align myself with the others?"

"Because you care about Tristan, too. I've seen the way you look at him, heard the way you talk about him."

She sighed and chirped a semblance of a laugh. "I have said my goodbyes to much dearer friends, Celestine!" Sadness suddenly marred her perfect face. "Ah, mortals have no concept of a true *end*."

"Where were *you*?" I asked, my abruptness intentionally calculated.

She winced in response. Surely, Bianca, the self-professed reader of all minds, had known of Nick's peril, yet chose not to act.

"Hardly *self-professed*, scumpa mea," she whispered. "I shall forgive your petulant manner; it would seem you are finally adapting the ways of your insolent brother. I don't have to remind you where that has gotten him!" She smoothed my brow, her hand then gently brushing my cheek. "As I have told you before, I do not always know Nicholas's thoughts. Even if I had I that ability, how could I possibly predict a capricious bolt of lightning when Nicholas, who was himself present, did not see it coming!"

"Why can't you hear his thoughts? Because you no longer care about *him*?" She didn't respond, but her expression told me all I needed to know; she would have left Nick in the water until the coroner arrived, regardless of how losing my twin might affect me.

"Razvan and I vowed both of you would remain mortal, Celestine!" she said in response to my thoughts. "Tristan knew this was non-negotiable."

"I don't believe you! I don't think you've ever forgiven Nick!"

"This has nothing to do with Vykoka and the attack! For God's sake, I think of Nicholas as a son, Celestine."

"Yet, *you* would have left him to die!"

"He *is* dead, something I cannot seem to make you understand! Your brother, as you knew him, is no longer. Those memories you hold so dear, treasure them for there will be no more. We have Tristan to thank for the hellish ones on the horizon."

Sobbing uncontrollably, I told her, "How am I supposed to live with this? Because of me, Nick, Tristan—"

"Calm yourself, Celeste. We mustn't let this destroy the rest of us," she interrupted, her tone comforting and reassuring. "Being mortal was difficult, Celeste. Oh, how I remember! But far less complicated because dead was dead, and the loved ones either survived such a tragic loss or they didn't. There were no difficult decisions. It is most unfortunate Tristan chose to intervene. Because of his reckless disobedience, possibly the most difficult decision awaits us."

"I don't understand! What about you and Razvan? Someone must have intervened."

Bianca intertwined her fingers, her eyes fleetingly glowing the color of a blood moon. "No one."

"Then how—"

"Decidedly different situations, ones I do not wish to discuss."

"Okay, then how did you two . . . die? Can you at least tell me that?"

"If you'd been listening closely, Celestine, you would realize your question answered."

No one intervened. "Then that can only mean one thing: One of those disgusting creatures attacked you!"

She raised an eyebrow, and I knew I had my answer. "Why are we discussing this, Celeste?"

"Because you two wouldn't be here right now if it weren't for that, and things worked out for you. If Tristan hadn't done what he did, I never would have seen Nick again."

"Nick," she uttered aloud, followed by a sinister laugh. She stared straight ahead, and I assumed she reflected on the past. "I'm surprised he has survived his adventures, outwitted death, until this most unfortunate happenstance. Do you recall the beautiful pond near the rose garden?"

I shook my head.

Bianca tapped a finger to her temple. "Ah, yes. Of course, you do not. Well then, I suppose I have a confession to make."

My stomach clenched as I imagined the possibilities.

Her eyes grew mysterious, and a thin smile stretched across her lips.

"Such things, traumatic occurrences and the like, are best not remembered."

My hand suddenly flew to my mouth, effectively burying a gasp.

"So, you're saying you did something to my brain; you erased a part of my memory?"

"But a snippet, Celeste! Heavens, you make it sound as if I'd performed a lobotomy!"

"Are you going to tell me what it is I can't remember?"

She sighed. "It was early summer, the summer after you and your brother arrived. Nicholas was supposed to be napping, but of course, the little demon sneaked out of the house. We discovered him and that dreadful yapping dog in his clutches, the one you and Nick insisted we tote back to New Jersey."

I hadn't thought about the Golden Retriever for years. "His name was Raff."

"Yes, yes, Raff. Ridiculous moniker, by the way. Nevertheless, the canine kept Nick above water until the fire department accomplished rescue."

"The fire department rescued him? Why didn't you or Razvan—"

"Suffer water of that magnitude, Celeste? I should think not!"

"Neither one of you can swim?"

"Pfft! Someday I shall explain an immortal's many perils."

"Why not tell me now?" I asked, not wishing to be alone, terrified Yesenia might return.

"Ah, where shall I begin?" she said, looking away. "I suppose, fittingly, with water. We require a purified form for bathing." I opened my mouth to ask her why, and she pressed a palm in my direction. "The reason remains a mystery. As you most certainly are aware, we keep our distance from all things equestrian and canine, werewolves being the exception when provided no other choice." She briefly studied me out of the corner of her eye. "We cannot bear children. Perhaps I should rephrase this—we will not bear children. Those who choose to do so produce offspring who lack souls."

"How do you know they lack souls? How can you be sure?"

She tipped her head toward her shoulder and served me a sarcastic smirk. "To us, it is as obvious as a child born without a limb. As with our aversion to water, the reason for this anomaly eludes us." She waved her hand, undoubtedly cognizant of the sadness suddenly overwhelming me. She smiled and interlocked her fingers with mine. "Do not look so forlorn, Celeste. It is no matter when I have you and Nicholas, my darling!"

I looked away and whisked a tear from my eye. Changing the subject, I said, "How many other things have happened that you chose I not remember?"

She pressed my arm. "You say you remember Raff."

I nodded.

"Do you remember what happened to him?"

I didn't.

"Do you wish to know? Think carefully, darling, before you answer for I will never tell you a lie."

I considered the possibilities and shook my head, preferring to remember Raff as I did.

~

I COULDN'T SLEEP. I sneaked from my bed and snugged in close to the twenty-five-foot column just outside my bedroom door. From there, I could see the expansive foyer beneath and

Tristan as he entered Razvan's study. I tiptoed downstairs and put an ear to the closed mahogany doors.

"The Omniscients will decree your punishment," I heard my father say to Tristan. "I need not tell you that the presumption is for a punishment most severe."

"I am ready, my King," I heard Tristan murmur.

I could hear footsteps pacing the floor. I assumed they belonged to my father. "If it were only possible to shroud this night's event from the others! I am certain you realize your importance to me, to us all."

"Harsh penance is most welcome and deserved. I ask only for your forgiveness."

"I have faced many difficult decisions. However, never have I encountered one more distressing." My father's voice cracked, and a heavy silence hung over the house. "If only it were possible to forget your assistance at my side throughout these many centuries, and the countless occasions our enemies would not only have obliterated our kind but also the humans we vowed to protect. This, Tristan, I attribute to your fearless dedication."

"'Twas an honor to fight alongside you."

CHAPTER 12

"*J* should think if you have learned but one thing this night, Celestine, it would be obedience," I heard Bianca say a split-second before she instantaneously appeared alongside me, just outside my father's study.

My heart still feeling as if lodged in my throat, I managed, "You only forbade me to go anywhere near Nick. I didn't realize you expected me to stay in my room!"

Her eyes flashed, and I immediately recoiled. "That is, precisely, what I expect. Now return to your room, Celestine! A heavy sadness is at hand."

Regardless of Bianca's instruction, I knew I couldn't rest until I laid eyes on Nick. I felt the familiar tickle again, the feeling as if a headache lay dormant, cranial nerves twitching just enough to serve as a precursor.

"What do you think of your brother now?" Bianca asked, telepathically allowing me a glimpse of Nick, as he lay writhing and cursing in a cage below.

I shook my head hard in a ridiculous attempt to eradicate such an impossible, dreadful image.

"It's likely he will never follow the Code. If that should happen, we will have but a single recourse; an option much more compassionate than that which you have borne witness. I would admonish you to take Nick's present affliction into account when the inevitable happens. Commit it to memory, Celestine! And in the end, you shall find a determination to annihilate Nick most merciful."

Shaking, I wrapped my arms around my body. "Did this . . . happen to you?"

"As I said, Celestine—as with everything else in his life, Nick continues to resist. Therefore, he's essentially caught in a world somewhere in-between that of the mortals and that of the immortals."

"Please, won't you give him more time!"

"Time is not a luxury. We must consider the possibility of Nick's escape." I had only just completed the thought when Bianca said, "You will not spirit your brother away! Don't be a fool, Celestine! Nick would most certainly destroy himself following a murderous rampage to include every human with whom he came in contact, as well as those only recently transitioned. You must take me at my word!"

"Please, Mom! Maybe if I talked to him—"

Bianca gripped my forearm violently, her touch so cold that purple welts formed immediately.

"Your safety is our greatest concern! Can you not understand that, in his current state, Nicholas perceives you merely as easy prey; a most delectable feast? And that is why your father has directed Lazarus to watch over him, ordered him to never leave your brother's side."

Slapping tears from my eyes, I said, "So it's already been decided? The Realm's intent is to destroy my brother?"

She wrapped me in her arms and stroked my hair. "Don't despair, my darling," she whispered. "We have yet to abandon Nicholas."

I'd always found her consolation comforting, and I stayed there in her arms for what seemed like not nearly long enough. Unwilling to surrender this rare and total tranquility, I hesitated.

"I see that now your thoughts have shifted to Tristan."

I looked up at her, my eyes begging the only answer I wanted.

"It is done."

I jerked free out of her reach, as if that possible.

"What's done?" I shrieked, my pulse marching loudly against my eardrums.

"Calm yourself," she murmured. "Razvan managed the impossible . . . amending the most important of the ancient doctrines." She bowed her head and seemed conflicted. "For, of course, your father's obligation to Tristan stretches beyond the battles they have fought side by side."

She glided across the colorful, mosaic tiled flooring, effort-lessly, the hems of her long skirts making a swooshing sound, and I caught of whiff of myrrh, an ancient herb to purify the dead.

"Do you remember the story I told you of Julius Caesar and Servilia?"

I nodded and curled my lip. "How could I forget."

"This was the night your father faced a decision most daunting, a consequence of Tristan's misbehavior. For you see, upon discovering his mistress's tryst with Tristan, Julius bathed his feared and renowned sword with Tris-tan's blood. One of Servilia's servants, possibly one who had inhabited the infamous bed I've previously described, set out to collect Razvan, clandestinely, of course. Although this was a night long ago, it continues to haunt your father, as his decision to offer Tristan the Adaptation was not one made easily. To the Realm's surprise, the Counsel allowed unexpected and utmost leniency of this; something of which I am certain they shall never replicate."

"But why are you telling me all of this," I asked, certain

her decision to share such personal information could some-how, someday, affect me.

"Should Tristan disobey the covenant again, Razvan will not be able to save him." A question was on the tip of my tongue. Bianca pressed a palm in my direction, and I knew she intended I only listen. "What chance do you suppose Tristan has at success should your eternity come into question? There-fore, if you truly care about Tristan, Celestine, you will forsake any notion of playing the odds."

I got her message loud and clear: Stay away from Nick.

Bianca shook her head. "No, scumpa mea, I remain unconvinced of your complete comprehension. Despite endangering his survival once again, Tristan will undoubtedly be compelled to protect you should Nicholas escape. He will find himself at a great disadvantage, Celestine, as he will no longer be able to know Nicholas's thoughts."

I had never realized he could. If that was true, apparently, he'd always been able to read mine as well! I flushed at the possibility. I shook my head, trying to come to grips with Tris-tan's capabilities and those of Razvan, Yesenia, and all the others. I had thought my mother was the only one with that particular talent.

She laughed suddenly and reached for my hand. "Do not dismay, my darling. A great deal of effort is required to accomplish this feat, and like mortals, we have our fair share of those either too self-absorbed or much too indolent to make such an attempt."

"But if Tristan once could read Nick's thoughts, why can't he now?"

"For the same reason your father is oblivious to Tristan's. Debated by many, this remains a phenomenon, the unproven explanations most complicated. Suffice it to say, Tristan will be of little use to Nicholas. As I said, Razvan has designated Lazarus Nicholas's chief-guardian. You alone," she began, an eyebrow nearly contacting her widow's peak, "and largely because Yesenia cannot be trusted, will become Tristan's priority—despite my contrary opinion."

I was both relieved and apprehensive. My feelings for Tristan were intoxicating and, obviously, quite dangerous.

But why could Tristan no longer read Nick's thoughts or Razvan Tristan's?

Bianca sighed, after which a marble column wobbled slightly, then rolled her eyes. "Why, my pet, do you persist in torturing yourself with the answer to such an impossible riddle? This is the way it has always been: Neither the Maker can know the protégé's thoughts nor his protégé know his."

"Is there any hope for Nick?"

"Time will tell, Celestine."

CHAPTER 13

*B*ack in my room, I could hear Nick calling my name, punctuated by his anguished cries, the metal covering the vent ducts rattling in response to each ear-piercing screech. I screamed into my pillow, my teeth gnashing together. When the sounds became more like a pathetic moan, I repeatedly called Bianca's name.

After getting no response, I shouted for Tristan. Suddenly, silence permeated every corner of the house. Was I the only one who perceived absolute silence as deafening?

I thought I heard footsteps outside my door. Throwing the purple coverlet—boasting all the constellations—aside, I slid from the bed. I tiptoed across the room, listening for any errant sound. Nick wailed my name again, just as he did the time he fell off his bike when we were six, or the time he waded too far out into the Atlantic Ocean without his life preserver. I whispered his name, then tried the door, antici-pating that Bianca had locked it from the other side.

Discovering it unlocked, a mishmash of emotions over-whelmed me, and I stood as though anchored to the ground. Fear of what awaited me advocated I stay in my room, prefer-ably within the confines of the closet. A sense of sibling oblig-

91

ation urged me to move my feet, through the door and down to the cellar.

Nick called for me again. With unsteady footing, I crept into the hall. Taking the stairs to the first floor, my feet testing each step as one might a field filled with landmines, I arrived to find the rooms deserted. Standing just outside the door leading to the basement, a ripple of frigid air suddenly swirled around my ankles. My heart thudded against my chest, and I inhaled, wondering if an exhalation would ever follow. Nick howled my name in that way he'd always done when he was terrified.

I crept down the stairs slowly, consistently peering over my shoulder. When I reached the bottom, I flicked on a single fluorescent light that hummed an eerie static in response, like a captive insect struggling to free itself from a net. A shrill cry permeated the large, dank space, and I tripped over a drain cover, staving off a nasty fall by clutching a suit of armor I doubted a replica. Fighting the temptation to backtrack up the stairs, I prepared myself for what lay beyond the eight-by-ten-foot wired cage.

I smothered a scream when my eyes fell upon Nick's nearly transparent skin, and his mouth twisted into a contemptuous snarl as sharp incisors dripped thick green mucus.

"Go!" he warned, his tone desperate and unfamiliar.

I called his name softly, and he crossed the space between us in the blink of an eye. He plowed repeatedly headlong against the cage, and the heavy-gauge steel anchors loosened upon impact. The structure continued to rock, and he screeched a decibel so ear-piercing I covered my ears and bolted for the stairs. Just as I reached the narrow landing, Yesenia wafted through the closed door.

She lifted her head over her shoulder as if it were no longer attached to her body. I gasped, then took a step back, nearly missing the stair below. Turning to face me, she revealed an expression so unexpected and gruesome, I grabbed hold of the banister to prevent a fall.

"Where do you think you're off to?"

"My room," I said, mustering as much defiance as I was capable. "Where are my parents?"

She licked her lips, the rims of her eyes intermittently polychromic. "Six feet under in a Kansas City cemetery. But then, that wasn't my doing. I would have at least granted them immortality." She licked her lips, forming a hideous smile. "Yes, my dear Celeste. Had I my way, your pitiable parents would have spent eternity in a cage; their blood spilled at my beck and call."

She drifted toward me, and I toppled down the stone stairs.

Nick continued to rock the cage, his face morphing from the Nick I'd always known to one I didn't recognize. I staggered to my feet, determined to make a break for it because suddenly, everything made sense. Yesenia was both Razvan's and Bianca's *Maker*. That's why neither of them sensed her abuse, why neither ever came to my defense. I debated whether or not to tell them as I pushed past her, taking the stairs two at a time.

"You actually think they will believe you?" she shouted after me.

I turned to face her contemptuous grin, her thin lips morphing into something reptilian.

"I have deceived the most brilliant minds for centuries. Madame de Stael, Galileo, Blaise Pascal, Gottfried Wilhem von Leibniz, Emanuel Swendenborg, even Da Vinci!"

Because it was obvious her objective was to keep me there regardless of my behavior, I smirked. "You forgot to mention Einstein."

"Einstein's IQ was but one-hundred-sixty," she said sneering. "He was hardly in the running." She came closer, and I narrowed my nostrils in a lame attempt to ward off her musty, icy exhalations. Then I blacked out.

~

Consciousness wormed its way back in just as Bianca appeared at my bedside. I didn't remember anything past my encounter with Yesenia in the basement.

Concern crisscrossed Bianca's face. "Are you ill, Celeste?"

I shook my head.

"You look positively pallid," she said, unconvinced, and pinched my cheeks with painful enthusiasm.

"Where's Father?" I hoped to not only change the subject but also learn Tristan's whereabouts.

Her lips pursed, and she averted sad eyes.

"Where would you think, Celestine?"

"With Nick?"

"Yes, with Nick."

"Is everything all right?"

She produced a tiny laugh. "As much as can be."

"Are they here?"

"No, they are not."

"That's all you're going to tell me?"

"Your father feared for Nick's safety and has taken him away."

I bolted upright.

She pushed me toward the pillow. "He will return when the time is right."

"Why would he fear for Nick's safety?"

"This is an opportunity the others have long awaited," she explained. "It is in Nick *and* Razvan's best interest to return to the old country. There, the Omniscients can offer protection and the degree of guidance Nicholas's current situation warrants."

"Who are the Omniscients?"

She placed a cold, inflexible hand over mine, her protracted fingernails nearly slicing the bedding.

"Our Elders, each one monumentally erudite."

"And what if they can't . . . help Nick?"

Bianca's eyes softened. "Ah, mortals! Such angst wasted on conjecture. I'll make you some tea," she said and forced me back into a prone position with no physical interaction whatsoever.

"I don't want to sleep," I argued, certain that was exactly what I could expect after a cup of her tea.

"Very well. As you wish." She swiped her lips across my sweaty forehead. "Until your father returns, matters of the Realm require both Tristan's and my attention. Rest assured, Yesenia will be close by. Despite your differences, your well-being is a task she will not take lightly."

A surge of cold air suddenly ravished the room, and Bianca's long auburn curls billowed behind her. She lurched forward, her black eyes piercing mine. "What is it, Celeste?"

I stayed quiet, my head swimming as she again attempted to annex my thoughts. With my father away, I thought it best not to broach the subject of Yesenia's wrath.

CHAPTER 14

*A*fter Bianca left my room, I slept a few hours, awakening to the sensation that I wasn't alone. An apprehensive glimpse toward the ceiling confirmed my suspicions.

"We didn't have the opportunity to finish our little chat," Yesenia stated contemptuously, her every word frostbiting my lungs.

I resisted the temptation to yank the covers over my head and instead snarled in her direction, feeling like a miniature poodle staving off a Rottweiler.

"I forget how easily frightened your kind becomes," she added, followed by insane laughter. "Forgive me, Celeste." Her words oozed sarcasm as she wound a handful of my long blonde hair around an arctic finger. "I assumed you would require comforting. That is why I am here." Leaning over me, a syrupy string of drool lingered, then plopped, landing just below my nose. "After all, it's most unfortunate such urgent circumstance did not allow you the opportunity to bid your dear brother farewell. Awe, horrid plight! With the deck stacked against him, it's quite possible, probable in all reality, you shall never have the opportunity."

I narrowed my eyes, convinced Yesenia—with her preter-natural abilities—could hear the sound of my heart thudding against my chest.

"Please leave my room."

She sucked her fangs, hovering closer still.

"Dear, dear, Celeste, I should be here in the event there is news of Nicholas's demise. The first twenty-four hours are, after all, Nicholas's most vulnerable."

"Why are you doing this? I thought you liked Nick!"

"I have nothing against the little Prince," she said with a malicious grin. "That's what he is now, you know . . . if he survives. The Insatiable Prince Torok."

Courtesy of Yesenia, 3D images of Nick hunting, then murdering humans filled my head. I rolled over and covered my ears. A split-second after that, she appeared on the oppo-site side of the bed.

"Awe, you are distraught! Did Bianca not explain the tribulations your brother must face?"

"I'm not listening to you anymore! Get the hell out of my room!"

"In due time," she spit and continued her oppressive explanation. "It is likely a rebel, such as Nicholas, will never adhere to the Code. The Toroks will never trust him—that I can promise you—particularly when it comes to the welfare of their dear, dear Celeste. Forgive my bluntness," she said, lowering her eyes and feigning benevolence. "Alas, it is my duty, as your provisional nursemaid, to offer a clear under-standing. Although his mortal heart still beats within his breast, many fledglings undergoing the change do not survive such an agonizing transformation. I would elaborate, but such horror is difficult to put into words."

When noticing the tears tracking my cheeks, she declared victory with a macabre grin, then vanished, leaving the shut-tered windows to clatter and the paintings on my walls askew. Every collective memory of my brother continued to play like a slideshow in my head—adventures we'd shared before kindergarten, the two of us playing on the beach, whether building sandcastles or simply racing the tide back to shore.

Other memories came, too, of challenging one another at various video games, rollerblading, tennis, skateboarding, even surfing. Sadly, I attributed these vibrant memories to Yesenia's sadism.

Hours later, I heard familiar voices and stealthily escaped my room. The interior shutters were closed, the heavy velvet draperies secured, and the bickering within my father's study, all were an indication the Realm had not retired at sunrise. I hugged the wall, just outside the study door and listened.

"Nicholas is resisting the change," I heard Stelian tell Bianca and wondered why my father's chief assistant was here, rather than by my father's side.

"Of course he is!" Bianca blasted.

"He is strong," Stelian went on to say, devoid of any emotion. "He will survive provided . . ."

". . . the Elders choose not to intervene," Bianca said, completing his sentence.

Stelian laughed hollowly. "Should they agree, a corrosive warning shall undoubtedly accompany such a consent!"

I heard Bianca puff her cheeks. "Once again, Nicholas has placed the entire realm in great jeopardy. Sometimes, I think if not for Celestine—"

I squeezed my eyes closed and covered my ears, success-fully drowning out the possibilities. *If not for Celestine, Nick would no longer exist,* or did she intend, *Nick would no longer threaten everyone else's existence?*

Stelian shifted his weight, the sword always in his company swinging, then coming to rest against his hip. "I thought you should know Razvan has yet to make his own decision regarding the Adaptation."

Following a protracted silence, Bianca said, "But without it, Nicholas will surely perish!"

"Forgive me, Mistress," Yesenia interrupted, "but surely our Master isn't considering it!"

"Why would he not? Nicholas is now the Prince, after all," Stelian replied, in an almost condescending tone.

"Regardless, a ridiculous risk, I should think!" Yesenia chimed in.

Once again, I considered Nick's fate. And yet again, I wondered if he'd have been better off if Tristan hadn't intervened. I'd spent hours self-reflecting, going over and over the what-ifs. Hadn't I been incredibly selfish, subjecting my twin to a world of chaos and uncertainty, possibly eternal damnation?

A few minutes passed, and Bianca broke the silence, which lay dormant beyond the door. "Tristan, perhaps you can offer perspective. After all, it is you who must bestow this preposterous preferment."

I had thought they'd sent Tristan away! A gasp escaped me; one so loud, it echoed throughout the long hallway. Thankfully, Tristan uttered a torturous sigh simultaneously.

"Perhaps, but I shall never defy Razvan nor question his judgment."

Yesenia sounded a belligerent laugh. "Never, you say? Do you not hear the absurdity in that statement?" By the shadows falling on the floor beneath the door, I knew she'd crossed the room. "For it is *you* who has wholly defied him!"

If Tristan responded, I never heard his reply.

"If he drinks what is Tristan's," Yesenia ranted, "Nicholas's power will surge, exceed that of his Maker, quite possibly that of our Masters! With all due respect, dear Mistress, can we afford to gamble our existence on such an unstable prodigious leviathan?"

"The decision is not yours to make," Tristan interjected, possibly directed at both Bianca and Yesenia.

Yesenia spoke again. An arctic mist billowing from under the door seeped into the hallway.

"Then spill your blood and fill that treacherous chamber, you fool! I have exhausted my caveat!" Afterwards, by the silence that engulfed the room inside, I knew she had gone.

I bolted at nearly a full run toward the sitting room. I slunk down opposite a wall of photographs, studying one of Nick and me, our first photo session as Toroks. Even as a small child, I looked as though the entire weight of the world rested upon my shoulders—sunken, hollow eyes, not even the semblance of a smile, while Nick appeared much as he always has, carefree and ready for mischief. The photos, arranged in chronological order, spanned the length of an entire wall and represented a timeline of our lives.

Coming upon the most recent addition—our graduation photo—I brushed a finger over Nick's phenomenal dimples, his perfectly sculpted nose, and marveled at his dazzling smile. The hank of blond hair, always present despite the best of efforts, swung low over his right eyebrow, a testament to his rebellious reputation. I closed my eyes, committing the photo-graph to memory, determined to remember Nick no other way.

Reluctantly, I wandered over to the table and picked up the photograph of my biological parents. Immediately, memo-ries of my time within the Circle engulfed me: 1997, Kansas City, the courthouse partially ablaze. The searing heat from numerous fires burning within and the choking smoke and dust made it difficult to breathe, difficult to see more than an arm's length in any direction. Through a smoky veil, a gaping hole in one side of the building allowed visual access to the street below. There, bodies lay scattered, most of the victims motionless. The Harvesters' preternatural screeches filled the air as they scavenged the building, determined to exsanguinate each and every mortal. Savagely attacking, their grotesque fangs punctured throbbing veins.

Razvan, Stelian, Tristan, Ariel, Paulo, Lazarus, and Lucas suddenly swept in. These men—most of whom I had known much of my life—transformed into shapes unfamiliar, shedding any semblance of a human form. Lazarus was the exception, outfitted in a suit of armor. They worked in pairs: Stelian alongside Razvan, Ariel with Paulo, and Lazarus with Lucas. Only Tristan fought alone. I realized their strategy as they overpowered one Harvester after another, successfully flinging them through any available opening and into the harsh sunlight. Their mournful cries, as their shapes contorted and smoldered, competed with the horrified screams of the observers lined up and huddled in small groups along the sidewalk outside. Within minutes, a hush fell over the crowd as the First Responders sidestepped pile upon pile of dust; the only thing that remained of the Harvesters.

Bianca, Trandafira, Yesenia, and Maria assisted the surviving mortals, instructing those able to walk to seek refuge in the sunlight. Then they turned their attention to those with the gaping wounds inflicted by the Harvesters. The first time I witnessed the event, I assumed Bianca anticipated further attacks when she instructed her warriors to drag the wounded nearer the opening. I shook my head, not wanting to remember the rest, now knowing full well what had really happened.

But the image persisted: Yesenia and her warriors launching wounded victims, including my biological parents, to the ground below, where—screaming and convulsing—those not-so-long-ago mortals disintegrated into ash. Now more than ever and largely because of what had happened with Nick, I completely understood that Bianca had no other option. The tragic chain of events had left the wounded in a state of limbo, not mortal and not immortal but something far more frightening; something in-between. Wracked with an onslaught of uncontrolled sobbing, I didn't hear her come in.

"Do you know how old that is, Celeste?" Bianca asked, intentionally misdirecting my focus to a map once belonging to Christopher Columbus.

"Over 500 years old," I sniffled, welcoming her distraction.

"Yes, my darling. Henricus Martellus drew it in 1491."

I nodded. "In Florence. I remember."

"Thus, Henricus was of Italian heritage?"

"No, he was German," I answered correctly.

Bianca applauded, as vibrant bursts of color coursed over her pale skin. "Yale *thinks* it has the original," she giggled, "but *we* know better." Her eyes flashed the way they always did when reflecting on something exciting from her extraordinary past. "Do you remember the stories I've shared of Christopher?"

I nodded, resisting a sigh.

"He was such an anxious little man," she said, happily reminiscing, "and always searching for something. Oh, to be with Columbus when he made his discoveries!"

I rested my chin on my palm, anticipating a lengthy discourse.

"King Ferdinand, you see, forbade any women aboard, the notion undoubtedly inspired by his wife, Isabella. Oh, how she would rant about women distracting the sailors! So, of course, one dare not consider stowing away."

I tugged at her sleeve. "Mom, you don't have to entertain me."

She chirped a sad laugh. "Celeste, you are much too intuitive for your own good." She glanced at the photograph. "I am sorry things could not have turned out differently."

"I know."

Her dark eyes shone cold, intermittent sparks flickering across the sclerae like comets in a game of tag while her pursed lips promised a lecture. "And *I* know you were listening outside the door. I also know you paid Nicholas a visit."

"I'm sorry, but Nick—"

"Nonetheless, you were forbidden. Perhaps now you can understand why."

I dipped my head and hoped I wouldn't always remember Nick that way. "What exactly is the Adaptation?"

"A mistake," she said, her stern words reinforced by a frosty glare.

"That's all you're going to tell me?"

Her spine stiffened, as she slanted eyes my way. "Do you really want to know?"

I nodded but heard myself swallow.

She sighed, microscopic crystal-like pellets crackling and popping, before evaporating altogether.

Witnessing the torment in her eyes, my heart ached. I'd expected the strange fog that usually accompanied her speaking of something painful, but not this.

"If you must, I shall attempt to describe it in layman's terms. Nicholas requires sustenance, something we cannot provide through customary means."

I knew that she was referring to the blood from Torok Laboratories—the source of the Toroks' seven-figure income and social prominence. I had figured out, long ago, the only reason the lab existed was to supply blood for members of the Realm, not to provide the world with state-of-the-art testing.

"So, Nick has to get the blood from Tristan?"

Bianca folded her hands in her lap, nodding sharply.

"Why Tristan? Why not you or Father, or one of the others?"

"Only the Maker should oblige."

"I don't understand."

"Darling, consider a pure formula versus a watered-down variety. The Maker-to-Fledgling transmission is not only the purest form but the most successful. This is how it has always been with our kind."

"What about the Harvesters?"

She curled her lips and flicked her wrist. "Consider them nothing but a pack of mutts. A most irreverent and heathenistic tribe! They will drink whatever is presented to them."

"What happens if the Elders prevent Tristan from giving Nick his blood?"

"We will not disobey their decision."

"So, you and Father won't give Nick your blood, and he'll die? Is that what you're saying?"

Bianca looked away, but I recognized fear and desolation in her eyes. "As it appears that is the word you most identify with, then yes, he will die. We shall have little choice but to destroy him."

"Then Tristan must give it to him!"

She hovered near the window and seemed to leisurely survey the enormous English garden bursting with peonies, hollyhocks, delphinium, lavender, and wisteria. It was obvious she was holding something back. She must have read my thoughts because she said, "Not to worry, Razvan will state his case, the Elders will agree, and your father will oversee the ritual."

"Has Tristan even done this before?"

"That is a matter most confidential. Even *I* am not privy to that information. Let us speak of something else."

I balled my hands into fists and rocketed upright. "Why won't you explain it to me?"

"Dear God, Celeste! Why must you torture yourself?" She gave in. "It is known as the Dark Deed and suitably so! Success depends on both the Maker and the fledgling. Tristan shall offer his blood to Nicholas. Whether he accepts it or not is wherein the problem arises. While I have the utmost faith in Tristan's abilities, I cannot say the same for Nicholas. He has not been and presumably never will be cooperative. If he refuses or consumes too much too quickly, Tristan will have little choice but to destroy him."

Hundreds of ice pellets suddenly shrouded the majority of her body, crackling and popping, while her eyes oozed blood.

I'd only seen her cry tears of blood on one other occasion: the night Vykoka and his pack nearly destroyed my father. Because I knew vampires only cried blood when inconsolable, overwrought, or essentially on the brink of a nervous breakdown, I grabbed her hand. "Mom, I'm sorry. Please—"

She pulled away. "Let's change the subject, shall we?" she said and turned her back to me again. Her shoulders shook as she gulped deep breaths, exhaling a frozen mist which covered the window in a layer of ice.

I racked my brain, desperate to come up with a distraction.

"Earlier, when you mentioned the old country, did you mean Romania?"

Bianca whirled to face me, her lips twisted into an awkward grin, and she opened her arms, cupping her fingers in my direction. I obliged and crumbled comfortably in her embrace.

"At least you didn't refer to my homeland as Transylvania. Oh, what does it matter, anyway? You won't find the old country on any map, Celeste. Not even your *Google*."

"But I want to know."

She sighed and appeared to consider. "Are you familiar with Admiral Richard Byrd?"

I nodded, vaguely recalling a few lectures in a history class.

"Then you're surely familiar with his expeditions involving the South Pole."

"Wait!" I gasped, pulling away, just enough so that I might study her eyes, suddenly recalling more details involving the explorer. "You're not saying the Hollow Earth actually exists?"

Bianca's melodic laughter once again filled the room. "Fortunately for the Omniscients, the mortals attributed the Admiral's claims of a mountain of coal sparkling with diamonds, yet unseen specimens of gigantic proportion, lakes, rivers, and lifeforms inside the earth to nothing more than hallucinations caused by the carbon monoxide toxicity he suffered during the expedition."

"So, he actually flew into a—"

"Cavity, a hole in the earth," Bianca interrupted. "A hidden city, to be more precise, and appropriately coined the Great Enchanted Earth."

"And these Omniscients hide out there?"

"To hide would suggest they are afraid of something. I can assure you, Celestine, the Elders are afraid of nothing."

"So why hasn't this enchanted earth been rediscovered?"

"Many great minds knew of its existence. The admiral was but one."

"Why would the others keep it a secret?"

"They never had the opportunity to publicize their finding," Bianca told me, and I knew by her sinister expression that the Omniscients had seen to that.

"What about Admiral Byrd? Why was he allowed to leave?"

"The admiral never departed his plane, so the opportunity to forever silence him never arose. For you see, he discovered the Great Enchanted Earth from the cockpit."

I ran her description of this unknown land over and over in my mind until my head throbbed. Unconvinced, I asked her, "How is that possible? I mean, seriously, mountains *under* the South Pole?"

"We are not discussing a city block, Celestine, rather four-thousand miles in its entirety."

"So why didn't the Admiral land his plane? It sounds like he had plenty of space."

"A very intelligent man, the Admiral, most intuitive," she said more to herself. "Because, you see, despite the Elders' assurance—by means of a telepathic transmission—that he had nothing to fear," she paused, a tight smile teasing her lips, "I don't think he believed them."

CHAPTER 15

"I'm going to the stables," I told Bianca. The thought of riding my Arabian stallion wasn't terribly appealing, but I knew that was one place she wouldn't insist she tag along. Not only was the sun nearly at its peak, but the horses terrified her.

Both Nick's horse, Rebel, and mine, Zeus, had destroyed the corral's enclosure the few occasions Bianca came within a hundred feet. The last time she abruptly materialized, Doctor Platt—the local veterinarian—had to sedate them. For the horses' welfare, I had begged her to keep her distance.

I curried Zeus and cleaned his hooves, although he required neither of those things; the stable master had arrived with impeccable references and always attended to every detail. Customarily rewarded for his good behavior, I collected several apple treats from a nearby bin and recklessly allowed Zeus to feed directly from my fingers. My cell sounded a snippet of *Crazy* by CeeLo Green, but I ignored Aubrey's call. Predictably, she followed up with a text.

Where have you been?!!

Lying to Aubrey wasn't easy. She should either become a

fortuneteller or apply for a position at Homeland Security. I've never been able to pull anything over on her, the exception being the truth surrounding my anomalous parents.

Nick's sick. I'm sick, I texted. *Hoping to see you by Friday.*

WTH? she texted back.

Flu. DON'T come over! If only the Torok household really suffered such a benign calamity.

Get better. Hugs.

I returned my phone to my back pocket and thought the interaction was much too easy. Knowing Aubrey, she was already seated behind the wheel of her '89 Chrysler LeBaron convertible and headed north, her purple hair soaring behind her, stopping only long enough for her to recover a couple of renegade hair extensions or reapply blue lipstick.

As I was listening for Aubrey's Chrysler charging up the drive, I returned Zeus to his stall, and Nick's horse nudged me again. Rebel, a Friesian, was a massive blue-black stallion, one of only three left in the world, as bullheaded as he was beautiful, almost as if he understood the rarity of his existence. Aside from his temperamental disposition, his size was equally as detrimental to his handlers, coming in at seventeen-hands —sixty-eight inches tall—at last report. To look him squarely in the eye, I needed a stepladder. Although his value exceeded one-million dollars, to Nick and me, he was priceless.

"I know, boy," I whispered, stroking his nose, my fingers gliding over the velvety texture. "I know you miss him. I miss him, too." Spending time with Nick was the only thing the horse enjoyed more than his gourmet treats. Swiping a rampant tear from my cheek, I led Rebel back to his stall and latched the door. He whinnied, low and mournful, and I slipped back in and plunked down in the far corner. He joined me there, nestling into a bed of straw, resting only a portion of his massive head against my thigh. I wondered if he too reminisced, remembering the exciting times with Nick, as we rode over acres of Torok Land, jumping fences and traversing creeks, the banks made slippery and perilous by periodic rainfall.

Just as Rebel closed his eyes, his soft snoring upsetting several blades of straw, he suddenly sprang on all fours, and his tiny ears—the only thing small about him—twitched a warning. Managing to maneuver out of his way in time, I remained in the corner, cooing softly and encouraging calm.

The sudden ear-splitting and unseasonal sound like ice contracting, then cracking, filled the barn. Cautiously, I eased a path between Rebel and the door, all the while whispering words of reassurance.

The needlepoint ivy, covering the majority of the large, old wooden structure, suddenly expanded, each bough twisting as its shadowy tentacles multiplied, and the inexplicable vegetation quickly obscured every window and both doors. The wind came up, its hurricane force whipping the phenomenal feelers free, and as I watched, the unfettered appendages took on the appearance of angry black crows.

The gale-force wind increased and, even though I'd grabbed hold of a support beam, my lower torso pitched north as the southern gust whistled through the barn; the continuous rumble similar to that of a freight train. Frantically clinging tightly to the beam, I curtained my eyes against the swirling debris. A few long minutes later, the tempest ended as abruptly as it had begun.

Surreptitiously peering out the nearest window, I tracked those things resembling crows to the woods. They perched on nearly every tree, like spectators at a sporting event, somehow unaffected by the hurricane-force blast. Their calls were atypical, not the usual mix of gravelly caws and clicks, but rather sinister and manic cheers. At least one hundred or more of these winged creatures suddenly swarmed two much larger soaring objects seemingly engaged in a vicious battle, bringing to mind a bizarre flash mob.

The wind further receding, I scaled the old wooden ladder,

which led to the hayloft. Once there, and not satisfied with the limited view, I mounted a newer, aluminum ladder and, rung by rung, made my way to the observation deck constructed years ago for Nick and me. From there, one could see for miles; in typical Torok splendor, the observation deck not only resembled a lighthouse but came equipped with a pair of Celestron Skymaster binoculars, as well as an Orion Refractor telescope. Mercilessly squeezing the binoculars, my sweaty palms marring the gutta-percha leather-like shell, although I was able to, transiently, glimpse my subjects, my mortal eyes were incapable of following such mystical momentum. Stunned deer appeared awestruck, the herd creating a safer distance just outside the woodlands, where these timid animals seemed to commiserate with the smaller woodlanders. Raccoons, squirrels, and chipmunks squatted alongside one another, while a few red-tailed hawks, three or more red-shouldered hawks, a barred owl, a great-horned owl, and a sprinkling of cardinals and blue jays huddled together near the trunk of a large oak tree. Each appeared to study the sky as if debating what kind of unworldly aberration had decided to invade their sanctuary.

The violent clash overhead increased, and the animals stampeded, the raptors and songbirds rocketing overhead in the opposite direction, the sudden cacophony of flapping wings nearly as loud as a hovering helicopter. Frightened, my trembling fingers lost their grip, and I dropped the binoculars, as the adversaries emerged from the woods, shrieking as they attacked one another, their battle far from over. One appeared to dominate the exchange, having intentionally lured its opponent from the shield the forest's canopy provided. The confrontation continued.

For nearly twenty minutes, unearthly laments followed thunderous crashes. Smashed repeatedly against tree trunks, through tree trunks, and finally overtop the tallest branch, the defeated one lay motionless, while the victor gloated over the remains before emerging through a wall of fire, its shadow diminishing the sun overhead as it soared toward Torok Mansion.

aking my way toward the house, three Torok guards approached wearing resolute expressions, further enhanced by draping dark hoods. "Our mistress insists on your return to the house," one said, his eyes darting from me to the woods and back to me again while the other two guards continually scanned the perimeter.

I nodded, resisting the urge to ask them just where they thought I was going, as I now stood only feet from the house.

Bianca suddenly appeared, her skin a sickly combination of gray and green, her eyes an odd color, one I'd never seen nor could accurately describe.

"You were wrong to deceive me!" she roared, her words echoing from her position under the courtyard awning and across the meadow, causing a covey of quail to attempt sporadic and clumsy flight. "Why would you conceal Yesenia's behavior? Never keep something of such significance from me again, Celestine!"

I swallowed past the lump in my throat while tipping my head toward the woods. "That was—"

"A solution to your problem: Yesenia will be a threat no longer."

"She's gone? For good?"

"We believe she was destroyed. Time will tell for I have borne witness to her escape of things equally lethal. She very well may be but licking her wounds as we speak." Bianca went on. "My instincts convinced me of something long amiss between you and Yesenia. Therefore, soon after you departed for the stables, I enlisted my power of observation, and discovered Yesenia's determination for you to never return. It would seem her objective was to startle the horses, which in turn would trample you beyond recognition. Only the Divine One knows what else lay in store for you from that point onward."

"She wanted me dead?"

Bianca clasped her hands and nodded. "Such a waste," she said more to herself. "Oh, the battles we fought side-by-side! The triumphs we celebrated!" Tristan appeared, suddenly, at her side. "Yet, she betrayed us all," she said more to Tristan. "The timing could not have been worse! Razvan is certain the others will come for us, and now we are missing one of our most formidable warriors." She took Tristan aside, and I strained to hear their exchange. "When you return from the Old Country, you must take Celestine to Kansas City. This night," I heard her say, afterwards dismissing him with a flick of her hand.

I planted my feet and set my jaw. "No, I won't go! Please don't make me." Her brows furrowed and, a blink later, I found her standing directly before me.

"You must! This is not up for debate."

"Let me go to Nick. Father can protect me there."

"Ha! A mortal in the company of the Elders? Impossible, Celestine! A lamb among lions, I should think! Even your father would be incapable of offering protection. You will depart for Kansas City and return only when I grant such a return safe."

"I'm sorry, Mom, but I won't," I said through blinding tears. I ran inside, my feet landing on every other stair, and hid in my room. I was sitting on my bed, brainstorming a way to change Bianca's mind, when a suitcase soared across the room, landing with a loud thump at the foot of the bed. Drawers suddenly flew open on their own accord from which several pairs of my favorite jeans sailed through the air, landing neatly folded inside the luggage. I was awestruck, rattled, but mostly annoyed because I knew everything I'd rehearsed, every debate I'd devised, Bianca also knew and had already vetoed them. I sulked downstairs, locking myself in the Music Room.

In an attempt to control the rage seething within, I ran my fingertips across the grand piano's ivory keys, reflecting on much happier times. I closed my eyes, forcing countless memories of Bianca's patient instructions, and more importantly, I thought of just how much she'd always meant to me. Something beyond the bow window caught my attention, and for a moment, time seemed to stand still as I admired the grotto—an artistic focal point for the picturesque waterfall— as if seeing it for the very first time. Nick and I had played there almost daily in years long gone; him splashing, me squealing with delight.

I passed Trandafira as I left the room, fixated on concluding my farewell ritual. She looked at me, as she always did, with the same sympathetic expression I'd seen when I was held captive within the Circle. I'd always had the distinct impression she believed mortals and immortals shouldn't cohabitate, but never more so than now.

Entering the large formal dining room, I vividly recollected Nick swinging back and forth, suspended from the gaudy chandelier—a gift for Bianca from France's King Louis XIV. Because Nick had chosen to utilize the small winding staircase leading to an exterior balcony as a catapult, Bianca demanded that the staff immediately dismantle the entire structure. I'd cried when Bianca ordered the staircase removed, and I often wondered why they hadn't done away with the chandelier instead.

From there, I sauntered toward my mother's workshop, a loft converted in grand eighteenth-century style, more specifically, Rococo, and easily accessed by the stairs leading from the main sitting room. The color scheme was pastel, the furnishings framed with the traditional gold, a Torok favorite, which dominated every ornate painting's frame and nearly every ornamental mirror. Strands of the eye-bleeding garnish metal persisted within the tapestries snugging every wall. When I closed my eyes, I could almost smell the piney aroma of turpentine infused within the oil paint, odiferous and mysterious, and hear Bianca's melodic humming lulling me to sleep as she painted, mostly English landscapes. I decided this was my favorite part of the house, the place I felt most safe. Tears welled in my eyes, dripping then pooling onto the nineteenth-century Persian-Tabriz-Haji-Jalili carpet, and I fled the room.

Relishing the coolness as my fingertips lovingly dusted the marbled tabletop within the gleaming and majestic entry hall, I studied the chandelier overhead, originally belonging to Anne Boleyn.

Embellished with a myriad of precious stones: diamonds, rubies, emeralds, sapphires, and the finest pearls, the fixture was not only breathtaking, but a work of art. According to Bianca, the candelabrum—as she refers to it—Anne never intended as a gift. It came to Bianca, fortuitously, the result of a grave misfortune. Suspecting King Henry VIII's interest lay in another, Anne enlisted Bianca to merely hide it, determined that the king should not toss her aside empty-handed. Days later, he ordered Anne beheaded.

Because Bianca had safeguarded Henry from a Spanish assassin, Henry allowed her to keep the chandelier. And, because she had to delicately stave off his many unwelcome and repulsive advances, Bianca felt she'd more than earned it.

"Ah, so this is where you've run off to," Bianca said from behind me.

"I guess I wanted one last look around."

She held out her arms. "Come here, child. Do you think I *want* to send you away? It is for your own good, Celestine. Can you not see that?"

I followed her to a sofa, which—according to legend—had once belonged to Marie Antoinette.

"Mom, will I ever see Nick again?"

"The situation with Nick is not progressing as we had hoped."

LATER, as I was seated at the kitchen island mindlessly picking at the generous serving of beef Wellington Trandafira had placed before me, I sensed Tristan nearby. When he appeared suddenly, we exchanged only a brief sideways glance. As he and Trandafira immersed themselves in quiet conversation, I attempted to decipher consequential words.

"It's time, Celeste," Tristan said, matter-of-factly, as if Kansas City was a death sentence.

"Isn't Bianca going to tell me goodbye?"

Tristan shook his head, and I knew he was hiding something.

"Is she with Nick?"

"It's time," he repeated.

"Why won't you answer me?"

With his prolonged sigh hanging in the air, he was across the room one moment and at my side the next, as if he were some sort of Marvel superhero taking flight. Towering over me, his body contacting mine, I suffered a sudden chill, so intense my chest ached, and I began to shiver.

"Yes, your mother is with Nick, Celestine! May we go?"

"Why is she with Nick?"

"Celestine, are you such an imp that you cannot grant Nicholas your mother's transitory attention?"

Trandafira shook her head, an expression of utter disgust distorting intense features. Clenching my fists, I spoke directly into his face, unaffected by the sudden pinkish hue transforming his skin.

"This has nothing to do with jealousy! I'm worried about my brother! No one's telling me anything."

Tristan sighed. "Perhaps, that is because it would be of things you would rather not hear."

"What about his transformation? Did you give Nick your blood? Can't you tell me at least that much?"

"It is time, Celeste," he repeated.

"That's not an answer, and I'm not a child!"

Tristan's eyes glowed a warning. "If I hadn't, Nicholas would have destroyed himself. After great deliberation, it was your father's decision. Bianca is there now to comfort Razvan . . . not Nicholas. Should your brother choose to disobey the Code, the Omniscients will have no other option but to destroy both him and—"

"And who? My father? You?"

He grabbed my elbow.

I jerked free, landing a vicious glare. "Okay! Let me get my stuff."

"Your stuff is in Kansas City."

"How?"

He laughed. "Celeste, have you never learned the extent of your mother's powers?"

I remembered the clothes spilling from my drawers and packing themselves. "So, she just has to blink, maybe wiggle her nose, and tangible items travel through, what, a bizarre time warp to wherever she wants?"

He wrinkled his nose in disgust. "You make it sound as though she is a circus magician. Bianca possesses telekinetic ability. Most of the ancients do."

"Do you?" He was poised to answer when I pressed my palm in his direction. "Never mind, I don't want to know."

"It is time to depart, Celeste. I would recommend that you close your eyes until I say otherwise."

I should have listened to him. Not long after he took me in his arms, I passed out. When I came to, I saw stars—actual stars, up close and personal—and the Sea Ferry miles below as it crisscrossed the Atlantic en route to Manhattan. I blacked out again. When I regained consciousness, we had arrived in Kansas City, the Sprint Center directly below us.

CHAPTER 17

Kansas City
Two Years Later

"So, what made you consider law enforcement?" Captain Burke asked, crinkling up his nose as he looked over my paperwork.

"My dad was a cop," I told him and wondered if his inhospitable demeanor was just his usual or if he felt I was too young, too petite, too female, or all of the above. My thoughts shifted to Nick. He was the one who'd always wanted to become a cop, though the routine blood tests and complete physical might now be an obstacle.

Burke gave my dossier another glance and whistled long.

"Your father was Russ Crenshaw?"

"Yes," I said, disguising a smirk. Now I had his attention. The decision to retake my biological parents' surname, surprisingly, hadn't been an easy one. Fearing for my safety, the Toroks insisted, as if a simple name change could protect me from their enemies.

"We were rookies together," he said a beat later, shaking his head as if to awaken memories. "Geez, that's been ages ago."

"Yeah, I really don't remember much about him."

"That's right," he stammered and cast his eyes on his desk. "You must have been just a baby when . . ."

He didn't finish the sentence; he didn't need to.

"Terrible day. He was a good friend and a better officer." Almost as an afterthought, he added, "Your mother was a lovely woman."

"Thank you," I muttered, wishing he'd change the subject.

Eventually, he resumed eye contact. "Wesley Gates and Billy Mooney still sit on Death Row for their part in the bombing, if it gives you any comfort. Gates's scheduled execution is next month; Mooney's two weeks from then. And," he said, disdain eroding his sharp features, "their appeals have been exhausted. This time it is going to happen."

I nodded and bit my lower lip. If only he knew the real story. While it was true that Gates and Mooney caused the explosion, most of the building's inhabitants would have survived if not for the Harvesters.

Burke emitted a soft whistle. "From what I see here, you were the top cadet in the academy. Impressive, particularly since we've had many very promising contenders this year."

"Yes, sir. Thank you, sir, er, Captain."

"Well, that should do it, Crenshaw. I like to welcome the rookies personally, so *welcome*. Roll call begins at 0800. Don't be late," he added with a forced smile.

"Yes, Captain," I said and made a break for the door.

"Where you headed?" a voice called behind me as I made a beeline for the bathroom.

I immediately recognized Ethan Brandenburg from our time at the academy. He was tall and muscular with perfectly chiseled features. Nothing about him was soft. His light brown hair with its warm reddish hue further accented eyes the color of rich moss.

"Think they'll make us partners?" he asked, not giving me an opportunity to answer. "I mean, they should. Don't you think? After all, we ranked top of the class."

I ranked top. You were runner-up. "They'll partner us with a T.O. first."

His lips twisted into a sarcastic grin. "I meant once the training officer sets us free."

I shrugged. *Not if there really is a God.*

"If they do, I promise to keep it professional," he quipped like he was all that.

I sneered and pushed past him. "That's big of you," I said over a cold shoulder.

"Just messing with you, Crenshaw. Lighten up! Come on," he said, jutting his chin toward a breakroom. "Coffee's on me."

"The coffee's free," I said, landing a sneer.

CHAPTER 18

"*Y*ou want to know where I live?" I eyed Ethan suspiciously, not particularly wanting to reveal my address, which seemed ridiculous. He was a cop after all, capable of accessing information much more invasive than a simple address. "About ten blocks, northwest," I eventually revealed.

He whistled, the sound both long and annoying. "You live in one of those renovated warehouses?"

Winging both nostrils, I executed a dramatic sniff, suddenly feeling defensive.

"Seriously? The rent's, what, a couple grand a month?"

We'd been walking side-by-side, though I'd tried several times to race ahead. Now, I stopped short.

"Didn't anyone ever teach you it's rude to ask those types of questions?"

He shrugged and graced me with another dimpled grin. "I call it polite interest."

"And I call it none of your business."

He laughed, long enough to give me a clear view of perfect teeth. "I've always wanted to see inside one of those lofts."

"Yeah? Call a rental agent," I told him then sprinted ahead.

He caught up effortlessly and tagged my arm. "How about I drop you at your place?"

"No, thanks."

"Look, I go right by there. I won't even ask to come in."

"I'll take the bus."

"Suit yourself," he told me, pitching his arms sideways.

I watched him strut in the opposite direction as the bus, *my* bus, careened toward the stop four minutes ahead of schedule. I made a run for it and reached the back bumper, a split-second after the doors closed, and the final passenger had boarded.

Rummaging through my purse for my cell phone, my intent to sequester a cab, I nearly jumped out of my skin when someone blasted a horn behind me. Turning, I landed a vicious snarl when I recognized Ethan behind the wheel of a pristine, red Chevrolet Corvette.

"Get in," he said like I wore a collar and tags. He revved a motor twice the size of his ego.

"No, thanks!" I shouted through a pelting monsoon.

"It's raining."

I jammed a hand on one hip and swept a river from my eyelashes. "No shit."

He inched the car closer and threw the passenger door open.

"C'mon! Get in."

By the time we reached my apartment building, for the first time in my life, I severely doubted my intuition. My perception of Ethan hadn't been exactly spot-on. The car belonged to his sister, Kourtney. He was borrowing it until he had enough money saved to buy an SUV. Why an SUV? Because he needed something to transport lumber for the Houses for Humanity Project—when he wasn't busy rescuing stray animals. I kept the conversation steered toward him, for obvious reasons, and was surprised how quickly we'd arrived at my apartment.

"I'll pick you up tomorrow morning—7 a.m., sharp. Don't keep me waiting," he added with a dimpled grin.

I thought about the outrageous amount of money I spent on cab fare and nodded in agreement, throwing in a little shrug to disguise my gratitude. I hesitated but finally asked, "Would you like to come up for a few minutes?"

"Next time," he told me and sped off, the tires splashing water onto me and the sidewalk.

I couldn't decide if I was annoyed or relieved.

Once inside, tapping my foot, I waited for the elevator, which probably hadn't been up to code since President Harry S. Truman laid his hand on a bible. Ten minutes later, I mumbled something vulgar I'd picked up at the academy and took the stairs.

By the time I reached the third-floor loft, I was still thinking about Ethan and what he must look like out of uniform. I turned the key to my apartment, surprised to find Tristan tucked away inside. Dressed in a black, bicep-gripping tee and jeans so tight they could very well be out-lawed, he leaned against the counter separating the small living room from an even smaller kitchen. He didn't appear happy. Just the sight of him made me forget all about Ethan.

"Things are complicated enough as it is, don't you agree, Celestine?"

"What are you talking about?" I asked, feigning ignorance.

"Ethan," he said like he was identifying raw sewage.

"What about him?"

He arched an eyebrow, which was explanation enough.

"He's a fellow cadet. I missed the bus, so he gave me a ride. What's the big deal?"

"You are attracted to him." This was not a question.

"You're jealous?" I asked, immediately wishing I could take it back. The past two years had been both excruciatingly frustrating and painful for both of us. Shakespeare couldn't have written this kind of romantic tragedy. I know because Tristan was once his friend and has told me as much. The chemistry between us was undeniable.

To combat any urges Tristan may or may not have had, he either spent a great deal of time away from my apartment or he played the Atom Trick which, as Bianca once simplified for me, was the ability to appear invisible. I think it was probably the latter; the apartment always seemed filled with his unique scent of forests, streams, hot rain, and sex. Dead silence continued to inhabit the room and spilled out of the partially opened window. When I dared to make eye contact, I wished I hadn't. Once again, I had wounded him, the hurt apparent in his haunting blue-grey eyes.

"What do you want from me?" I managed to push past swelling emotion. "You're the one who says . . ."

". . . we can never be," he finished for me, his expression communicating the kind of pain only hopelessness brings.

"Look, he's just an associate, another cop," I tried to say unemotionally, but even I heard my tone skyrocket to a higher register. I pressed my palms toward him. "Look, Tristan, am I hoping for some kind of normal future? Yeah, I guess I am. Unlike you, I have limited time on this planet, and I don't have any more to waste."

"Celeste," he murmured, bowing his head, a single tear splattering on his Converse sneaker.

I wanted to run to him, but instead, I twisted around, planning to lock myself in the bathroom. I pivoted last minute and faced him, but not until I'd injected eight fingernails into my navy-blue trousers and promised myself I wouldn't cry.

"I love you, Tristan. I always have, for as long as I can remember. Before I even knew what love was, and it's killing me that we will never—"

He rocketed to my side, took me in his arms, and held me there. Then he kissed me, releasing me long after my pulse quickened, my thighs quivered, and I struggled to breathe. Our first kiss. I experienced a type of elation I had never before known. I could die, right then and there, and that single kiss would have made death worthwhile.

"I'm sorry, Celeste," he whispered through the dense fog suddenly surrounding us, his words falling on my lips as my head continued to spin. And then, just as he always did when things got interesting, Tristan vanished. Only this time, he had actually kissed me. And I wanted more.

I WAS BLOTTING my eyes and adding another soaked tissue to the pile on the counter when an arctic blast infiltrated the forty-by-sixty-foot living space, my ficus tree wilting instantly.

I suppressed most of my rage and whirled ninety-degrees to discover Fane, Bianca's most annoying Kinsman. It wasn't only that I couldn't tolerate Fane and his dramatics, but his presence made it abundantly clear Tristan didn't plan to return. My shoulders drooping, my face contorted into a scowl I hoped not permanent, I stomped across the loft and slammed my bedroom door behind me, as if that alone would keep Fane out.

"I like this even less than you do, dear girl," Fane sang after drifting through the adjoining wall. "So, let's try and make this deplorable situation work. Wait! Did I say, deplorable? Silly me! Well, that simply won't do. I surely meant, ghastly. Yes, yes, that's much better, for this is a most ghastly situation indeed!"

The thing about Fane is that he became an immortal shortly after his twenty-third year on earth, which was sometime during the mid-sixteenth century. So not only was he male and perpetually twenty-three, but he both relished and practiced the sexist traditions of the time. Which I found peculiar, taking into account he is the most effeminate male I have ever met.

"That's the problem, Fane. It won't work," I said, pivoting in my bed so that I faced the wall.

"Tsk, tsk! But a bump in the road, as I see it. Perhaps an updated hairstyle would improve such melancholy." Fane paused, tapping a finger against his chin. "But I digress. To categorize that which is on your head as a style is a perversion of the word, I should think."

I rocketed upright and thrust an index finger toward the door.

"Get OUT!"

"Ah, me, if only I were so entitled. Alas, my mistress informs me I am here for the duration."

I tugged a cell phone from my uniform and called Bianca.

"Celeste, you know this is for your own good," Bianca lectured without as much as a hello.

Of course she knew why I was calling. Aside from her supernatural powers—the ability to access my thoughts despite the twelve-hundred miles that separated us—she surely must have anticipated how I'd feel to have Fane invade my life!

"Unless you want to discuss Tristan's motives for surrendering his post, Fane's involvement is now a moot point."

"All right!" I said, moderating my outburst to a whisper, after a glance in Fane's direction assured me he found the whole situation much too entertaining, "but why couldn't you have sent Lazarus or Trandafira?"

"They are both indisposed, I'm afraid. Little about your brother has changed," she told me, her tone effectively communicating exasperation. "Immortality being the concession, of course. He's still stubborn, defiant, and much, much too energetic for his own good. He is quite a handful, Celestine."

I didn't envy her situation. Nick was a handful before he became the equivalent of a phantom monster.

"I want to see him. It's been two years, Mom. Two long years."

"It's not possible! Razvan would never allow it."

"Why?"

Bianca suddenly entered the room and oxygen, as I knew it, made a hasty momentary retreat.

"Come, Celeste," she whispered, serpent-like fingers cupped in my direction. Sullenly, I took a seat beside her, harboring a strangled breath.

After a silent exchange between Fane and Bianca, he left abruptly, though the vapors outlining his silhouette stuck around a few more seconds. This peculiar anomaly isn't traditionally a vampire thing, at least not to my knowledge, but rather an annoying display of showmanship, totally unnecessary, and just another way for Fane to get under my skin.

Bianca threw her head back, her long hair sweeping the bedding, and sniffed the air, her nostrils opening then closing like a Venus Flytrap.

"At long last, we find ourselves alone! I sent Fane rather than Trandafira because he is not capable of managing Nicholas. Your brother's powers surpass most, much like—"

"Yesenia's," I interjected.

She tucked her chin and narrowed piercing eyes. "A reality most repugnant."

"Yet, you tried to destroy her."

Bianca shook her head.

My jaw dropped at this revelation. "So, it was Trandafira?"

"Yes, with great regret because, you see, their friendship spanned the ages, despite the occasional bickering." She chuckled, then looked away and seemed to study her hands, as a nearly indiscernible sob caught in her throat. "Yesenia left us little option."

I breathed in until my lungs felt as if they might burst and held my tongue. I was glad Yesenia was gone.

"About Nick . . . I want to see him. He won't hurt me, Mom, I know he won't."

Bianca threw her arms in the air. "Positively daft, Celestine! Why not throw yourself in the path of a runaway horse! You know not of what you speak." Bianca sighed, exhaling tiny ice pellets, which flickered and flittered on bands of sunlight trespassing floor to ceiling windows. "We are unwilling to take that chance, Celestine."

I skyrocketed upright, clamping my mouth shut, fearing regrettable words might escape. I ran to the door, tense fingers strangling the knob.

"Celeste," she purred from the bed, "come, sit beside me. For I do not think it is only this separation from Nicholas that torments you so."

"I'm in love with Tristan," I blurted without turning around. "If I can't be with him . . ." I sank to my knees, clutching my stomach, and unleashed a burst of sobs that robbed me of the shallowest breath while competing with silent, angry screams. Gasping for air, my breath stuttering with each inhalation, I caught a whiff of something sickly-sweet reminiscent of something dead or decaying, as a powdery substance not unlike a mixture of dust and ash dotted the skin on my arms like murky raindrops.

"My darling," Bianca croaked above me, her voice suddenly aged and unfamiliar. "Can you not see your despair is but mine."

I raised my head slowly, afraid of what I might see. Bianca glided toward me like a kite deprived the mandatory breeze, her skin washed implausibly gray, her lively eyes lying hidden behind an opaque white veil. My mouth opened in a soundless scream as when I was a child held hostage within a terrifying nightmare. Recoiling, I scrambled across the room on all fours, burrowing myself in a corner.

"Do not be afraid, my darling," she said, her words stilted as she pushed each one out as though her last. Her once beautiful face was now wrinkled and slack, her full lips suspended like a rooster's wattle. It was as if I was bearing witness to someone's terminal illness, not in a span of time but instantaneously. Suddenly, she crashed to the floor, writhing as though on fire.

Rushing to her side, I screamed for Fane, for Tristan, for anyone. She reached for me, her appendages more like claws than hands. "Mom! What's happening! What do I do?"

A strange sound came from outside the windows, much like the reverberation of whirling helicopter rotors. Winged creatures, outside one minute, inside the next, surrounded us. Pushing me aside, one appeared to examine Bianca with a glowing cylindrical tube that resembled a lightsaber or a glow stick. One turned to look at me and must have telepathically communicated with the others because they all joined ranks, creating a blockade while ruffling their glossy, satiny, jet-black feathers. Attempting to bulldoze my way through and failing, I ducked beneath one of their wings, which could easily span six feet, and my eyes fell on a withered corpse. Bianca.

The congregation of creatures communicated in clicks and high-pitched tones, two of whom appeared engaged in a volatile argument. Unsure of what they were, whom they represented, or what they had planned for my mother, I tearfully demanded an explanation. One turned to look at me, its nose resembling more a beak, and I instantly backed away. I was suddenly unable to move or speak; I suspected this one of their preternatural capabilities. In unison, and like puppets on strings, the winged creatures ascended effortlessly into the air, and I watched them spirit Bianca away.

Fane materialized immediately, cloaking me within his multicolored layers of silk, velvet, and satin, his demeanor subdued and strangely comforting.

I shook my head, still unable to speak, as if someone had glued my lips together.

"This shall pass, dear girl," he said, patting the top of my head like I still wore diapers. Noticeably impatient, he sighed and mercilessly tapped his foot.

I wagged my jaw side-to-side, then tried opening and closing my mouth.

"Who were they?" I finally managed to say. "Where have they taken her?"

"Pfft! Why, those were the Elders, you silly ninny. Not to worry. She is in the most excellent hands. I shudder to think what may have been had they not rescued her! For it is only the almighty Omniscients," he said with some disdain, "who are capable of reversing a storm most fecal, such as this one."

I arched a brow, but he was right. This was a shitstorm. A chill ravaged my spine, remembering Bianca's appearance. "She looked—"

"Dead?"

I nodded and heard myself swallow.

"Ah, yes. A most proficient description, lass. I have only known this to happen on but one other occasion. An attempted suicide, if you can imagine one in the blood inviting death. Quite the quandary, I dare say. The Elders intervened and, presto," he said, snapping his fingers, "the ridiculous fellow was as good as new."

"This was my fault," I said, wringing my hands and pacing the room.

"Your pain is her pain, as they say. For her sake, dear girl, I hope you have transcended your little nervous breakdown. At the moment, our beloved mistress is powerless to assist herself, and I mean that in the most literal sense."

On the verge of tears again, I said nothing.

He pulled me closer still, his hair reeking of a musky pomade.

"Aw, do not despair. The wise ones will see to it she recoups all that she has lost. You on the other hand can never recoup that which was never yours. Can you not see, poor girl, that a tryst between you and the gallant Tristan is not to be?

This infatuation must pass. Can you imagine a union without children, a world in which you abandon your mate in a blink of an eye? For you see, to Tristan time is relative; he lost his true love centuries ago, yet the wound still gapes as if inflicted yesterday. Why would you willingly bestow another such curse on the poor fellow? If you won't think of yourself, you must consider Tristan."

ane brought me breakfast in bed; a curious concoction of grapes, some type of seeds, what I perceived slices of bacon, and a cup of tea smelling noxiously medicinal.

"Bianca is fine, I assure you, and sends her love." After performing an unexpected pirouette, Fane chirped, "A rose by any other name," as he plucked an odd flower from the air: a peculiar melding of a rose and a daisy. "Ah, Shakespeare . . . a blowhard by any other name, I should think! He squirted meaningless drabble more often than a babe its waste, I dare say!" Fane's hand flew to his collarbone. "Forgive my speaking ill of the dead, but surely Hippocrates would agree that William was the fundamental specimen as his most unnerving habit mimicked logorrhea like no other!" I knitted my brows while sniffing the surprisingly fragrant flower. "Oh, silly me, I've thrown you a curve! Do allow me an explanation. Logorrhea: excessive and often incoherent wordiness."

"Oh God," I muttered, hitching myself more upright. "Well, you're the expert." I ignored Fane's pouty expression. "If Bianca's fine, why isn't she here? I want to see her."

Fane shook his head, corkscrew curls flying this way then

that. "I'm afraid that is out of the question. I have my orders, and while I'll be the first to admit I often enjoy a degree of aggressive canoodling, a robust flogging is most certainly not a part of my repertoire. Therefore, for my sake, I implore you but obey this simple request!"

"I want to talk to her. I *need* to talk to her."

"Impossible."

"You said she was fine, so why—"

"Yes, yes, I did say that. Perhaps, adequate might have been the wiser choice. She has yet to regain her full powers."

"Even more reason for me to see her with my own eyes."

"She's across the country, dearest simp! As things stand, she's nearly as helpless as a common mortal." Fane threw his head back and chortled. "What would you have her do, hop an Amtrak or board a plane? I'm afraid the circumstances dictate me her surrogate." My head swam as I attempted to track Fane's movements. He was standing beside the bed one second, lounging upon it the next. "Let's try it, shall we? Close your eyes, Celestine. Pretend I am Bianca."

I set the tray off to the side. "I don't think so. Thanks for breakfast, but I'd like to be alone now."

"Perhaps later, after we've had our little chat. Do you think you are the only one to ever suffer such heartache?"

"I'm not discussing this with you."

"No mortal has ever survived a tryst with our kind. Were you aware? That is why Nicholas has been such a handful, the little womanizer." Fane covered a gasp. "I see, by your astonished expression, no one has ever explained this to you!" He bolted upright, an eager expression stretching his lips and widening his eyes. "Oh! Whoa to me, the reluctant volunteer!"

I pressed both palms his direction. "No, no way! We are not doing this."

"Although I did say no mortal can survive a night of passion with an immortal, that's not to say one could not, provided the immortal demonstrates a modicum of self-restraint. But, you see," Fane said, stretching a wicked grin, "that's just not in our nature."

"So, let me get this straight: Most vampires are incapable of having sex without——"

Fane flicked his wrist. "Yes, yes, without feeding simultaneously." He sighed and popped upright. "Do not judge us, fair lady. For who is in their right mind once taken to the point of ecstasy!"

∾

UNABLE TO CONTACT Bianca telepathically for the third day, I dug out my cell phone while waiting for my training officer outside the police garage. Trandafira answered, and she too assured me that my mother was on the mend. Reading between the lines, I got the impression she thought it best I didn't disturb Bianca for a while.

Not a day went by that I didn't miss Tristan. To counteract my depression, I threw myself into police work, even moonlighting as a security guard on my days off. On one occasion, I was sure I saw him and spent the rest of the day like a zombie, the fog never lifting completely.

Though I refused to accept a future without Tristan, I agreed to go out with Ethan. We always had a good time, whether it was taking in a movie, having a beer with the guys at *Unbroken*—a club mostly cops patronized—or cultivating our shooting skills at the range. At first, I was relieved he didn't seem interested in taking things any further. But after a few months of dating, I seriously wondered if he was physically attracted to me. Or if any man was. Tristan rejected my advances, and Ethan apparently wasn't inclined to make any of his own.

"Time to gas up," Randy, my T.O., shouted, jarring me into total awareness. When we arrived at the gas station, Randy cocked his head toward the pump, which was his way of telling me he intended to stay in the warm vehicle while I froze my fingers off. Resisting a little harsh commentary, I stepped out into the brisk, autumn wind and snugged my collar.

"Shouldn't you kill the engine?" I yelled at the back window. When he either didn't hear or chose to ignore me, I grabbed the cold nozzle and unconsciously counted as the seconds and the numerals on the pump ticked by.

I was choking on exhaust fumes while Randy drained a sixteen-ounce root beer wedged between his sausage-like fingers, wincing when he tossed the empty can over his shoulder and into the backseat. Although it wasn't in my job description, after each shift, I was the one forced to remove mountains of food wrappers and pop cans from the patrol car. Shifting my weight in a useless attempt to block the wind, I silently cursed Randy and the slow-moving dispenser. The tank filled about as quickly as my savings account.

I heard the driver's door open and glanced Randy's way. After he'd wedged nearly two-hundred pounds from the driver's seat, I noticed he'd drawn his gun. He snapped his fingers to get my attention and gestured toward the building.

Through the plate glass window and between tacky advertising posters for Mountain Dew, chili dogs, and motor oil, I could barely make out two silhouettes, one on the business side of the counter, the other on the customer side. The revolver the robber held, however, was quite distinguishable. My first robbery-in-progress caused my heart to pound and my survival instinct to kick in. Fighting the urge to curl up in a fetal position, take cover, and stay put, the consequences of a bullet whirling its way through one of the gas pumps and causing a massive explosion occurred to me. Staying low, I practically belly-crawled behind another vehicle, distancing myself from Randy. Not attracting any gunfire, I then planted both feet at the corner of the building where anyone inside couldn't possibly see me.

Popping his head from around the opposite corner of the building, Randy signaled for me to go around back. Duck walking to the rear door, I discovered it slightly ajar. Sweeping it quickly to the wall rather than chance a succession of creaks and groans, I tiptoed inside a storeroom housing floor-to-ceiling cases of beer, pallets of bread and assorted snacks, and cartons of cigarettes, some stacked haphazardly like dead soldiers on foreign soil. A shot rang out, and I shouldered open the *Employees Only* door, just enough to allow me a clear visual of the gunman.

The store manager and the assailant began a life and death struggle for the gun. The assailant appeared to be winning, and I knew this didn't give me much time. Expelling a long breath, I clenched my teeth, eased the door open further, and slipped in, unnoticed. I propelled myself across the floor—recently mopped and about as slick as a skating rink—toward the rear aisle. From there, I spotted suspect number-two, cramming everything he considered of value into a faded-denim backpack. Crouching low with arms extended, and as rigid as forks on a forklift, I set up the shot. Zeroing in, the sight from my police-issued Glock 22 trained on his head, I was about to take the shot when his partner shouted.

"C'mon, Zeke! There's a freakin' cop outside!"

"I see them, and you just said my name, dumbass!"

My eyes settled on his sawed-off shotgun, and my rookie ass froze. About that time, two patrol cars careened to a stop outside, and Dumbass made a run for it. My training kicked in, and I rushed to the front of the store like it was a finish line. The store manager took advantage of the distraction and chose cover between two soda machines, which drew Zeke's attention from the action playing outside to my location.

Both the robber and I ducked down, neither he nor I had a decent shot at one another. What I did have was a bird's-eye view of the situation outside. With the officers and assailant number-two at an impasse, bullets raining in both directions, I was the only cop afforded the opportunity to end the deadlock. I took aim and fired through the glass window, hitting the target in the shoulder. Losing the grip on his gun, and with blood seeping toward his fingertips, he yelped surrender.

Zeke was apparently more optimistic and refused to abandon his hiding place. I shouted a warning, informing the officers of the perp's location, and Randy and four uniformed, outfitted in respirators, swarmed the interior. Randy pitched a canister of tear gas over the Formica counter into the assailant's temporarily lair. Hacking, cursing, and shielding his face with his shirt, he surrendered within seconds and begged Randy to recite his Miranda Rights outdoors.

"Well, well. If it isn't Zeke Jones," Randy said, once he'd checked the suspect's ID. "You just saved us a trip to the east side, Zeke. There's a warrant out for your arrest. That wouldn't happen to be your buddy, Lenny Schmitz, in the ambulance, would it?"

I resisted the urge to tell Randy the name Dumbass better suited the suspect. A sharp nod from one of the arresting officers confirmed suspect number two was, indeed, Lenny Schmitz.

"Seems it's our lucky day, Crenshaw," Randy said to me. We've got a warrant for that one, too." He signaled to an EMT. "Rinse her eyes, will you? Good job, Crenshaw," Randy said and clapped my back hard. "You just scored your first collar."

"I know my rights," Zeke cried as one of the officers forced him into our patrol car. "And they don't include being taken to jail in a garbage truck."

Randy snickered along with the other officers. "I think he just insulted my car."

"I'll get the statement from the store manager," I told Randy, hitching a thumb over my shoulder toward the sidewalk outside the store. Halfway there, out of the corner of my eye, I saw movement and was sure I'd caught a glimpse of Tristan.

~

By the time I reached my apartment building that evening, I had three things on my mind; a shower, food, and Tristan, not necessarily in that order.

The elevator doors opened, and I gasped when I found Tristan waiting in the hall.

"What are you doing here?"

He said nothing as my heart flip-flopped, only stared at me through those hypnotic eyes of his.

"Seriously, I hadn't expected to ever see you again," I said with a hand on my hip, aware I was flaring my nostrils. "Isn't that why Bianca's saddled me with Fane?" I was faking indifference, but I had a feeling he wasn't buying any of it. I knew he could tell that his mere presence brightened my world; the cascading autumn leaves were suddenly much more vivid, the air crisper, and my life worth living.

"They had guns," he said, his intense eyes piercing mine, the distance he put between us shredding the tiny slice of hope I'd clung to since seeing him last.

I laughed, my laughter both pathetic and soulless. "I'm a cop. It comes with the territory."

"Then I suggest you reevaluate your vocation. It's much too dangerous, Celeste."

I looked up at him without lifting my head. "Why do you care, Tristan? I'm no longer your problem, remember?"

"Do you wish to die? Is that it?"

I shook my head, my eyes now locked on my tactical boots, but I resisted the urge to say, *What's the point?* "No, Tristan. I want to live, really live, not just exist as you and the others would have me do!"

He wagged his head and grabbed my wrist.

"It's much too dangerous, your mortality is too fragile and but a blink in time!"

"That's my point," I said, studying the perfect angle of his jaw, the flawless slope of his nose, and the artistic bow of his lips. "*This* is it for me. I don't have the luxury of hoping next century or the one after, maybe, just maybe, I'll fulfill my destiny, my desires. I'm in love with you, Tristan, and we're wasting precious time."

He shook his head and looked away. "Come home where we can protect you, Celeste. The threat in New Jersey is over, and Nick is manageable. Why would you not wish to be closer to your brother, to Razvan and Bianca?"

"What about us? Will *we* be closer? You know what I'm asking, Tristan. Is there a future for us?"

"I cannot afford another mistake, Celeste."

My heart stopped, and I backed away. The words caught in my throat, but I eventually said them. "So, you think being with me would be a mistake?"

He reached for me, his cold fingers closing around my hands. "Bringing Nicholas back from death's door, allowing his adaptation, it was all a grave mistake! He sensed your danger today and nearly relapsed. He attacked two mortals. Had it not been for Trandafira—"

"Oh, my God! That's horrible. Is he—is everyone all right?"

"Bianca has seen to it the mortals remember nothing of the attack, so yes, all is well."

I nodded in relief. I assumed Bianca had utilized Ad Deiectioneum—the Purge, as she called it, but I didn't see the point in asking him to validate my assumption. "You didn't answer my question, Tristan: Do you think being with me would be a mistake?"

"Why do you persist traveling this road, Celeste? You know it is forbidden! Our being together could end your days as you know them."

I laughed at the absurdity and pulled away. "End them, then! Please! End these days filled with nothing. No joy, no promise, no anything!"

"I cannot!"

"Then tell me you don't love me, Tristan, and I'll never again mention a future in which we'll be together."

"You once told me you couldn't live without Nicholas. Yet, that is what you are doing. Is it not? Come with me, Celeste. Don't allow that all I have done is for naught. Come home."

My forehead scrunched, my fists digging into my thighs, I said, "Do you love me? Tell me, Tristan!"

He dipped his head, anguish marring his exquisite face.

"I don't wish to hurt you, Celeste."

"Too late," I said and left him standing outside the elevator.

CHAPTER 20

*I*t was nearly 3 a.m. A teeth-chattering chill annexed my bedroom. Half-awake, I drew my knees to my chest and tucked the covers under my chin, the combined scent of lavender, lilac, and myrrh awakening me fully. Just as I suspected, Bianca hovered overhead. I blinked, and she was gone.

I lay there, my hearing long ago trained at identifying the subtlest of sounds. Although the room was eerily quiet, no sign of even the most elusive shadow, I knew I wasn't alone.

Just as a phantom cloud appeared, I lunged for my gun.

"They don't give you nearly enough credit," Fane said, the dense fog shrouding his body dissipating, droplets at a time, with each word he spoke. "Even if I do say so myself, I'm as quiet as a church mouse and every bit as light on my feet."

I didn't have the energy to point out his feet seldom contacted the ground. "Why are you here, Fane?"

Running his fingers along the top of my dresser, he displayed an index finger covered in dust, then uttered disgust.

"Mortals. Such vile, nasty creatures," he said under his breath. "To answer your question, it assuredly is not to get your house in order, in a literal sense. And quite the shame for you that I am not." He expelled a long sigh. "Five centuries walking this repulsive planet, and my master has reduced me to a common babysitter."

"I don't need, nor do I want, a babysitter. Please leave!"

"Believe me, no one's more dismayed about this predicament than I. Such a waste," Fane continued unfazed. "And to think some decades past, I was often compared to Elvis Presley."

I snorted; the kindest response I could manage.

"More recently," he went on, "while on the streets of Manhattan, everyone mistook me for Tom Cruise."

I rolled my eyes to which Fane sniffed loudly, acknowledging my sarcasm. "Do I need to point out that you're two to three feet taller?"

"In all fairness, if memory serves, I suppose I hardly resemble him. If either of us is to consider this a compliment, I should think it Tom."

"You said if memory serves? When was the last time you saw your reflection?"

Fane expelled a long, dramatic sigh, and swept a fistful of curls behind one ear.

"Rome: August 18, 1516, following the signing of the Concordat of Bologna." He slanted sad eyes in my direction. "I had decided to join in the celebration and was staggering out of a pleasant, little tavern. This but another argument against public drunkenness."

He was on the verge of tears, and I immediately regretted my intrusion. "I'm sorry I shouldn't have asked."

Fane flicked a wrist. "No need. I'm living proof, well, proof anyway, that we all must pay for our transgressions. My recompense came in the form of a most handsome vampire, whom I perceived, in my inebriated state, but a harmless, infatuated Frenchman. My God, he was beautiful. Adonis in the flesh, he was. Oh, such a night of splendid lovemaking I have not known since! Often, I think walking this earth as an immortal was but a small price to pay for such a wickedly delicious encounter."

I clawed at the skin between my thumb and index finger, my eyes downcast. Fane's eyes weren't just a window into his soul but, like most vampires', more a floodlit stage.

"I had stopped to admire my reflection, you see . . . Oh, what does it matter! I doubt I've changed a lick," he said cheerily and twirled further revolutions without coming in contact with the floor.

Sympathizing, I managed a painful, frozen smile.

He plopped down on the bed. "Why, oh why, will you not consider returning home, precious lass? For my impetuous sake, if not for your own! This wretched city so lacks a robust nightlife."

"Because I have a job, Fane. Besides, there's plenty of nightlife."

Fane rolled his eyes and yawned exaggeratedly. "Ah, yes, the infamous Birthplace of Jazz! Well, dear girl, I've been to the *Blue Room* and found it appropriately named. Sad does not begin to describe it. And, while we're on the subject, I should think the state more suitably referred to as Misery."

"For your information, Kansas City, Missouri also happens to be Walt Disney's birthplace. And Ernest Hemingway began his journalism career here."

"Hemingway, pfft! Until he'd consumed his first pint, he could bore one to tears! Some would argue his prose often achieves a similar result." After some apparent deliberation, a smile mutilating his lips, he added, "Though I must say, I relished the insults he would bestow on Steinbeck. Oh, how John's face would flush unbridled rage! I believe he would have challenged Ernest to a duel had it been fashionable."

I stifled a yawn; I'd heard about the row between Steinbeck and Hemingway on more than one occasion. And because it suddenly occurred to me who better than Fane to glean information from, I leaned into him, steepling my fingers.

"So, did you and Tristan know one another at that time?"

Fane withdrew instantly and flittered over to the window. "Humph! I should have known you have little interest in *my* illustrious, historical past unless it pertains to him. Oh, by all means, let's talk about Tristan, the magnificent! Please do tell me all about Tristan," he trilled, mocking me. "He is so hand-some. He is soooo charming. He positively puts a skip in my step, a waddle in my caboose. Do, do, do tell me all about Tristan!" Winded, he collapsed on my bed, his arms outstretched, knees drawn to his chest, eyelashes fluttering flamboyantly.

"Fine, don't tell me!" I said, jabbing him with all ten toes.

Fane shot upright and patted a ridiculous top knot in place, then batted layers of false eyelashes, crisscrossed his hands like an overindulged child, and scissored his legs together, all in one theatrical motion. "What would you like to know?"

Displaying what I hoped he interpreted as indifference, I shrugged. "When did you and he first meet?"

Fane tap-tap-tapped a fingernail against his upper lip.

"Well, let me think. Ah, yes! December . . . 26, 1776. Yes, I am quite certain it was about the time George Washington crossed the Delaware River." While I gaped, he pitched the same finger in the air. "Oops, perhaps I have confused George with Thomas and the occasion with the Signing of the Declaration."

I pressed a hand in his direction. "Hold up! Are you talking about Thomas Jefferson and the Signing of the Decla-ration of Independence?"

"Yes," he said, laughing until he snorted, as if suddenly reflecting on much more. "Oh, how Martha hated the man!"

I attempted to erase the crease deepening between my

eyebrows. "Wait a minute. You're referring to Martha Washington?"

Fane misinterpreted my question because he said, "For heaven's sake! It was Thomas she loathed, not good old George."

I was fairly certain my eyes bled intrigue by this point. "What did she have against Jefferson?"

"Dear girl, where, oh where, do I begin? There were so many reasons."

Wiggling until I'd found a comfortable position, my butt snuggled into the pillowy mattress, and anxious to hear more, I cupped my fingers in a sort of give-me gesture.

"As you insist. Undoubtedly, the thing that most ruffled her feathers, and do pardon the pun, was Thomas often declaring he much preferred Dick's—his pet mockingbird—company to that of George's. On more than one occasion, he inferred both George's brain of equal weight as the bird's. As if that was not enough, the disastrously Thomas dabbled in adultery, bribery, and the harvesting of opium, which may explain his proclivity to go about the oval office with Dick perched on his shoulder excreting poop while providing vocals as Thomas sawed away on his cherished violin. Ghastly, I dare say! Had Beethoven had the foresight, he surely would have severed his own hands and gouged out his eyes rather than create such glorious masterpieces only to have them perverted in such a way!"

I laughed until a coughing jag sprayed Fane with spittle, which prompted him to distance himself and raise an artistic eyebrow. I opened the drawer to a bedside table and pitched him a tissue while mumbling an apology.

"So, Tristan was at the signing of the declaration?"

"Heavens no, I should think not! Where on earth would you get an idea like that?"

I felt my teeth grinding together. "Because earlier, you said that very thing!"

"Ah, I did, didn't I? Yes, yes, Tristan had found favor with Polly, and only an armed brigade could keep him from the famed Monticello! Suffice it to say, Thomas was on to him, you see." Fane threw his head back, producing shrill laughter. "I suppose it takes a scoundrel to know one. He guarded the poor girl like she was the crown jewels. And to think, Tristan infatuated with someone so pedestrian! I suppose she was pretty enough if one prefers a dull onyx to a sparkling diamond."

I threw up a hand. "Okay, who was Polly?"

"Why, Thomas's daughter, of course." He paused, just long enough to tap a sickeningly long fingernail against a jagged tooth, producing a sound similar to a razorblade scraping against glass. "I digress. Her given name was Mary. Later in life, most referred to her as Maria. It's a wonder the poor woman knew who she was!"

I swiped a hand across my forehead and took a calming breath. "Oh, for God's sake! What does that have to do with the declaration?"

"What does it have to do with it, my good woman? Absolutely everything! Had it not been for Tristan and his opium antidote, the document might never have seen the light of day! What with Thomas's initial contribution the equivalent of a horrid love sonnet, which, more than likely, he plagiarized from the incessant ramblings of his bird, Dick!"

I took a minute to massage my temples. "Let me get this straight. Tristan was responsible for parts of the Declaration of Independence?"

Fane shook his head. "He only sobered Thomas. But to Tristan's credit, rather than housing a deplorable, nonsensical, verbose edict, the National Archives stores the grand proclamation we're familiar with today. Hip hip bloody hooray for Tristan."

Swiping loose strands of hair behind my ears, I said, more to myself, "That's pretty damn impressive."

Fane pursed his lips and slanted mischievous eyes in my direction. "Of course, you would think nothing less. It's not as if he parted the Red Sea."

I covered a gape with a sweaty palm, then remembered the facts he'd shared earlier. Fane hadn't existed until the sixteenth century, so he wouldn't have any firsthand information to offer on the subject of Moses.

"I can see it in your eyes; you want to know all you can about Tristan's entanglement as it applies to Polly."

"Not particularly."

"Then suffice it to say, Tristan saved his allegiance for the royals and the battlefield. He left his loyalty at his many conquests' bedchamber door. Polly was but a notch on a disintegrating bedpost."

I puffed my cheeks, suddenly wanting to sleep away this conversation. "That was a long time ago."

Fane clucked his tongue. "A leopard doesn't change his spots, dear girl."

I yawned and hitched a thumb toward the door. "I've got to get some sleep."

"Humph! As if I need a door," Fane sang and vanished flamboyantly through a wall.

WITH ALL THE fissures in the plastered ceiling above accounted for, I rolled out of bed two hours before my alarm was set to sound and stumbled toward the kitchen. Twelve ounces of stout caffeine beneath my gun belt, I waited outside for Ethan.

Twenty minutes later, I glanced at my watch and dug my cell phone from the sheath on my belt, just as Ethan's Corvette tore across the parking lot. The passenger door swung open.

"Get in; we're going to be late."

"No kidding."

"Sorry, somebody's water heater blew, and I had to install a new one."

"This morning?"

"No. Last night. Luckily, I made it to the hardware store before it closed."

I gave my head a shake and tried to put the limited pieces together. "So, if it happened last night—"

"I overslept." Ethan glanced in my direction, his bloodshot eyes settling on mine. "You don't look like you're doing much better."

I couldn't very well tell him that a chatty gay vampire kept me awake most of the night. "I had a little trouble sleeping."

"So, Celeste, if you're not doing anything this weekend, we could use an extra hand."

"The Houses for Humanity thing?"

Ethan nodded, his eyes focused on the road.

"I would, but I've got security detail this weekend."

"There are more important things in life than money, you know."

"Yeah, try telling my landlord."

Ethan shrugged it off. "How's it going with your T.O.?"

I told him about the armed robbery.

His eyes darted in my direction, his mouth hanging open.

"Well, thank God you're okay!" He reached for my hand and covered it with his. "I wouldn't want anything to happen to you."

CHAPTER 21

I threw my purse in my locker, pinned on my badge, and attempted to forget Ethan's ambiguous confession. His words may have been generic, but his tone was anything but. He was into me. I was into Tristan. I had enough stress to deal with after learning about Nick's attempt to murder innocent people following the robbery. I didn't need some colleague, no matter how charming and attractive he might be, distracting me from things far more important. And how can anyone possibly be a cop *and* play it safe, anyway? My anxiety increased as I considered Nick's predicament had Trandafira not managed to subdue him. I suspected the Realm would have destroyed him. Rubbing my temples, I paced the spotless concrete floor. Then I balled my hands into fists and considered pummeling a locker or two.

Nick. Always trouble. Always screwing up my life. He was the reason I was here, away from Razvan and Bianca, away from Tristan.

I blinked away tears and felt guilt's heavy weight as the truth edged its way from deep within my subconscious. If I could alter the events that took place on graduation night, I would. I choked back sarcastic laughter. Of all the people in my life, it was Yesenia who was the first to make it all crystal clear.

My brother died that night. The thing that inhabited his body now wasn't Nick and was about as familial as a rabid stray dog.

~

SIX HOURS into a relatively uneventful day, I watched Randy inhale a Cinnabon as we patrolled the city's east side, beginning at the 6300 Block of Prospect and all points north. Once we'd ended some hair-pulling between two homeless women over a three-wheeled cart, Randy made a leisurely left turn onto 59th from Prospect and headed west. Amid beautifully preserved three-storied homes, boarded-up structures attested to the community's blight.

Close to the Paseo Boulevard, dispatch radioed a possible jumper at the Research Medical Center. Randy activated the lights and sirens, then executed a U-turn and kissed the curb outside the main entrance off Meyer Boulevard, alongside the KCFD's Engine-3317. I exited the vehicle first. From the reflection thrown off the gleaming paint of the fire truck, I noted the usual lookie-loos lining the perimeter of the hospital, the local press sandwiched in-between.

"Up there," Fire Chief McClellan said, indicating what resembled a fractured component of Notre Dame's Bell Tower. Securing a pair of Bushnell binoculars from the patrol car and squinting through the lenses, I tracked what appeared to be an early-twenties male in colorful garb including a long, red cape.

"What's the plan, Mick?" Randy asked the chief.

Chief McClellan scrubbed his bald head and instructed his firefighters to back the truck to the center of the building. "You're up, Wilson," he said, tipping his glimmering white hat to a young athletic type about my age.

Randy shook his head, a pudgy thumb thrust inside a trouser pocket. "There's no way to apprehend the jumper from the inside?"

"Look, Randy, you wanna see him splat all over the pavement on the Channel-5 News? I know what I'm doing here. It's not my first rodeo."

"I'm just sayin', Mick. The ground is soaked. I don't see—"

"Get that truck moving!" McClellan said and spat a stream of chewing tobacco within an inch of the toe to Randy's worn boot.

Randy took a defiant stance with arms crossed tightly over his barrel-chest. "The Medical Director's not gonna like having to replace all that sod." To me, he said, "He'll play hell finding a tow truck big enough to pull that pumper out when she gets stuck. What's that lunatic wearing anyway?" he said and jerked the binoculars out of my hands. "A Spiderman costume?"

I didn't answer and instead distanced myself from both Randy and the Fire Chief, ducking the string of news cameras.

"Come on, man! Let's see if you can fly," a bystander heckled, and Randy was on him before I could blink. Snugging both hands behind the agitator's back, Randy said, "One more outburst like that, and let's see if you can afford a lawyer."

With the ladder raised above the seventh floor, Wilson ascended as if he were a chimpanzee and the rooftop a mere step or two above ground.

A cacophony of cheers echoed through the promenade when he reached the top; dying like an infant's cry once plugged with a nipple when the jumper engaged Wilson in a precarious game of tag.

"Roder," McClellan boomed, "get up there and help Wilson restrain that maniac!"

"You got it, Chief," a sandy-haired firefighter said, flexing his muscles and an inordinately stroked ego for the cameras.

Nearly to the top, Roder lost his footing, and the crowd gasped in bursts of oxygen-deprived waves.

Grasping a ladder rung with only one hand, he swung his torso left then right, and eventually secured both feet on the ladder.

I scoured the car for a second pair of binoculars. Finding a pair missing only the strap, I scrubbed the lenses in time to witness Roder and Wilson apprehend a grinning but volatile, lanky male, who appeared to be high on something other than the Research Medical Center.

Into his walkie-talkie, McClellan instructed Roder and Wilson to escort Lanky through the rooftop entrance and from there, the main entrance.

"Looks like you've got her under control," Randy said to the chief. The two men shook hands, and then Randy nodded from me to the patrol car. I happily complied, flinging myself inside just as a reporter barreled her way through a crowd now grudgingly disbanding.

Randy, postured stoically behind the wheel, grinned and breathed life into the impressive 3.7-liter Ford Interceptor AWD cruiser with a simple turn of the key. A blink later, he stationed the patrol car along the redbud-lined Meyer Boulevard.

"What are we doing?" I said, craning my neck in time to see Engine-3317 sputter, its tires churning as it made little headway along the tall, sodden grass.

"I wouldn't miss this for the world," Randy said, popping the lid of his third Pepsi.

"Seriously?" I said, my patience exhausted. "I thought we were all in this together."

"Hey!" Randy admonished. "Just because I didn't start the fight doesn't mean I don't intend to win the war."

COUNTING the minutes until my shift's end, I unleashed a long sigh when we spotted a toddler teetering down the center of a busy side street on our return to the precinct. Randy stopped the car a safe-enough distance away, and I jumped out and scooped-up the wide-eyed, soiled child. Her expression was an enchanting mix of both surprise and exuberance. We scanned the neighborhood for panicked mothers. Finding none, Randy and I began a resentful and time-consuming door-to-door inquiry. Fifteen minutes later, after disturbing an irritated young woman's afternoon nap, I surrendered the baby while Randy imparted a stern lecture upon her.

"Write up a report," Randy barked after we'd tumbled into the patrol car.

I grabbed the clipboard and pen.

"Not a formal one! I just want a record of this, that's all. Because if it happens again, we're calling Family Services."

"That's it? Someone endangered this kid's life, and that's all you want to do?"

"Take a good look around, Crenshaw. Most of these women are single mothers. For all we know, that one there," he said, jabbing a finger at the residence we'd just vacated, "works two jobs, and that's just to keep the kid in diapers. Maybe she needed more than a few hours of sleep and didn't intend to doze off."

ETHAN WAS WAITING outside the Corvette when I clocked out two hours later. "Hungry?" he asked and swept the passenger door open.

"Hmm, yeah, I guess."

"That's good because we're going to dinner," he said and strolled around to the driver's side.

"Where?" I said as I swung inside, bumping my knee against the glovebox.

"I was thinking Chaz on the Plaza. Good music, better food."

My jaw dropped. Chaz wasn't only considered one of the best restaurants in the city but was also known for its romantic ambience. I wanted to tell him I wasn't interested in a romantic dinner. Not with him, not yet anyway. Instead, I said, "Dressed like this?"

"Why not?"

"It's upscale, frequented by women who wear designer clothes and the men who design them. I want to have a relaxing evening, Ethan, not endure prying eyes and judgmental looks."

Ethan took his eyes from the road, looked at me, and shook his head. "Who's being judgmental now?"

"Look, I'm sure most of them are lovely people . . . I'd just feel more comfortable at the Cheesecake Factory tonight, all things considered."

He smiled, flashing perfect teeth. "Okay, but I'd think you'd want to watch your weight."

"Excuse me!"

"It's your call. But I don't want to hear any complaining when you can't fit into that wedding dress you've probably already picked out because of all that cheesecake."

"*What* are you talking about?"

"You know, you walking down the aisle; me, waiting at the altar, all sweaty and eager."

"You're insane!" I said, as the streetlight glowed red.

"Yeah, well, we have that in common." He leaned across the console, his right hand at the nape of my neck, and kissed me. The sexual tension between us hung heavy and sultry in the unseasonably warm air.

As we turned onto 47th Street, I pretended fascination in the Bromsgrove Guild fountain depicting Neptune riding three horses, then the breathtaking buildings exemplifying Spain's iconic architecture.

"Is there someone else?" Ethan suddenly blurted as he inched the Corvette into a narrow parking space inside the Giralda Parking Garage—modeled after the Giralda Tower; Seville, Spain—and cut the engine.

"No," I lied, avoiding his eyes.

He waited for me at the rear of the car and took my hand, escorting me from the rooftop parking lot to the pedestrian stairwell.

"It's a beautiful night for a walk," he said, in an attempt to restore conversation. Tires suddenly squealed around the sharp bend outside the garage entrance just as we reached the bottom and exited the stairwell. Ethan grabbed hold of my arm and pressed me toward the building.

"Somebody's hungry," he said, a scowl directed at the driver behind the wheel.

The line outside the restaurant circled the block. A waiter, armed with an Apple iPad and a charming smile, took drink orders for the customers in line. I considered my second drink before the first had even arrived. Forty-five minutes later, we were finally seated.

After cramming in the last bite of Chicken Bellagio, our eyes met. Ethan's were twinkling in the low lights. I shot him a compulsory smile and quickly turned my attention to the windows and the traffic outside.

Ethan was great-looking, kind, funny, and ridiculously responsible. But he was looking for more than an occasional companion. I wasn't sure I could be that person. I wasn't sure I wanted to be.

CHAPTER 22

Five Months Later

*E*than asked me to marry him. Working side-by-side on Houses for Humanity projects, we had first become better friends, then something much more. I hadn't thought about Tristan for months. Well, at least not twenty-four/seven.

I paced the loft, more specifically the space along the row of windows overlooking the street below. Ethan was due any minute, and tonight he expected an answer. To my surprise, Bianca was apparently oblivious. I thought that impossible and tugged my cell from my back pocket. Hesitantly, I speed-dialed her.

"Celeste," Bianca greeted almost immediately. I heard the joy in her voice, the thing I loved most about her.

"Hi, Mom," I shouted over the commotion coming from her end. "Where are you?"

"Turkey . . . I regret to say there has been some trouble."

I covered a gasp, suddenly recalling *Breaking News* involving an earthquake.

"Is Razvan with you?"

"Yes, as are Tristan, Nicholas, and Trandafira."

"Really! Nick too?"

"Your brother has been a tremendous asset. A victor!" she exclaimed fondly. "His fate, it seems, was a godsend."

"The Harvesters?" I asked and felt the entire length of my spine shudder.

"We are at war, Celestine, one Yesenia appears to have initiated."

"But Yesenia was—"

"Destroyed?" she finished for me. "Regrettably, it appears her obliteration was unsuccessful."

"But I saw—"

Bianca laughed softly. "What did you see? Her presumed remains? You saw what she wanted you to see, as did we. Have I not told you of her powers? She is the mistress of deception. Save for the Elders, her sorcery is unequaled."

"But how do you know for sure she wasn't destroyed?"

Bianca laughed and arranged her long hair over one shoulder. "Time will provide the answer, my darling. For now, we have this under control. Let us not spend this time on Yesenia's transgressions. It would seem you have your own tribulation. No?"

"So, you *do* know about Ethan?"

Bianca giggled a melodic chorus. "Merely respecting your privacy, my love."

I took a seat on the couch, hugging my knees to my chest. I'd missed her much more than I'd realized. "You have nothing to add?" I said, smiling into the phone.

"I believe a June wedding a splendid choice."

"You're evading."

"I am doing no such thing. According to Fane, Ethan seems a fine young man, not entirely insufferable."

"Fane has never met him."

She cut loose gregarious laughter, and I could easily visualize her head tossed back, her long hair sweeping the backs of her knees, her eyes glinting mischief. "Ah, Celestine, so naive! It doesn't benefit you, particularly given your position within law enforcement."

I squeezed both eyes shut, my skin tingling with both rage and embarrassment, wondering just exactly what Fane may or may not have witnessed. There was plenty. Bianca laughed fervidly, undoubtedly reading my thoughts in their entirety.

"Trust your instincts, my darling; they have yet to fail you. And do keep a robe handy. Both of you."

Our conversation ended just as Ethan brought his car to a stop near the curb. My decision to marry Ethan had come suddenly and much more easily than I'd expected. Introducing my family to him would most likely prove tortuous.

Following a romantic dinner, a bottle of champagne, and a somewhat salacious public display, Ethan and I giggled as we bade the maître d goodnight. Once outside, he swept me off the ground and kissed me, stopping just long enough to allow a barrage of patrons past. We held hands after he'd swept his latest car, a Prius, into the Canterbury Lofts' parking garage and snagged a space. Once inside the loft, we picked up where we'd left off in the secluded booth at the *Café Sebastienne*. I suddenly sensed Fane nearby and applied the brakes.

"I understand if you want to wait," Ethan whispered in my ear, his breath hot, each word labored as we exploited my bed.

The tiny hairs on the back of my neck were at full salute. Now I was convinced Fane lurked about.

"I'll be right back," I assured Ethan, his expectant expression now a mix of surprise and disappointment. I opened the door to the bathroom where I found Fane, laughing annoyingly.

"He's a handsome brute; I'll give you that, but about as smooth as sandpaper. I have witnessed far more sophisticated techniques in a schoolyard."

"You need to leave," I whispered loudly. "Not just the loft, the entire freaking state!"

Fane dropped his deceptively conniving head. "Alas, perhaps, I shall." He tilted his head toward the bedroom. "Particularly given tonight's entertainment holds little promise. Most mundane, I would be willing to wager, even by a convent's standards."

"Out!"

Fane drifted closer to the door. "Perhaps your beau could benefit from my vast experience, hmmm? I shall make the inquiry."

I lunged for him, but my ten fingers grabbed only heavy vapor.

"Up here, dearest," I heard him taunt.

My homicidal eyes flew to the ceiling. I motioned him down. Mocking me initially, he eventually floated toward the floor.

"Look, Fane. What's it going to take for you to disappear?"

Fane tapped a fingernail against his chin. His eyes suddenly widened. "A trip to the amusement park!"

"It's seasonal," I replied glumly.

"Seasonal?"

I pushed the words through clenched teeth: "Worlds of Fun. It opens in late spring and closes in the fall."

"Opening day then, and by that, I mean night, of course. Agreed?" Fane held out his hand. I didn't shake it.

Although I couldn't possibly fathom why a vampire wanted to visit an amusement park, I didn't care. As long as he held to his side of the bargain and vacated the premises.

"Agreed. Now, go!"

When I returned, I discovered Ethan had peeled his shirt off, revealing a tat that read *Freedom*. Because he'd slipped under the covers now drawn to his navel, I couldn't be sure what else he'd shed.

I intended to find out.

But first, I had to be certain Fane hadn't double-crossed me. I smiled at Ethan and jerked a thumb toward the kitchen.

"Sorry, I need a glass of water . . . the champagne, I guess. You want one?"

Ethan shook his head no, smoldering eyes following my every move.

"I'll be right back," I promised as I backed out of the room.

Fane was leaning against the refrigerator, arms smugly folded across his chest.

"In need of a cold beverage? Perhaps some wine to settle virginal nerves? I know," he rambled on, popping a finger toward the ceiling, "you have discovered a desperate need for expert advice." Pushing off the refrigerator, he soared toward the bedroom. "To the rescue straight away."

"You go in there, and I swear I'll see that Bianca banishes you to some forsaken jungle!"

Fane sighed and feigned a dismal expression. "Truly, my intent is not to be a nuisance, but rather my abhorrence of solitude. I get quite lonely, you know."

I clamped a hand on one hip. "Get. The. Hell. Out!"

"If you insist!" Fane swooped closer and fingered my robe. "Exquisite fabric. By the by, whatever is it with you mortals and your propensity toward modesty?"

"Out!" I warned again. "Last chance."

Fane grinned slyly and flicked a wrist, menacing eyes all but guaranteeing havoc. "Before I depart, there's just one other thing."

"What?"

"Do remind me upon my return, to share a tiny little mishap which occurred earlier this evening."

My mind wandered to all things devastating, and suddenly, he was gone.

I slipped back into the bedroom and discovered Ethan rolled onto his side, facing the door, propped seductively on one elbow. His brows knitted together as he studied my robe, and I got the impression he'd expected me undressed. I kicked off my stiletto heels and slowly unbelted the robe. Ethan snaked out of bed and did the rest for me.

While his lips traced my right shoulder, he whispered, "Have you decided?"

"Yes," I gushed softly.

"Yes, you've decided, or yes, you'll marry me?"

"Both," I said, closing the space between us.

CHAPTER 23

At one a.m., I persuaded Ethan to go home. Of course, I couldn't give him a truthful explanation, how I didn't want my gay vampire guardian to offer any more suggestions regarding his lovemaking techniques. So instead, I cited much older, nosy, conservative neighbors as the reason. I lay awake for another hour, admiring my engagement ring. The diamond was small but brilliant and nestled in an antique marquis setting. Hugging myself and smiling until my cheeks ached, I eventually dozed off.

When I woke, Fane was waiting with some concoction he maliciously dubbed Phryne's-Morning-After Brew. I poured it down the drain.

"Humph! I have never suffered such insult!"

"I doubt that. And don't think I don't know who Phryne was."

Fane grinned. "I thought it most appropriate."

"Comparing me to some ancient Greek whore?"

"The term, I believe, was harlot, for those who desire historical accuracy."

I shook my head and, for a quick second, wished it possible for him to die.

"So tell me," he began with sickening excitement and a dramatic bat of thick eyelashes, "was it everything you dreamed it would be?"

I narrowed my eyes. "We're not discussing this."

"Embarrassed due to your lover's substandard boudoir skills, are you?"

I glared a warning, to which he merely batted his eyelashes.

"And whosoever could blame you! From what I had the misfortune of witnessing, your liaison was not one demonstrating the throes of passion, but rather the insufferable throes of apathy!"

Grinding my teeth, I threw my cell phone, nearly hitting him in the head.

"Enough, Fane! What mishap did you have yesterday?"

Fane cleared his throat dramatically and ran a finger along the surface of the countertop.

"Let me begin by saying, it is no secret that I have, most certainly, always adored elevators."

"Oh, God," I muttered and motioned for him to get on with it.

"And you know how impossibly slow that eternal thing in this building can be."

I felt my cheek muscles twitch. "And?"

"I may have grown tired of waiting and entered the contraption somewhat prematurely."

"And?" I was shouting now.

"It seems your neighbor, Mrs. Dumbfounder—"

"Oleander!"

"Right you are—Oleander. Well, it seems Mrs. Oleander inopportunely chose to descend the top floor within that dreadful metal box while I was embarking on my little shortcut."

I cradled my head and considered an Advil *and* a hotel.

"But not to worry," he prattled on. "She fainted, much to my advantage, allowing for my judicious escape."

"I get the sense there's a little more to it."

"Perhaps a smidgen," Fane said with an impish grin, pinching his thumb against an index finger. "As luck would have it, for an old woman, she has the most amazing recall!"

"And exactly how do you know that?"

"She's a sharer, too. Did I mention that? Every little experience, no matter how big or how small."

"Whom did she tell?"

"Does it matter? It seems, to me, we could better expend our energy by discrediting the old hag. That's it!" he exclaimed, treading air halfway between the kitchen and the loft entrance. "I'll initiate a few rumors straight away!"

"Oh, no! You will absolutely not! I don't want you within a hundred yards of my neighbors. Why can't you be a normal—"

He swooped beside me, creating a whooshing sound, and sent the mail resting upon the countertop airborne.

"Handsome, positively irresistible rascal?" he interjected.

"Leave!" I said, pointing to the door.

Fane sighed and smoothed wrinkles from tight leather pants dyed a bewildering and unflattering shade of Fuchsia. "As you wish!" Soaring toward a window, he paused in midair. "By the by, do forewarn me of any upcoming rendezvous with that flaccid beau of yours, for I shan't be there. I find the entire spectacle most anticlimactic. I dare say observing your pathetic tête-a-tête is as stimulating as watching Michelangelo's paintings dry."

I picked up a vase. "Fane, I'm warning you: Get. The. Hell. Out!"

≈

WALKING into roll call the next day, I discovered I was the first to arrive and took a front-row seat. As the rest of the officers filed in, I overheard several conversations. The discussion revolved around Turkey, more specifically, the unusual sightings noted there, and every nerve in my body seemed elongated like an array of overstretched rubber bands. A dynamic debate ensued, involving statements from several Turkish witnesses, most describing ill-defined, lightning-fast shadows.

Sitting a couple of chairs down from mine, one officer said, "What about that one guy who said, 'A pale man, draped in black, saved my life?'"

"Yeah, I heard that too," a female officer added. "Something about a hideous creature attacking him before this hero appeared out of nowhere?"

Seated beside me, Ethan coughed out a laugh. "Maybe it was an Akashita."

"What the hell's that?" asked the first officer.

"Some creature that materializes from a black cloud near water, usually a flood gate."

"That's just a freaking legend!" someone else chimed in.

"Your job is to hunt the bad guys here, in Kansas City," Randy quipped as he assumed his position at the podium and waited for the room to quiet, "not some phantom creature clear across the world. So, listen up!" Some whispered disparaging remarks, but Randy continued. "Officers Marks and Rajas will be assisting the East Division, along with me, Officer Crenshaw, Officers Mahoney and Decker, and Officers Sanchez and Kirkpatrick. The Milburn trial ends today and, while we don't anticipate any trouble, the commissioner wants additional police presence. Any questions?" Randy scanned the room for a show of hands. Seeing none, he said, "All right, dismissed. Stay safe out there."

"They'd better find him guilty," a female officer whispered behind me. "It was a clear-cut case of rape. That asshole gets off, just because he's the senator's son, there's going to be hell to pay."

~

RANDY COULDN'T HAVE BEEN MORE wrong. Less than an hour after the jury returned a "not guilty" verdict, the entire east side of the city became a warzone. Many detectives suddenly found themselves assigned to duties well beneath their paygrades, off-duty officers reported back in, and—for the first time, anyone could remember—officers utilized riot shields. When snipers began taking potshots at cops, tactical ballistic shields also accessorized the party.

I heard a bullet whistle past my head and eagerly snugged on a helmet. A moment later, I saw a cop from another precinct catch a round in the shoulder and dive under his patrol car.

So much for tactical vests.

Hiding as best we could behind shields, I—along with a dozen or so other officers—stormed a building where looting was in progress. Because this happened to be a gun shop, Midwest Justice, Sergeant Dickerson bellowed a lethal warning from a bullhorn. His warning went unheeded, and a Barrage of Blue stormed the store. Those who refused to comply encountered either tasers, rubber bullets, or both. Fortunately, for all, the majority of the mob decided not to call Dickerson's bluff and made a run for it.

Forty-five minutes and several arrests later, the volatile protest came to a bitter end. Officers from six precincts returned to regular duty, some bruised and battered, most weary, all grateful that no casualties had occurred on either side.

Officer Decker was returning the riot gear to his squad car when a bullet ricocheted off the trunk lid, grazing his left cheek. I saw him drop to the ground and roll toward the vehicle's opposite side. I assumed the shot came from the rooftop of Harry's Liquor Store, so I backtracked up the block to the corner and darted down the alley until I reached the rear entrance. Before gaining entry, I whacked the Glock's magazine hard to make sure it had properly seated.

I tiptoed up the metal steps and cautiously cracked the door ajar. The sniper was nowhere in sight. I opened it another twelve inches or so. An impressive *ping!* sounded off the steel entry. I ducked and radioed for backup. My pulse was pounding in both ears. Certain I'd heard footsteps—each one sounding more distant than the one before—I stayed low and charged from the door. Seeking concealment, I spotted a flue pipe and made a run toward it. Crouching behind it, satisfied I was now invisible, I took a deep breath, attempting to slow my heart rate.

The assailant grabbed me from behind and—after a brutal skirmish—confiscated my weapon. When he planted my gun against my skull, I froze. A few anxious beats after that, a shadow loomed overhead, and the suspect sailed sideways.

I went for my gun, now just to the right of my tactical boot, and spun, the gun accurately leveled despite trembling fingers.

Although his back was to me, I recognized Nick, his golden hair nearly to his shoulders, slumped over what I assumed the suspect. I called his name in a near whisper. He turned slowly, his errant and familiar smile grotesquely marred behind a veil of blood. Then he vaporized, discarding a nearly decapitated exsanguinated corpse.

CHAPTER 24

*W*ringing my hands, I paced a path on the rooftop, contemplating a plausible explanation for the horror Nick had left in his wake. I jumped when Tristan appeared near an outcropping by the door.

"We must act, Celestine," he said, effectively blocking my access to the body. "They're coming."

I listened, straining, but heard no one approaching.

"They have already breached the first landing," he insisted. The sniper's gun in hand, Tristan fired a round within a foot of my position, cupped the corpse's hand around the gun, then suddenly appeared at my side.

Somewhat disoriented by his rapid movement and still reeling from the gunshots fired, I stumbled in the opposite direction.

"What the hell, Tristan?"

"It is important your comrades believe he was shooting at you." Effortlessly, he wrestled the Glock out of my hand, aimed and fired a forty-caliber bullet, perforating the gunman's throat.

I covered a scream then grabbed his arm.

"Oh my God! What have you done?"

"What would you have me do, Celeste? Do you wish the police to discover exsanguination as this man's cause of death? Do you wish to explain that your brother is a vampire, thus the reason behind this man's inexplicable injuries? Turn around, Celeste."

"No!"

He glanced toward the rooftop's entrance. "Please, do as I say."

"Why?" I asked shrilly. My eyes darted toward the door. I heard them now, determined footsteps rebounding off metal stairs.

"As you wish." Tristan slashed his own carotid artery and blood gushed from his wound. Directing the stream to the corpse, he splayed it, artfully, around the sniper's head.

Unable to catch my breath and feeling as though I might vomit, I threw both hands in the air.

"Why would you do that!"

"I had to replace the blood."

"What if they test it?"

"They won't," he said and vanished just as law enforcement stormed the rooftop.

Back at the station, I coordinated my statement so that it matched the evidence. To my relief, there were no suspicious glances and no skeptical inquiries. I showered there, though no amount of soap and water could scrub away the things I'd seen, the massacre I'd allowed. I left word for Ethan with the dispatcher, informing him I'd chosen to grab a cab home. Feeling a full-fledged panic attack on the horizon, I knew I had to get out of the station. Because I wanted to avoid running into any of the other cops, I decided to wait at the corner.

Tristan crept up behind me, a decadent scent of frankincense, myrrh, and patchouli announcing his arrival.

"Celeste," he murmured through my hair. I waited, comforted by his smell, by his touch, but he stayed quiet.

I turned to face him, slowly, preparing myself for what always proved a heart-wrenching event.

"What will happen to Nick?" He seemed confused. "I'm talking about the Code, Tristan."

"Nicholas did nothing wrong according to Omniscient law."

"What do you mean, he did nothing wrong!"

"The explanation is complicated."

"Try me!"

He shrugged as if we were discussing the weather. "If one deserves annihilation, why would the universe make such a denial?"

"The universe! What does the universe have to do with it?"

"In our eyes, evil deserves the ultimate reprisal."

My mouth dropped open, and I shook my head in disbelief, resenting his preposterous justification and, even more, the effect he had on me.

Tristan nodded, robotically, as if his insistence might change my opinion. "In your time, so much effort is wasted on banter."

"Banter? Don't you mean, proper judicial course? As in abiding by laws and regulations?"

Tristan's daunting eyes continued to devour my soul, and I averted my eyes, silently damning him for making me want him, making me love him.

"Trials, prisons. Both are ineffective."

"So, you're saying Nick can murder—because that's what it is—anybody he wants to, as long as it's someone who deserves it?"

His skin becoming more transparent, Tristan snugged his hood over his prominent forehead.

"Yes, uncomplicated and most effective."

My eyes probing the cracks in the sidewalk while my fingernails dug into my hips, I said, "Unbelievable!" Out of the corner of my eye, I noticed a cab inching along the curb. "I can't deal with this. I'm going home!"

～

THE SUN WAS SETTING, the moon subtly competing, when I sulked from the cab. The evenings were still chilly with spring in no hurry to hand over the reins to summer. I tugged my Levi's jacket closed. The wind picked up suddenly, and I quickened my steps.

Rounding the laborious stone portico, I caught a whiff of canine adrenaline and felt the urge to run. The pack of wolves surrounding me, the alpha wolf, Vykoka, prepared to charge. The others simply observed, content to lope a tight circle with predatory grace. Taking a defensive stance, I brought my right arm up, and my forearm caught the brunt of the attack.

Fraught with panic and putting all my weight behind it, I dropkicked Vykoka's frothing shark-like teeth, and the alpha male retreated. Keeping an eye on the pack, I ran backwards, then dove into a dumpster, just as he prepared a second strike, and slammed the lid shut tight. For nearly fifteen minutes, I stayed put, surrounded by reeking garbage, a few dilapidated lawn chairs, and what I suspected a rodent or two. Convinced the pack didn't intend to give up, my fingers retrieved my cellphone from a back pocket, and I phoned Bianca.

"You must be in the elevator," she said, her angelic tone still comforting, regardless of the circumstances.

"No, a dumpster just outside my building."

"Hardly the explanation I would have anticipated."

"And I've got company."

"That would explain the urgency. Darling, I am listening."

"It's Vykoka, and he's not alone."

"Of course, he is not alone, the coward! Sit tight, my pet. We are nearly there."

Brushing off rotted vegetation, an assortment of limp

documents, and several things that moved, I knew members of the Realm had arrived. I covered my ears when earsplitting screeches, growls, and other indescribable sounds punched the still, night air.

Because I had to know what was going on outside the dumpster, I pinched the lid open. I recognized Vykoka, foremost. His fur bristling and sharp incisors snapping the air beyond a snarl, he launched an unfathomable distance from a dead stop. Landing in close proximity to Bianca, she whirled round and round, bringing to mind the Tasmanian Devil or film clips documenting a violent tornado. In the midst of her revolutions, Vykoka disappeared, and I assumed her extreme velocity had sucked him inside. My eyes wide, I covered a gasp when bits of fur showered the parking lot as if hairy confetti and chunks of flesh hit the pavement with a sickening thud. The remainder of the Realm battled the rest of the pack with far less dramatic flair, most opting to meet incomprehensible strength with a supernatural force far superior, essentially disintegrating the preternatural canines upon impact. They greeted some of the heartier wolfish opponents with unforgiving fangs, which lanced gamy, rancid-smelling fur. The vampires decapitated each one of the disabled werewolves. Then with their eyes glowing red, members of the Realm aimed the equivalent of lasers with pinpoint accuracy, and the werewolves burst into flames. The few wolves still in the fight encountered reptilian monsters of extraordinary size with gigantic mouths housing teeth comparable to those found on excavator machinery. I must admit that upon witnessing the terrifying metamorphosis, I considered closing the lid. The violent conflict was over within minutes, and I wondered how the Realm had ever considered Vykoka and his pack much of a threat.

Alerted to the shrill arrival of police cars, my eyes flew to Bianca, who met my gaze, then instructed me to close the lid. Which was fine with me; I did not intend to involve myself in explanations, particularly after the rooftop incident.

Thirty minutes later, several vehicles roared to life, and I heaved the lid open, squinting as a parade of taillights created a colorful procession. Once it had reached the corner, I wrenched myself out.

"This is the end, Celestine," Bianca said from her perch on a limb above me. "You must come home."

Other than a small pool of blood on the pavement, the parking lot appeared as it had before. "What happened?"

"Ashes to ashes, my darling."

"So, they what, just disappeared?"

Bianca flicked her wrist, and I may have witnessed an eye roll. "What does it matter?"

I noted curtains from a second-story window slide from wrinkled fingers, and I knew Mrs. Oleander had placed the 911 call. "Mom, let's talk inside."

She was waiting for me with chin in hand and keen raptorial eyes when I entered the loft. "You have nearly ended your life twice today. I simply will not tolerate any further recklessness, Celestine!"

"*I* nearly ended my life twice today?"

"Perhaps I should have rephrased it. Nevertheless, it hardly changes a devastating outcome, now does it?"

I plied both hands on my hips.

"Speaking of devastating outcomes . . . I saw Nick today."

"Of this, I am most aware, which only emphasizes the urgency that you abandon this utter nonsense and return home."

"I saw Tristan, too . . . after Nick murdered a man." I waited for some kind of response, but Bianca remained dormant, like a volcano on the verge of eruption. "He told me about the Code."

"That has little to do with you and the current situation."

"It has everything to do with me!"

Bianca stiffened as she clasped her hands. "The Code allows for the destruction of all unworthy mortals or immortals, a much-deserved obliteration."

I sputtered a laugh. "Well, I'm a cop, whose job is to arrest murderers; mortal or immortal."

Bianca's grin was both transient and impish. "Immortals you say? To do so would prove very unwise. Perhaps, you should embrace the Code, Celestine. Common sense would dictate that it only serves to simplify your duties."

I threw both arms sideways. "Simplify! So what, you expect me to stand by and watch civilians slaughtered?"

She clucked her tongue, crimson pooling in her eyes, like rays from a sunset cast upon the water. "Surely, you of all people can make the distinction between a criminal and an innocent civilian."

I shook my head. "They're all innocent, Mom, until proven otherwise!"

"Such preposterous dribble!"

"I always thought you—of all people—would never lie to me. I believed you when you told me the Realm received their sustenance only from the lab. So that's what you did; you lied to me!"

"Those words never crossed my lips, Celestine! This you assumed. I have never deceived you!"

Pressing my palms toward her, I backed away, feeling both repulsion and betrayal.

"Pack your things! You are returning home where we can protect you."

"The hell I am!"

"Stop behaving like an insolent child! Putting some distance between you and this day's events is most rational."

"I'm not a child, something I can't seem to make you understand."

She vanished, and I twirled several revolutions in an attempt to locate her.

Her hair still swirling, she reappeared, her nose nearly contacting mine. "*We* make the world a safer place, Celestine."

I shook my head. "*My* world was doing just fine until *yours* entered it."

Clutching her heart, with a poof, she was gone.

~

THAT NIGHT I dreamt of Nick, as we were long ago, carefree and inseparable. His blond head bobbing, his jaw set in that determined way I'll always remember, his beautiful eyes gleaming as he pulled me along in the little red wagon he referred to as my princess chariot. Managing a steep incline, Nick stopped to catch his breath, his feet braced solidly against the sidewalk, his tan forearm tense and quivering in response to the effort required to keep the wagon from sliding downhill.

"Lesty, I can't hold it!" he said, between grunts and groans, his angelic face contorted in fear and exhaustion. "I can't hold it!"

Losing his grip, the wagon slid backwards, picking up momentum as it clipped along. Striking a rise in the concrete, I sailed headlong into an oak tree bearing our initials, and I awoke with a start. I saw Nick, but this time in the flesh and hovering overhead. We stared at one another for some time.

Nick finally spoke. "They don't know I'm here."

I assumed he meant our parents. "What are you doing here?" I whispered, not wanting to wake Ethan.

Nick shrugged. "I just wanted to make sure you're all right."

I slipped from the bed and gestured toward the living room. Nick followed. Without prompting, he took a seat beside me on the sofa and slung an arm around my shoulders.

"Is this about today?" I said. "Because I understand why you did what you did. I don't like it, but I understand it."

Nick shook his head. "Like I said, they don't know I'm here."

I twisted around to face him, and his arm slipped away. "Is something wrong? Are they all right?"

He pressed a palm in my direction, offering a curt nod.

"Earlier tonight, Mom was attacked."

I gasped, mostly because of the disclosure and partly because I hadn't heard Nick refer to Bianca as Mom for years.

"Oh God! What happened?"

"Yesenia ambushed her over the Atlantic."

"When she was returning from Kansas City?"

Nick nodded. "She's pretty fucked up, Celeste."

CHAPTER 25

I popped upright. "That's all you're going to tell me?"

"Her face and most of her body look like a friggin' road map. She's missing some hair. I hardly recognized her. She's really weak. Dad insisted she drink his blood, and most of the superficial lacerations were already healing when I left the house. So, that's a good sign."

"Was Yesenia by herself?"

Nick shrugged. "I did hear Mom tell Dad that Yesenia destroyed a few Harvesters who attempted to join in."

"That's weird." Nick looked confused, so I elaborated. "I guess I just assumed, we all assumed, she'd aligned herself with them after that fight she had with Trandafira in the woods outside the stables."

Nick nodded. "I heard about the time she came after you in Rebel's stall. I guess you know he hasn't been the same since."

I didn't know. I shook my head, and my heart sank a little.

Nick must have sensed my sorrow because he said, "He's fine, Celeste. As long as I don't ride him anywhere near the woods."

He clasped my hand, a little too firmly. I withdrew immediately, my fingers aching as if frostbitten.

"I still don't understand why Yesenia attacked the Harvesters."

"She wanted Mom all to herself and, when they decided to horn in, she kicked their asses." He offered a weak grin. "From what I've heard, Mom did a lot of ass-kicking herself. Yesenia got the worst of it."

"But she's wasn't destroyed?"

"No, which is why I'm here." He slanted stern eyes in my direction and set his jaw. I found his tone similarly aggressive. "If Mom hadn't been in Kansas City, it wouldn't have happened. You need to come home, Celeste. We've got enough shit to worry about."

"Oh, don't you dare put this on me, Nick!" I said, not caring if I woke Ethan. "This is bullshit. Mom's always putting herself in danger, involving herself in this battle or that. And Yesenia could have sought her revenge at every turn."

I thought Nick's eyes might bore a hole through me, his beautiful blue irises suddenly a black onyx, kaleidoscoping to gold then silver sporadically, and I considered distancing myself. I heard Ethan stir in the bedroom and lowered my voice. He'd never met my brother, and this sure as hell didn't seem the optimal time. I folded my arms across my chest and tipped my head toward the door. "You need to go, Nick."

∾

FANE KEPT me apprised of my mother's recovery, and while I wanted to see her, I thought it best I keep my distance for now, particularly after our last conversation. While I waited for Randy to saunter out of the Men's Locker Room, instead of phoning her, I made reservations at *Garozzo's*, Ethan's favorite Italian Restaurant. All of a sudden, my cell sounded *Crazy* by

CeeLo Green, and it took me several minutes to make the connection. I hadn't heard the song nor heard from Aubrey in years.

"Where are you staying?" I asked, following the obligatory greeting.

"Nowhere, I just got in," she said past a wad of gum, and I visualized her tugging on an oversized earring.

"Why are you in Kansas City?"

She laughed, and it occurred to me how much I'd missed her.

"Some things never change. You're the most direct person I know."

"That's like the pot calling the kettle black."

"Celeste, you're the only person I know who uses those dumb shit, archaic phrases."

"Are you still living in New Jersey?"

"Nah, let's just say I'm still looking for my true calling."

"What does that mean exactly?"

"Bumming around the country. Don't judge, Celeste. You've always had your shit together."

"Did you get your degree?"

I thought I heard her laugh. "I lost my scholarship before the end of the first semester."

"Aubrey," I chastised softly.

"It turns out college isn't all it's cracked up to be. They actually expect you to study. Enough about me! Why'd you leave New Jersey and without a word?"

I rubbed a guilt-stricken eye. "I should have kept in touch."

"You think!"

"You could have called me, Aubrey."

"You're right," she said. "I love you, Celeste, but I always felt like such a dumbass next to you. So, after flunking out of college—"

I suffered a pang of guilt, then just as quickly dismissed it.

I wasn't responsible for Aubrey's lack of motivation.

"How'd you end up in the Midwest?" she asked after a loud pop, and I knew she hadn't lost her penchant for bubble gum.

"I got this job offer . . ."

"I bet you're a schoolteacher," Aubrey said and laughed.

"No actually, I'm a cop."

"No shit!"

"Afraid so. So, what are you doing here?" I said, wanting to divert her attention.

"I've got this job interview in Wisconsin—cheesy, huh— and thought I'd look you up along the way."

I rolled my eyes and, subconsciously, grinned a half-grin. Aubrey hadn't changed a bit.

"No, the job interview isn't cheesy, but I can't say the same for your sense of humor." A loud pop once again blasted my eardrum, and I exhaled some aggravation. "Nice to know you're still keeping the chewing gum companies afloat."

"I quit smoking, so I'm going through like twenty pieces of this stuff a day. My teeth may rot to hell, but at least I won't get lung cancer, right? Hey, I was hoping we could meet for lunch, Celeste," she said, her tone almost sentimental.

I glanced at my watch and made a mental note to text Ethan regarding our usual lunch plans.

"Sure, why not. Where are you now?"

"At the Nelson Art Gallery. I've heard it's a *must-see.*"

"Do you know where the Country Club Plaza is?"

"Just came from there. It almost measured-up to all the hype."

I gnawed on my lip, resisting a snide comment. Cynicism was an unattractive trait Aubrey apparently had not outgrown.

"I'll meet you at the corner of Broadway and Main at noon, near the fountain with the horses spewing water."

"I'll be the one riding the horse."

"And I'll be the one with handcuffs, ready to cart your ass off to jail."

"You were never any fun, Celeste."

"You were fun enough for both of us." I caught motion out of the corner of my eye; Randy gesturing manically. "Gotta go. See you then."

AUBREY NEVER SHOWED. My calls to her cell phone went unanswered. I was annoyed, confused, and somewhat worried. When Aubrey made a commitment, she stuck to it, the exception being college. Maybe she was lost. I considered that, but her GPS wouldn't have failed her. Besides, she would have called. By twelve-thirty, I'd nearly convinced myself she'd simply changed her mind; probably found a hot guy and had lunch with him instead. If that was the case, the Aubrey I knew wouldn't have bothered to let me know. Judgmental, inconsiderate, selfish Aubrey; there was a reason I'd always been her only friend.

I blew the whole thing off, didn't think any more about it until shortly after 5 p.m. when I returned to the station. The Sixth Precinct had found a charred car in an abandoned industrial section, two blocks north of the Missouri River. I insisted they run the New Jersey license plate, which confirmed my suspicion, and I requested my superiors instigate an APB for Aubrey Swayze.

"Looks like a carjacking," I heard one of the detectives say as he leaned against the doorway outside the Captain's office. I shuddered when he drew out a sigh and said, "Young, attractive woman. Having her car stolen is the least of her worries. I doubt they're done with her yet; or that this is going to end well."

Gangs were responsible for nearly half the city's crime. Gang initiations were as horrific as they were infuriating to the police, and the suspected situation at hand, involving Aubrey, followed a consistent and unfortunate pattern. My assessment coinciding with that of the detective, I knew we had to find Aubrey quickly, and I hoped she'd be alive when we did.

"Take Rodriquez and go lean on the Ninth Street Ghosts," Captain Burke barked. "Haul in their leader—"

"Alphonse Marquez," Detective Markowitz interjected.

"Yeah, that's right . . . Marquez. Get his ass in here. Oh, and Detective, the kid gloves are off. This being a tourist, the mayor will want answers and a suspect or suspects in custody yesterday."

Detective Markowitz nodded, quickly turned on his heel, and left the room when Burke arched a brow and leveled stern eyes, tipping his head toward the street.

I rapped on the door molding, hesitant to step in, unannounced.

Burke looked up from his paperwork. "What do you need, Crenshaw?"

"I'd like to be in on this, Captain."

"Why's that?"

"Aubrey Swayze is a friend of mine."

Burke plucked a piece of paper from his desktop, then straightened his reading glasses. "That's right. You put out the APB."

I nodded. "She was supposed to meet me for lunch."

His expression softened, and he rotated his pen. "That why she was in town? To visit you?"

I shrugged and willed away a tear. "I suppose it may have been a primary reason."

"Let the detectives handle it," he said, tossing the pen off to one side. "Aren't you just coming off a shift?"

I nodded, squaring my jaw. "She is a friend of mine, sir," I reiterated.

Sucking his lower lip, the captain seemed to deliberate.

"All right, Crenshaw, just don't get in the way."

CHAPTER 26

e found Aubrey's body just before 10 p.m. in an abandoned house near Eighth and Hardesty. Her jewelry was missing, her wallet, and most of her clothes. I slunk to the dusty, filth-covered floor, covering my face with both hands.

Rodriquez stooped beside me and clasped my forearm.

"You should wait outside," he said, helping me to my feet. "And watch where you're walking. See those hypodermic needles," he said and made a wide sweeping motion.

To Detective Markowitz, he said, "Give Forensics a heads-up . . . and see that no one compromises the scene until backup arrives," he added, jerking his chin toward the growing crowd now gathering on the sidewalk. "Give him a hand, Officer . . ."

"Crenshaw," I managed, my eyes burning with the threat of tears.

I overheard Detective Markowitz tell another detective who'd arrived on the scene, "Those arrogant bastards tagged her. We've got them now."

"Like it's ever been that easy," the other detective said. "Some up-and-coming defense lawyer, trying to make a name for himself, will spew this was all a setup by a rival gang, most likely the East Side Marauders."

Markowitz shook his head. "DNA will likely prove otherwise," I heard him whisper. "Looks like those assholes were sloppy."

~

I PUT in for a two-day leave. Although Aubrey and her mother had never been close, I wanted to be the one to tell Lacey Swayze her daughter was dead. By the time the airbus circled for a landing at Newark Airport, I almost wished I'd agreed to let the Asbury Park Police Department deliver the bad news.

Once I left the Avis Car Rental lot in an ocean-blue Ford Focus, I limped through rush hour traffic, arriving in Asbury Park an hour later. I recognized Lacey Swayze's tired and rusted Toyota Corolla, taking a much-needed rest on two narrow strips of grease-stained concrete. The house remained the same soul-sucking green color I remembered, and although it was nearly noon, a porch light glowed indifference. Forcing myself from the car, I took a deep breath and rapped on the tattered screen door, a loose piece of mesh fluttering as if to say it had long ago surrendered. Their Yorkie, Guinevere, yapped an unimpressive warning. I must have shifted my weight five times before Lacey tentatively swept the door open, but only a few inches.

Her expression convinced me she wasn't in the mood for company.

"Celeste?" She said, with an air of surprise and annoyance.

"Hello Mrs. Swayze. Can I come in?"

Her hard, oppressive stare was like a slap in the face. She was almost as hospitable as a hostage-taker. "Aubrey's not here."

"I know. I'm here to talk to you."

"I was just getting ready for work," said Lacey, her tone implying I was much more than a minor inconvenience. "What are you doing here? Didn't you move to someplace in the Midwest?"

I nodded, gulping air. "Kansas City. I'm a police officer there."

"Congratulations," she said flatly, "but like I said, I need to get to work."

Executing a fixed stare, which I assumed would convey I was about to share some devastating news, I said, "This will only take a minute . . . it's about Aubrey."

She tightened the knot to her worn pink chenille bathrobe, closing it over a prominent and colorful orchid tattoo, and swept the door open, just enough for me to squeeze through. Once inside, I realized her invitation apparently didn't extend past the foyer.

I nodded toward a dilapidated, faded floral sofa covered in stacks of crumpled gossip magazines and patches of dried dog urine with a splash of fresh cat vomit here and there.

"Can we sit . . . just for a minute?" I said, removing a stack of *National Enquirer* tabloids and taking a seat.

She threw her arms to her sides, before referencing a watch Aubrey had given her years before. "One minute, that's it!"

I sat facing her and pressed my palms together.

She puffed a dramatic sigh, and I recognized the stench of stale tobacco smoke, whiskey, and strong coffee. "Well, what is it? Is Aubrey in some sort of trouble?" Before I could answer, she asked, "What has she done *now*?"

"Aubrey came to visit me . . . in Kansas City . . . on her way to Wisconsin for the job interview."

"Wisconsin?"

"You didn't know?" I wondered why I was surprised.

Lacey shook her head and, again, checked the time.

"We were supposed to meet for lunch."

She dropped her hands in her lap and arched a heavily penciled brow. "So?"

"She never showed."

Lacey launched upright and swept a pack of Marlboros from a *Reader's Digest*, tossed haphazardly atop a nearby TV-tray table. "What do you want me to do about it? You've come all the way to New Jersey to tell me that? I've told you, she's not here."

"I know where she is," I said, lowering my eyes.

CHAPTER 27

I don't think Lacey Swayze realized how much her daughter meant to her until she'd learned she was dead. I consoled her as best anyone could, considering the circumstances, and couldn't help feeling it much more than she deserved. Aubrey hadn't always been just a latchkey kid, but the housekeeper, cook, ambulance caller, and gardener to boot. After I explained to Lacey that Kansas City would release Aubrey's body as soon as the investigation was complete, I gave her my cell phone number and told her she could call me anytime.

Winding through Asbury Park, I veered toward Ocean Avenue, still uncertain whether I wanted to detour toward Pier Point, more specifically Torok Mansion. Leaving much-less-impressive real estate behind, rows of stone-and-lapboard mansions—extensively spaced and all sporting six-car garages with an unrivaled view of the Atlantic—dotted the costal four-lane boulevard.

Possibly long before I'd pulled onto the winding lane, situated between flowering trees and enormous shrubs, Bianca had been eagerly waiting, just inside the Toroks' laboriously paved courtyard.

"You're here," I said simply, reluctantly climbing out of the Ford.

"As are you," she replied. "Perhaps you were hoping otherwise?"

I shuffled my feet, my approach numbingly slow. "I'm sorry I haven't called. You look well, Mom."

She said nothing, content to study me through her gleaming, all-knowing eyes, and I tried not to flinch.

"Nick came to see me after your attack, but I guess you know that," I said and self-consciously scrubbed my toe against the brick pavers.

"Nick came to see you?"

"You didn't know?" I said, dumbfounded.

Bianca chirped a laugh. "I venture to say I was not myself for a few days."

"I'm sorry that happened, Mom. Sometimes, I think if I hadn't . . ."

She interrupted with a brisk wave of her hand. "Darling, do not go blaming yourself. Yesenia caught me off-guard. That is what it amounts to. She shan't be so lucky next time."

I stared at my feet as sadness overwhelmed me.

"Aubrey's dead," I told her.

"I know," she purred and held out her arms.

Of course, she knew. I ran to her, content to let her hold me and whisper the kinds of things mothers whisper when their children are bordering on an emotional breakdown.

"She was always so insouciant, so trusting," Bianca whispered through my hair. "*Too* trusting."

I pulled back and deliberated a much-overdue apology. "I'm sorry. I didn't mean the things I said the night you came to my rescue."

Bianca flicked a wrist. "Water under the bridge. I suppose it is time I acknowledged the fact that you are now a mature, intelligent young woman, quite capable of managing her own affairs."

"Where's Father?"

"Syria," she said caustically and arched a brow.

"Oh . . ." was all I could manage. The current turmoil in that country made stateside, gang-ravaged cities seem more like paradise. I studied her concentrated gaze, falling somewhere beyond the pristine lawn and the horizon, and I was certain she witnessed everything now occurring within Syria.

"Both he and Nick should return by dawn," she offered moments later. "Won't you stay?"

I WOKE to a room left unchanged since I'd departed for Missouri. The Torok house was always perpetually dark, and it was often difficult to distinguish night from day, particularly upon awakening from a deep sleep. I lunged for my cell phone, the bedside alarm clock—an annoying blur of green digits—and I was surprised the time was now 9 a.m. Although I assumed the remainder of the household lay nestled in caskets or had yet to return home, I had a hunch Bianca waited patiently downstairs in the shuttered parlor, armed with a glass of orange juice and more motherly advice.

Reaching the bottom stair, I realized my mistake. The solemn voices became louder as I rounded the arched entryway to the long shadowy hallway, which led to my father's office. Peering discreetly around the doorway, I saw Nick first. He seemed taller, more muscular, exceptionally handsome, imposing, and surprisingly sedate.

"Total annihilation," I heard Razvan tell Bianca. "Nick and Tristan were both relentless."

"So, the threat has been extinguished?" she pressed.

"For now," Nick said, in a tone as alien to me as a family day at the beach. As I listened to him describe more of the situation to Bianca, he sounded articulate, mature, humble, and compassionate, all qualities I'd always felt he'd never possess.

"Casualties?" Bianca queried.

"Tens," Razvan told her. "If we hadn't intervened . . ."

". . . it might have been hundreds," Nick finished for him. "Possibly, thousands instead."

"Dreadful." Bianca's tone turned cheery when I walked into the room. "Good morning!"

Nick glided toward me, effortlessly. "Celeste! My God, you look older!"

He was teasing, but I'm sure he was most aware time would forever be my enemy but not his. His smile disappeared, and he pulled me close, curtaining sad eyes. A moment passed, and the old Nick returned, sniffing the air, overzealously, like a dog scrutinizing a guest. I instinctively pulled away.

"Relax," he said, laughing. "I'm just messin' with you!"

I smiled up at him, recoiling somewhat as he brushed glacial lips across my cheek.

"Some things never change. It's good to see you, Nick."

Nick pulled me close. "It's good to see you too. Dadcula over there laid down the rules; otherwise, I would have always been close by."

Razvan crooked a finger in Nick's direction as if to invite a physical confrontation. Then, to my surprise, he rolled his eyes and laughed. "Pfft! *Dracula*—Such a Godforsaken book!"

Bianca twittered, adding, "I hardly think the comparison of your father to that ridiculous impotent figment of Mr. Stoker's imagination fair, Nicholas. The pitiful Mr. Stoker was as versed on our kind as a shepherd is to erecting pyramids."

Razvan snared her by the waist and whispered something she must have found flush-worthy.

"Dearest Celestine, how wonderful to have you home!"

I broke away from Nick and kissed my father's cheek.

"But not for long, darling," Bianca informed him.

"Is this true?" he said to me.

"Aubrey died . . . was murdered. I wanted to tell her mother in person. Now, I have to get back."

"Such horrible news. I do wish you would reconsider, Celestine. Your mother worries so."

"Sorry to hear that, sis. Need any help?" Nick offered.

I envisioned Aubrey's murderers attempting to wrestle free from my brother's preternatural jaws.

"I think we can handle it. Besides, it looks as though you've got enough going on."

Nick grinned. "I've become quite the world traveler. Last month, Afghanistan; yesterday, Syria."

Bianca's eyes suddenly flickered, then glazed over, the typical precursors she suffered when telepathically witnessing bloody chaos. Razvan and Nick waited with heightened senses, leaving me to wonder what part of the world was now involved in a horrid catastrophe. She recovered moments later, her eyes shedding a crimson border, a pool of saliva marring perfect teeth.

"Celestine, it seems we shan't be far afield. A tornado has scattered much of Joplin, Missouri." All three crooked erudite noses westward. "One can positively smell the carnage."

CHAPTER 28

"The district attorney is concerned there's not enough evidence," Captain Burke informed me in an apologetic but resentful tone.

"But I thought the DNA . . ."

"The prosecutor has concerns that it won't hold up in court," he told me, scowling now. "The investigation has turned up, let's just say, controversy regarding Ms. Swayze's sexual escapades."

I narrowed my eyes involuntarily. "Can you be more specific, Captain?"

He puffed his cheeks, rounded his desk, and leaned against it, cupping the edge with all ten fingers. Pretending interest in something over my head, he said, "All right, Crenshaw. The prosecution has discovered that your friend had a reputation for being quite the . . . party-girl."

I considered Aubrey's promiscuity. "But the DNA proves a connection. A timeline!"

He held up a palm. "That may be true, but the defense attorney will argue that Ms. Swayze was a willing participant, given her promiscuous reputation. He'll insist she gave consent. I can almost hear the summation now: *After the victim*

*enjoyed the company of several men to include my clients, she had the
misfortune of entertaining one too many, a man other than my clients; her
murderer.* The district attorney won't touch this case unless we
have more compelling evidence. So, what we need," Burke
returned to his seat, tilting forward in his chair, "is more
evidence tying Aubrey to the Ninth Street Ghosts, after the
fact."

"Like what?"

"Her wallet was missing. Possibly jewelry from what we've
gathered. Find a connection between those missing items and
the gang, and we've got an airtight case."

BACK AT THE PRECINCT, I headed toward the canteen, where I
victoriously grabbed a bag of pretzels from the vending
machine and a Coke, nearly giving up after the machine
rejected a few one-dollar bills. Entering the squad room, I
noted Randy was still engaged in a conversation with his
confidential informant, so I nibbled on a pretzel impatiently,
distancing myself further when he graced me with a scowl.

Gripping the desk phone like a hand grenade while
his scuffed tactical boots marred a desk placed there during
Herbert Hoover's presidency, Randy continued to grill his CI
for any word on the street. Meanwhile, I scoured the internet
for any social media accounts Aubrey may have had. Discovering a Facebook account, I accessed it and scrutinized her
profile photos. In every photograph, she wore the gold
bracelet her father had given her for her sixteenth birthday. A
pearl ring, surrounded by diamonds and once belonging to
her grandmother, caught the light and glittered on her right
ring finger. A gold crucifix, also diamond-studded, hung on a
gold chain suspended from her neck. I saved the relevant
images, afterwards enhancing the photographs before printing
several copies.

Randy's chair screeched across the tile equally abrasive, and I tossed the half-empty can of Coke and discarded the deflated bag of pretzels.

"That asshole actually thinks he can play me," Randy said, after he'd returned the desk phone handset to its cradle. "But after I reeducated him on his pissant role and reminded him of his unending reservation at the Jackson County Correctional Facility, it seems it was enough to jog his memory. Grab a vest. Those Troost Avenue thugs have nothing better to do but use cops for target practice."

Randy and I decided to begin our investigation at two of the more infamous pawnshops, one located at the corner of Thirty-first and Prospect Avenue, the other at Thirty-ninth and Troost Avenue.

With Randy shadowing, I barged into the Gold Post on Prospect and took a step back when the shop owner, four-hundred pounds of bad news, swept an impressive shotgun from under the counter and laid it topside.

"What can I do for you, Officer?" he patronized past two enormous gold teeth.

Narrowing my eyes, I plastered the counter with three enlarged photographs. "Anybody bring any of these items in?"

Without as much as a glance, he shook no.

"Look again," I demanded without blinking.

"You got a warrant?"

Randy stepped forward and fielded the question.

"No, but she can get one. In the meantime, it'll just be you and me. And, since we will have inconvenienced a judge anyway, maybe I'll have a look at all your inventory. Maybe compare it with some home invasion catalogs and some local smash and grabs. Hope you got insurance to cover your losses."

The owner whisked a tray from the bottom counter and plucked out Aubrey's bracelet. From the safe, he collected her grandmother's ring.

"I sold the crucifix," he volunteered with a ragged sigh. "Holidays, ya know?"

"Yeah, sure, I get it," Randy quipped. "Nothing says *I love Jesus* quite like stolen shit."

"We want the names of the sellers," I managed through grinding teeth. "A photocopy of the transaction will do."

Bad News hesitated until Randy made a move for his handcuffs.

"Okay, okay," he said, pitching both hands toward the ceiling. "I gotcha Barney Fife."

He strolled over to a file cabinet covered in filth and cartoonish-nude-women stickers and riffled through equally shabby documents. Finding what he was looking for, he crushed one against smudged copier glass.

When he returned with three separate records, Randy looked them over. "Now, I want their legal names."

"Those is their legal names!"

"You ask for ID?"

"Shit, man, what you think?"

Randy read from the document detailing the ring sale. "Jimmy Bswaggin." Then he recited the name of the bracelet seller. "Lionel Richie." He studied the third document and chuckled. "Get this, Officer Crenshaw: Jason Voorhees. Well, what'd ya know? And here I thought he only existed in the movies. Guess he's not content with just slicing folks up, he robs them too." I resisted an eye roll while Randy whacked a jewelry case with his nightstick, and I took a few steps back, surprised the glass hadn't shattered.

"Unless you want your freaking life to turn into *Friday the 13th*, I suggest you tell me what I want to know. Otherwise, I'm gonna haul your ass in." Getting no response, Randy shrugged. "Doesn't matter to me. I get paid either way."

Although Bad seemed to be considering the odds, sixty-seconds later, we had our suspects' legal names: Jimmy Johnson, Lionel Williams, and Jake Roberts.

"Hey," he said as I stepped out the door, "you didn't get that from me. Snitchin' is bad for business."

"I'll bet," I said and came to a dead stop alongside Randy. Riotous laughter rolled out behind us.

"Nice ride, Five-O," Bad snorted past a belly laugh.

While we were inside, someone with an artistic flare had tagged the patrol car. Krylon spray paint cans, once containing every primary color, littered the curb. The mess still wet, I suggested a car wash at the next corner.

"Slap on some gloves and put those cans in the back," Randy barked. "With any luck, those jerkoffs left prints."

Farther down the block, Randy careened the tatted Challenger into what was once known as Slick as Glass; the G and the second L either surrendering to years of neglect or a very dedicated vandal with a juvenile sense of humor only an absentee mother might find witty. Braking abruptly and backing from a booth littered with broken glass, Randy brought the car to a stop within a rust-covered stall shedding pock-marked pavement. The change machine compromised by thugs, I pocketed the three dollar bills I'd intended to use and ransacked my pockets for quarters. Randy did the same. Coming up empty, I spotted another battered machine at the end of the row.

As I passed the last stall, I noticed a woman prewashing a Silver Cadillac Escalade, and my eyes settled on a diamond-studded crucifix peeking from behind her faux-fur jacket. With a sharp inhale, I approached her.

"You mind telling me where you got that necklace?"

"Let's say I do mind."

"I'll need it," I said, wiggling my fingers. "It's evidence in a homicide."

"The hell," she said, simultaneously diving inside the vehicle. She attempted to start the engine. When it failed to respond, she ran out of the car to make her getaway only to trip over the garbage in the parking lot.

"Put your hands where I can see them."

～

WITH LISA JACKSON IN LOCK-UP, and now armed with proof our three DNA donors had once held Aubrey's personal belongings, Randy and I—in the company of four well-trained officers—went on a scavenger hunt for our three homicide suspects. Randy's snitch, a reluctant but reliable informant, had suggested Lula's Pool Hall at Twenty-first and Prospect. Surrounding the crumbling, flamingo-colored two-story brick and stone building with plywood for windows, Randy and I assumed the lead.

Jimmy was the first to fire, one bullet grazing Randy's head. Jimmy was a lousy shot; it was a big target. Crippling the gang member with a round from my Glock, Lionel and Jake flung their hands in the air, and our backup swooped in and disarmed all three.

"Looks like we got them," Randy said behind a rare and fatherly smile. "Sorry about your friend, kid."

Our carwash collar, Lisa, received a ninety-day jail term and a year's probation for resisting arrest and possession of stolen goods. Aubrey's killers weren't that lucky. Because the bullet the coroner plucked from Aubrey's skull matched Jimmy Johnson's Midnight Special, and he'd already racked up three strikes, this a first-degree murder indictment, the jury awarded him the death sentence. Accomplices to the homicide, Lionel Williams and Jake Roberts both received life sentences with no chance for parole. I doubt Aubrey was satisfied.

While I waited for Randy to testify in another trial, I decided to call Aubrey's mother and inform her of the convictions. No answer. No surprise.

CHAPTER 29

Three Years Later

$\mathcal{I}$ shuffled into the station an hour early, the sun not due to arrive for hours. My intent was to avoid anyone and everyone. The dark circles beneath my eyes throbbed, and my throat was scratchy and dry. Last night had marked our first and possibly our last wedding anniversary. Instead of celebrating, we'd had the same argument after leaving the restaurant. Ethan had thought it a romantic idea to include his mother and sister, and now, as I neared my desk, I caught myself shaking my head, still reeling from his ridiculous decision.

With them all sitting rigidly in the booth across from mine, hesitant and looking one to the other like cowardly soldiers embarking on a suicide mission, they had executed their attack. Resisting the urge to get up and leave, several times, I ultimately played the firm hospitable diplomat, convincing them both that Ethan and I should continue a conversation involving our personal matters privately. And by 2 a.m., I'd made my position perfectly clear.

I didn't intend to quit my job and raise baby after baby, particularly since I'd only just made detective, and despite Ethan's argument that we no longer needed my income to stay comfortably afloat. I didn't remind him that, if not for my financial contribution, he might never have finished law school.

My eyes glued to the case folder involving tens of missing children, I noted Ethan's photograph, and I tossed it into a drawer upon a heap of other things I either no longer or seldom needed. Twisting my wedding ring around and around, I knew there was no coming back from that explosive and bitter argument. I regarded Ethan's insertion of his mother and sister into such a private matter as a betrayal. And I knew, in my heart, Ethan would never see things from my perspective.

I considered returning home, but Ethan would be there since he wasn't due at the prestigious law firm—his name soon to grace the enormous bronze plaque above the reception desk—until 9 a.m. So instead, I persuaded myself upright and stumbled over to the outdated coffee machine, its splotchy, etched glass carafe testifying to years of abuse and neglect.

Suddenly inhaling an intoxicating mix of frankincense and everything erotic, I closed my eyes. I leaned into him and felt his body press against mine, and for an instant, both of us were willing victims to a destiny sanctioned someplace between heaven and hell. Not caring if I lived or died within that perfect, salacious moment, I felt every desire I'd ever experienced culminate, and my heart, thumping erratically, threatened to burst. My skin flushing amid mounting goose-bumps, I turned to face him.

A painful longing robbed me of the tiniest breath as I stared, spellbound, into his haunting eyes, and I couldn't move, couldn't speak.

"Celeste," Tristan whispered, his splintered breath teasing an involuntary response from every nerve ending. He whirled me around to face him, and I watched as he scanned the room and sniffed the air, his nostrils fluttering open, then closed. Possibly convinced we were not alone, he said, "Let us renew our exchange outside this wretched place. It reeks of sorrow and disappointment."

"All right," I said, still feeling catatonic, and I strung my purse over one shoulder.

Leading me by my elbow, Tristan whisked me into an alley at the corner.

I stood across from him, shifting my weight, wishing he hadn't come, wondering if he'd always possess the power to torment me like this.

"Why are you here, Tristan?"

"There are nearly one-hundred divisions of the Realm within this country alone."

"Yes, I've heard that," I said, my brows furrowing, my head pounding.

"Nearly every commander finds himself toppled from power."

I swallowed past a hard lump. "Where's Razvan? Is my mother all right?"

He looked away, and his eyes fluttered twice before they closed completely.

"Tristan! Are they all right?"

"At this time, they remain unharmed. They both wished nothing more than to counsel you, personally, but with Razvan and Nicholas leading the charge on the west coast and Bianca and Trandafira battling those murderous savages on the east, it was out of the question."

"Do you mean the Harvesters?"

"Yes, suffice it to say they have acquired an unprecedented following. A vast number now rallies behind them, massacring thousands of mortals, for whom we can offer little salvation."

"What does this have to do—"

"The missing children."

I covered a gasp and felt my eyes widen.

"These . . . these monsters are murdering innocent children?"

Tristan shook his head and reached out to steady me. "They are procuring them for living receptacles."

I realized I'd screamed the first few words, composed myself, and tried again.

"So, you're saying they plan to use these kids as a continual food supply?" When he nodded, I said, "But won't they become—"

Tristan interrupted with another headshake. "It is true that a most proficient technique need be implemented, but total survival, and as a mortal is possible, should they follow these constraints."

"You don't sound very convincing."

He sighed and scrubbed his forehead.

"It is only a matter of time. Such control will be short-lived, as this is unconventional conduct among irreverent fiends."

"We need to stop them!"

"Not *we*, Celeste. Need I remind you your bullets will only alert them of your presence!"

"Don't even suggest I sit this one out, Tristan. Protecting this community is my job, and I plan to do it! What about fire?"

"Have you forgotten our effort to destroy Yesenia? Such a strategy is now most certainly next to impossible when one considers the expansive number of our adversaries she has aligned herself with. Suffice it to say the odds lie not in our favor." While I considered another solution, he raised my chin, the suggestion of a grin teasing the corners of his mouth. "And a stake to the heart is nothing more than folklore."

"What then?" I said, slapping his hand away. "The Harvesters outnumber the Realm. You said so yourself!"

"I have a plan. Before presenting it to Razvan, I need something from you."

I threw my arms to the side. "Okay . . . anything! We have to save these kids."

"You must promise me you won't confront them until my return, iubirea mea."

My emotions raw, bordering on tears, I said, "Don't call me that."

His expression turned more serious, and a lost look marred his ethereal eyes. "How can I not call you *my love?* For that is what you are, Celestine," he whispered. "Though our destinies dictate we merely exist within the same world, it is enough. Every day when I wake, no matter the distance between us, I feel your presence. And without that, I am lost for all eternity. Please, Celestine, I beg of you; do not entertain certain death."

I backed away from him, my hands balling into fists. "I am not a helpless child nor a woman who needs a man to lead the way! And maybe just existing is enough for you, Tristan, but it's all or nothing for me! I'm tired of you moving into and out of my life. I'm sick and tired of wanting your arms around me, your lips against mine, you to see me for who I am. I am physically sick of wanting you!" Fighting tears, I folded my arms hard across my chest and turned my back on him.

He gripped my shoulders and twirled me around. Sinking before me, he grabbed my hands and burrowed his head between my breasts. "You must listen to me! I have had a foreboding; one I have had but once before."

I assumed he meant a premonition; probably one occurring before his wife's and son's deaths. I cupped his face, and when he raised his head—his eyes searching mine—I kissed him. His arms around me now, his frigid skin tempered my heat. He whisked me off my feet and carried me high above the city lights.

~

It wasn't until Tristan's feet touched down on the cliff above the Missouri River that I opened my eyes. A full moon was reflected on the river, the sound of the rolling water serenely splashing against the surrounding rock. Crickets chirped in the background, joining a chorus of humming mosquitoes, warbling nightingales, the raspy croaking of more than one night heron, and the incessant hooting from a chastising barred owl roosting nearby.

He set me down, his fingers surprisingly warm as they cupped my face. I pressed my body against his, wanting him, needing him to touch my soul. Our eyes met, and I saw a raw hunger in his unlike any I'd seen before. Our lips touched, his more hesitant than mine, as my fingers explored what lay beneath his clothes.

He pulled me into him hard and unapologetically, his arousal catching my breath, my body trembling in anticipation. He tugged my shirt over my head, and as he cupped my breasts, sparks erupted from his body, each more intense than the other, and wafted a decadent aroma of lust and everything forbidden.

He ripped off his shirt, eager to connect his skin with mine. One hand gently nestling my face, his other unbuttoning his Levi jeans, he whispered romantic and tantalizing thoughts in my ear, words I've dreamt he'd say for as long as I can remember. His mouth covering mine, he parted my lips with his tongue, and I tasted a blend of licorice and honey. I jumped when his budding incisors pierced my lower lip, and I took a step backward.

"Do you wish me to stop?" he said, his words blowing hot and sweet across my face.

I didn't, despite the fact that my life, as I knew it, quite possibly lay on the line. But Tristan's change of heart had taken me by surprise, and I wasn't sure I was ready. I took another step back, agonizing over my decision, every erogenous zone in my body alert and pleading.

He smiled at me as he waited patiently for my response, his herculean muscles breathtaking in the moonlight.

"I would never bring you harm, Celeste. Do you trust me?" he said, his gaze seductive.

"Yes," I whispered, then undressed slowly, aware his eyes were riveted on me while they devoured every inch.

As I stood naked, my body and soul bared, he lunged for me, cradling me in his arms before setting me upon lush grass. Then he made love to me with the kind of expertise I suppose I'd always expected but one I'd never experienced, delivering a kind of ecstasy so powerful, neither the past nor the future mattered.

He withdrew suddenly, his weight no longer upon me, and I opened my eyes to find him gone. I lay there, my body shuddering, greedily longing for more when the nearby timber lit up with a rosy hue, and a primal howl pierced the quiet. Moments later, Tristan emerged from within. He bent to kiss me and began gathering my clothes, afterwards tenderly dressing me. Sweeping me up, we soared high over the river to the Broadway Bridge. Setting me down a block from the loft Ethan and I now shared, he wiped a tear from my eye.

"Regrets?"

"Only that this didn't happen years ago."

"Were it in my power to stay . . ."

I peeled myself away, afraid we'd never see each other again.

"Please, be safe."

He brought my hand to his lips. "And you, iubirea mea."

I kissed him for what may very well be the last time and walked toward the loft entrance, my heart shredding with each step I took from him. I turned to wave goodbye, but he was gone.

I punched in the loft's entry code, hoping Ethan remained asleep. My cell blasted *Night Moves* by Bob Seger, and I fumbled the phone as I attempted to answer Bianca's call.

"Celeste! What have you done?"

CHAPTER 30

I backed out of the loft and took the call from the stoop.

"We're not talking about this, Mom."

"Celeste, you know this cannot be!"

"It's what I want, what I've always wanted."

"You have no regard for a marriage vow, apparently."

I winced, her words stinging my soul. "My marriage is over."

"Is it? How convenient."

"It's been over for a long time. Don't pretend you didn't know, Mom." She didn't respond, and I visualized her shifting restlessly, a sheepish smile contorting her lips.

"Of course, I did," she eventually sputtered. "But heavens, Celeste! You've scarcely been wed, what, an entire year."

"I made a mistake. I should never have married Ethan. I'm in love with Tristan. You know that! And nothing, no matter the repercussions, is ever going to change that."

"It's a mistake, Celestine! An abhorrence! Your father will be heartbroken. *I* am heartbroken. Do we mean nothing to you?"

"Don't you want me to be happy?"

"Of course, Celestine. That is all we have ever wanted. Oh, why did you not heed our warning!? Such a union has only brought heartbreak. If you will not think of yourself, won't you think of Tristan? You will cause him only pain. And with what lies ahead—"

"Mom, Mom," I said, attempting to calm her. "It's done."

"Are you aware he has already lost so very much? Utter torment he suffers to this day, Celeste, a heartache so devastating it has outlasted dynasties, plaques, every conceivable atrocity. And now, he must carry not only this albatross into the greatest battle the Realm has yet to face but the fear he may, once again, lose another he's come to love."

"What am I supposed to do, Mom? I won't just sit idly by while—"

"If what you say is true . . . if you do indeed love Tristan as you say you do, you must abandon your quest for the infidels responsible for the atrocities of late. To do anything less will put him at even greater risk!"

Pressing a palm against my forehead, I said, "I'm a detective, Mom. I can take care of myself."

She laughed, and I nearly bit my lip in two. "What good are your guns against the Harvesters, Celestine? Your mace or your tasers for that matter? Such absurdity!"

"I won't run or hide should they begin slaughtering cops or abducting more children!"

Bianca expelled a pronounced sigh. "Then allow us but time. Those still aligned with the Realm had plans to convene in Chicago. Perhaps Kansas City might be as strategic. I only ask that you await our arrival, Celestine, before you react impetuously."

I had no idea where to begin, so I agreed.

AT AROUND MIDNIGHT the following day, I slipped from the bed, threw on my favorite faded sweats, and tugged a *Rolling Stones* T-shirt over bed-ravaged hair. Grabbing my Glock along with an extra clip, I snuck out, trying not to wake Ethan snoring softly on the sofa.

Soft lights burned within an abandoned warehouse only two blocks from the loft. The perimeter was shrouded with the magical scent of myrrh and frankincense. I crept inside.

"President Niore of the United States," I heard Razvan say, "will soon involuntarily vacate his position, but before that happens, the world as all mortals know it will change dramatically."

Involuntarily vacate his position? I wondered if the Realm planned an assassination.

"And the Vice President?" I thought I recognized Paulo's voice.

Razvan's laugh was foreign to me, almost depraved. "The Vice President will gladly step aside, and the Speaker of the House, James Vanslyke, will be sworn in. I am certain you all are aware he is a member of the Realm."

Paulo spoke again. "And I am certain *you* are most aware the majority of the government officials are either mortals or Resistors of the Realm."

Rounding the corner, I scraped my arm on several exposed nails, and as it began to bleed, the entire congregation of one hundred or more sniffed the air and turned hungry, yellowed eyes in my direction.

"My daughter, Celestine," Razvan informed members of the Realm, more a warning than an introduction, as he beckoned me with cupped fingers.

I slunk inside, managing a wide arc around the vampires, and stood alongside my father. He reached inside his long coat, produced a monogrammed handkerchief, and wrapped my wound.

"Celestine is a detective with Kansas City Law Enforcement and will be a valuable asset in our foray."

"A valuable asset? Your daughter is a mortal, is she not?" one member gibed. Deafening laughter followed.

Razvan's eyes sparked annoyance, and the mob quieted. My attention cut to Bianca, standing in the third row. Before I could blink, she too appeared beside my father.

"Please tell us how it has come to pass, Commander, you learned of the President's involvement?" a bizarrely tall vampire with a permanently fanged grin queried from the first row.

"As centuries have taught us, Amadeus," my father began, "things are seldom as they appear. President Niore—Drakus, as some of you may know him—was the catalyst in this renegade revolution. Because he has gained tremendous strength by partaking in the supreme blood of the innocents, we must act now before forced to combat an army of equally treacherous foes!"

I assumed my father meant the missing children when he spoke of the supreme blood of the innocents, but decided it best to ask him later, once we were alone.

"Why begin our assault here?" Amadeus argued. "As we speak, the renegades continue a much larger siege in Europe."

"One would suppose his daughter is foremost in his thoughts," another uttered.

Bianca glided forward, the movement difficult to track, quick like a peregrine falcon. Beneath her translucent and golden squint lay growing rage and promised retaliation. The ends of her burnished long hair morphed into errant insects, redirecting dormant dust molecules and abandoned trash, while her lips shone red, slowly parting to reveal deadly incisors spoiling for a fight.

"Who are you to defy your commander?"

A much older vampire, his hair white and as thin as a spider's web, shot overhead and hovered above Bianca.

Beneath a nose crinkled in defiance, he jutted a crooked index finger in Razvan's direction and said, "He is not *my* commander! His most revered consort, Yesenia, destroyed my true master, and my presence here is but to seek retribution! I demand her whereabouts!"

Bianca tossed her head back, her laughter echoing throughout the warehouse, prompting squatting barn shallows into flight in their urgency to roost elsewhere. "And you fancy yourself capable of such a confrontation? To suggest such absurdity is to disparage your master, I should think!"

Razvan laid a hand on her shoulder and whispered something that encouraged her to take a step back. "Jasper, is that not what you are called?" The old man delivered a curt nod. "Rest assured, Yesenia's nights will soon come to an excruciating end, my friend."

The old man thumbed his nose, his intense gaze falling on those comrades reputedly both competent and bold.

"If rumor serves," he said, looking directly at Bianca, "that endeavor proved a disastrous challenge some years ago."

Bianca soared overhead. When within an inch of his nose, she said, "One learns from their mistakes, ancient one. The next time she crosses my path, I shall personally see to her demise."

CHAPTER 31

ith his feet sweeping a dusty path in a room once serving as a manager's office within the warehouse, Razvan paced.

"Think of these defectors as rebellious children, Celestine," he went on to explain. "Mutiny is an attractive lure."

Nick suddenly wafted through the door. "And why would one eat a hamburger when a slab of prime rib is much more satisfying?"

Both Razvan and Bianca frowned in annoyance and trained severe dark orbs his way. Grinning, Nick pressed both palms in their direction in a sarcastic show of surrender.

I ignored my brother and fielded another question to my father. "But why take kids? Some of them were only infants."

"A child's blood to us is pretty much the same as steroids to athletes," Nick intercepted, then winked in our parents' direction. "Not that I'd know personally, of course."

"So, the blood from a child makes these defectors stronger?"

Razvan nodded. "Precisely, Celeste, in every conceivable sense."

"Which is the intention," Bianca cut in. "These factions

212

have attempted to topple the Realm many times in the past and have failed wretchedly. They desire a New Order, one in which feeding off all humans is acceptable and does not warrant reprisal."

"So, if they're more powerful, will it be possible for you to defeat them?"

Razvan's eyes cut to Bianca. Neither of my parents expressed much optimism.

"We remain guardedly confident," Razvan eventually said flatly. "However, there is something we feel you should know."

I heard myself swallow. My ears rang as if unwilling to hear what came next.

"As Amadeus expressed, with abduction numbers far exceeding those in the States, we have no choice but to begin our counterattack in Europe."

"And because we know Yesenia's hiding out in France," Nick grinned and comically puffed out his chest, "Mom's gonna kick her ass."

Bianca slanted eyes in Nick's direction, as her finger waggled a warning.

"Alas, Nicholas, words often seem your greatest adversary." To me, she said, "Fane and a few of our greatest warriors will remain behind, Celestine. We cannot spare a larger number. Do your best to avoid engagement until our return." She drifted across the room and took my face in both hands. "Scumpa mea, honey, please, promise me."

Forrest Quaid, a veteran detective, and I had checked out the few leads surrounding the most recent abduction and came up empty.

Both equally despondent over our failure to find little four-year-old Natasha Windsor, we dove into the two other cases we'd been assigned.

"At least with this one, there was a witness," Quaid said, only mildly enthusiastic.

I pushed off my desk and bent to retrieve a pen. "Yeah, maybe we'll get lucky."

"The APB for a blue Nissan Rogue hit the airwaves right after the abduction, and an Amber alert went out for Bella Dawson, too."

That was good news. The expedient release of an all-points bulletin had benefited us greatly in the past. "Witness get a look at the license plate?"

Quaid shook his head no. Then I noticed him staring.

"Why don't you go by Detective *Torok?*"

Surprised, I failed to disguise my glare.

"I checked into your background."

I sat up straight, tapping the pen hard against the desk. "Oh?"

"Don't feel special. I research everyone I work with this closely."

I stared long into his blank, hazel eyes. "Maybe I should do the same. But don't you have enough to investigate?" I said, picking up a case folder and allowing it a hard freefall with a harder landing.

"So, why don't you . . . go by Torok? You haven't taken your husband's name either."

"If you must know, my father—my biological father—was a cop, here in this very precinct."

Quaid's eyes hadn't softened. "Ah, so you thought maybe that would give you a leg-up. Five years in and, *bam*, you're a detective. I'd say it worked, Detective."

I resisted touching my face. I knew it was nearly as red as Quaid's tie.

"Dedication and long hours—that's what worked, Detective."

He popped in a stick of gum.

"Okay, okay," he said, parking the wad off to one side of

his mouth. "Stranger things have happened." He chuckled and rolled his chair closer to mine, one wheel scoring the cracked tile. "What's wrong with your husband's name?" When I didn't answer, Quaid drum-rolled his knuckles on the armrest. "Nothing, and you'd like to keep it that way?" he added, grinning.

I rolled my eyes and returned the pen to the drawer, slamming it shut in the process. "That's hilarious, Detective. But take my advice; don't give up your day job."

He laughed, one hand slapping the edge of my desk. "I like you, Crenshaw. You've got moxie."

I crinkled my eyes and graced him with an insincere smile. "Well, now, I feel fulfilled." I grabbed my gear and started for the door.

"Where are you going?"

"To re-interview the grandmother. You coming or not?"

"I SUPPOSE it could have been my son, Jeremy," Jeanette Dawson told us ten minutes into our questioning.

Quaid ratcheted upright, pointing an accusing finger at Jeanette. "You're just getting around to telling us that?"

My eyes cut to him, and I pressed a palm toward the floor, hoping he would interpret that as a plea he back off. Speaking in what I hoped a soothing tone, I said, "Does he drive a blue Nissan Rogue?"

"Well, that's why I can't be certain it was him. The last time he dropped Bella off, I remember him driving a red car. A big red car."

"So, what makes you think your son might be involved?"

"I haven't seen him since Bella disappeared."

Forest mumbled something that sounded like, *Oh, good God!*

Waving a document in front of her face, he said, "This is your statement to the police: *When asked where the child's parents were, the grandmother, Jeanette Dawson, said, Bella's mother is in jail and my son, Jeremy, is out of town, Iraq, I think."*

Jeanette Dawson flicked her wrist. "My medication . . . it does things to my memory, sometimes."

"What do you take medication for?" Quaid asked.

"Well, they say I have Alzheimer's, but I'm sure it's the medication that causes it. I don't remember having problems before."

"Of course, you don't." Quaid fell back against a slip-covered sofa and raked fingers through short, graying hair. "So, your son, he's back from Iraq?"

"Oh, yes. I baked a birthday cake for Jeremy only last week. A chocolate one with sprinkles. Did I mention Bella loves sprinkles?"

An insincere smile plastered Quaid's lips, and I knew a sarcastic storm was brewing. "No, surprisingly, you left that out. Can you think of any reason Jeremy would leave town with his daughter without letting you know?"

Jeanette stared off into space. She abruptly refocused when Quaid cleared his throat loudly.

"Disneyland . . . That's it! Jeremy promised to take Bella to Disneyland."

I delivered a curt nod Quaid's way, letting him know I'd take it from here.

"We need to be sure. Did he give you a contact number? Cell phone? Hotel?"

"My address book is around here . . . somewhere." She patted my hand. "Would you be a dear and look in the kitchen?"

CHAPTER 32

"*I*'ll drive," I told Quaid.

"Suit yourself." He pitched me the keys and threw himself into the sedan. "You got a problem with my driving?"

"Yeah, as a matter of fact, I do." I thought I heard him chuckle. "Where to?"

Quaid thumbed through a report and recited Katie Bosworth's address, our third abduction victim.

"Another damn waste of time," he said more to himself. "Get this: *I thought I heard a noise, you know, coming from Katie's room, so I opened the door in time to see someone—something—carry her through the window.*"

"And you find something bizarre about that disclosure?"

"Oh, it gets better. When the investigating officer asked her which bedroom her daughter, Katie, slept in, she said: *The one at the end of the hall, on the second floor. This thing could fly.*"

The mother seemed perfectly rational to me, but there was no way I could tell Quaid that.

Situated in a quiet neighborhood, just off Rockhill Road and 59th Street, sat the Bosworth's residence, a nicely renovated, two-story stone bungalow. Immediately, the ample porch roof caught my eye, jutting just below several windows I presumed belonged to one or more bedrooms. Possibly, Katie's abductor was human, after all.

A middle-aged man, who looked as though he hadn't slept in days, answered Quaid's thunderous knock.

"Hello, I'm Detective Quaid, and this is Detective Crenshaw. We're here to follow up on Katie Bosworth's disappearance."

"I'm her father, Jon—Jon Bosworth."

He extended a clammy hand which Quaid reluctantly shook.

I heard sudden movement beyond the door, and I noticed Quaid's experienced hand fly to his holster. He relaxed some when a pale, haggard, petite woman with bloodshot eyes appeared from behind Jon and introduced herself as Maggie Bosworth.

I glanced at Maggie and immediately bowed my head. Her pain was palpable. "May we come in?"

Jon swept the door to the wall and stepped aside; Maggie latched onto him.

"Please, have a seat." Jon scraped trembling fingers through his dark, uncombed hair and ushered us toward the living room. There was no way I was going to separate Maggie from Jon, so I caught Quaid's attention and jutted a chin toward two chairs flanking the sofa.

Sitting across from the couple, I fielded the first question.

"Your description of the intruder was vague, Mrs. Bosworth. Can you provide any more detail?"

Her eyes darted to her husband.

"We know how crazy this sounds." Jon squeezed his wife's hand. "Go ahead, honey."

Maggie gripped her temples and cleared her throat. "I didn't get a good look at his face."

"So, you're certain the suspect was male?" Quaid asked.

Maggie seemed suddenly uncertain.

"I . . . I guess I assumed it was a man. I suppose it could have been a woman."

Presenting something I hoped resembled a smile, I said, "Totally understandable, Mrs. Bosworth. Just tell us what you saw."

She shook her head hard as if to jar her memory. "Oh, I remember! It was only a split-second. That's all it was, but I'll never forget it. He turned as if to look over his shoulder when I barged into the room. His skin was—" She yelped a strangled sob, and began to shake, uncontrollably.

"Go on please, Mrs. Bosworth. Help us find your daughter," I pleaded.

"His skin was . . . almost transparent. By that, I mean, I could see veins and bones." She buried her face in her husband's chest as if that would somehow shield her from the worst of the nightmare yet to come.

I vaulted from the chair and stooped beside her, cupping her knee.

"I know this is difficult, but if we're going to find Katie, you have to help us."

She nodded and hiccoughed a sob. "I ran toward him. I just wanted Katie! And then he—he flew through the window, taking her with him!"

"He *flew?*" Quaid asked incredulously. "You're sure he didn't *tumble* from the window onto the roof?"

Maggie shook her head. "Katie's bedroom is in the back of the house. There isn't a roof outside her window."

Jon spoke up. "This neighborhood isn't the best. We purposely chose that bedroom to keep our daughter safe."

I didn't see the point in questioning the couple further. The kidnapper's identification wouldn't be found in any database or even within the most comprehensive collection of pedophile mugshots. And no matter how proficient the detective, Katie's abductor was in the wind, untouchable by mortal standards.

But I continued the interrogation for protocol's sake. "Can you describe what the suspect was wearing?"

Maggie's hollow gaze fell on her husband, and he squeezed her hand. "Dark clothes; black jeans, I'm pretty sure, and I think you would call the shirt a tank top."

"Hair color?" Quaid asked flatly.

"I guess you'd call it purple. And spikey, you know, like the teenagers like it."

Quaid scowled, and we exchanged a combative stare. "Kinda like one of those rock stars?" he said and may as well have rolled his eyes.

Jon glared, and I quickly jumped in to diffuse the situation. "Did he have any distinguishing marks? Like tattoos or scars?"

Maggie's eyes widened.

"Yes, two small tears in his skin! Here," she said, tracing her jugular vein. "I noticed them because they appeared to rise and fall, you know, quiver. Almost as though something lay dormant beneath and was coming to life."

CHAPTER 33

I'd been avoiding Ethan as much as possible ever since the night I'd spent on the cliff above the Missouri River. I didn't want to hurt him. I loved him, just not in the same way I loved Tristan. Sitting across the table from him now, I knew the time had come for the infamous clean break. Excluding the old cliché, *But we can still be friends* from my overly rehearsed speech, I took a deep breath, ready as ever to launch the proverbial breakup attack.

"Are you still mad?" Before I could answer, he said, "I know you've been avoiding me. Look, Celeste, I shouldn't have ambushed you. At least not alongside my mom and sister. I am sorry about that."

Despite what I intended to dump on him, I wasn't willing to let him off the hook completely. "It was incredibly selfish, Ethan. But . . . I think it's great you have a family so invested. Family is a wonderful support system."

"Do you, Celeste?"

"Of course, why wouldn't I?"

Ethan pitched forward, his stare hard and accusing. "Why hasn't anyone in your family ever come to see you? For God's sake, not one of them even came to our wedding!"

"I told you they couldn't get away."

Ethan flicked his wrist. "Yeah, I know all about the Fortune-500 company. What about your brother, Nick? What is this now, his second or third tour in Iraq?"

"What is this, an interrogation?"

Ethan's jaw flinched, and I returned his cold, unwavering stare.

"No, Celeste. I'm trying to understand what's going on with you." He exhaled enough pent-up frustration for both of us. "It's not my intent to hurt you, okay," he said, extending a hand across the table, "but I have to say, biological or not, I think it's pretty shitty your parents couldn't take one day away from their company . . . corporation . . . whatever to attend their only daughter's wedding."

Unable—no—unwilling, to tell him the truth, I shrugged my shoulders instead.

He cocked his head and ran his fingers along the table edge. I winced, remembering those very capable fingers all too well.

"I'm just trying to get to the root of the problem," he said softly, apparently changing gears. "I have my own theory if you'd like to hear it."

I gnawed on my lower lip; this clean break was about to get very messy. Stalling, I nodded.

Ethan grew quiet, studying me a few minutes.

"Do you ever miss your biological parents? I mean, it's not about that, is it, Celeste? Some anniversary, maybe?"

I shook my head, embracing the lie I was about to tell.

"It's been so long. I barely remember them."

Ethan reached for my hand, and it took everything I had not to pull back. "I think I know what's bothering you."

"I don't think you do," I said, unable to look him in the eye.

He tilted his head to one side, looking at me as if I were an inhibited, coddled child. "You don't feel a part of anything.

Sure, there's work, and there's us, but I don't think that's enough for you, Celeste. That's why I was thinking maybe having a baby could change things."

I shook my head, setting both hands in my lap. "There's something I have to tell you."

"Is there someone else?" he said, as if it was a punchline, filling the silence between us as I continued to stall. As I summoned up the courage to lay all my cards on the table, he laughed suddenly. "Don't tell me I'm going to have to beat Quaid to a pulp." When I didn't respond, didn't even blink, his grin died, corresponding with the look of dread flittering transiently across his eyes.

"Yes, there is someone else," I told him. The words barely audible, I hoped he'd heard them. I didn't want to repeat them.

He ratcheted upright, quick, like a rocket from a launching pad. He tossed his chair against the front window, the crash so violent, I was surprised the glass remained intact. Turning in two tight circles before plastering one hand against a hip and pressing two fingers hard against his lips, he demanded my lover's name.

I shook my head, then executed a harsh stare; a warning he need calm down.

He thwacked the table, sending the salt and pepper shakers flying, and jabbed a finger in my face.

"And don't tell me it doesn't matter because it does fucking matter!"

"I won't talk to you while you're like this," I said, and clambered to my feet.

"Like what, Celeste? Betrayed? Screwed over? Played for a fucking doormat?" He threw himself to the ground and lay there, rigid and motionless, smirking like a child throwing a well-practiced tantrum. "Is this better, Celeste? Will you talk to me now?"

"I never meant to hurt you, Ethan."

He didn't move, save to ball his hands into fists. I thought to tell him I should never have married him, but that kind of disclosure would only escalate the situation.

"I have a right to know," he murmured, his breathing shallow, his eyes fixed on the ceiling.

"It's not anyone from the precinct."

"I have a right to know, Celeste," he repeated, his tone flat, his face expressionless.

I resisted going to him, kneeling beside him, cupping his face tenderly for the last time.

"His name is Tristan. I've known him all my life."

One hand flew to his eyes, pinching them closed. "How long has this been going on?"

Before I could respond, he sat upright, his face splotchy and red, his eyes adequately communicating intense loathing. He jumped to his feet and shoved a palm in my direction.

"You know what? It really doesn't matter."

I shuffled my feet and managed a quick nod. "I'm moving out. I'll come by for a few things later."

He shook his head, a sinister grin playing out across a tense mouth.

"I won't play the sore loser, and to prove it, I'll make sure you find all your shit boxed-up and waiting at the curb!" He strolled by me and flung the front door open. "I'd say I'm happy I met you, but that's the difference between us . . . When I say something, I mean it."

LATER THAT AFTERNOON, I huddled, transfixed, within a group of twelve or so surrounding Randy's computer as MSN blasted a *Special Report* from Rome.

"Did you see that?" someone yelled behind me, and Randy rewound the video.

"What the hell?" several officers cried in unison—Randy

included, his stubby index finger jabbing at shadowy images appearing helter-skelter across the monitor.

"What are they . . . birds?" a female officer asked, bobbing her head in an attempt to get a better look.

Nearly everyone contributed to the debate. Some said enormous crows, some said drones, while others insisted they were merely clouds distorted by satellite upload.

But I knew what the shadows represented and wondered which of them were my parents. By day's end, the debate continued. Aliens seemed to be the more popular choice, probably the more accurate assumption because that's exactly how I'd always perceived the immortals; a bizarre extraterrestrial life-form. Except, technically, vampires were no longer a living form of any kind.

I quickened my stride, anxious to leave the exhausting conversation behind. Throwing the precinct door open, Fane ambushed me, difficult to miss dressed in his favorite *I* ♥ *Cher* hoodie.

"That wretched Yesenia has escaped much-deserved annihilation but again!" he blared without even a *hello*. "The minx! That profane slut is like a despicable plague. Wreaks havoc and then *whoosh!* moves on to who-knows-where."

"Hi to you too. And why don't you tell me how you really feel?"

"What more is there to say, dear girl? That one is like a dreadful venereal disease; just as one is confident it has dispatched, *gadzooks!* it makes a most unwelcome comeback."

I shoved a hand into the hair on the top of my head and ruffled it, convinced I now resembled an excitable parrot.

"Oh, God! Spare me the drama, Fane. It's been a long day. What else is going on?"

Fane jutted his chin toward a cloudy sky, puffed out his lower lip, and jammed folded arms over his bony chest.

"I'm afraid I shan't be able to do that as it's quite dramatic."

"Look, I'm sorry." I took a deep breath, momentarily reconsidering my planned disclosure. "I'm leaving Ethan. I told him this morning. So, I don't have the energy for theatrics."

Studying me out of the corner of one eye, he said, "Understandable. Might I have the particulars?"

"No. Now, tell me what's going on."

Fane sneered insolently and perched one hand on a pointy hip. "It comes as no surprise our relationship is one-sided, what with me, the badgered sycophant and you, the ruthless intimidator."

I took a step in his direction. "Fane, I don't have time for this."

He seemed hesitant to elaborate. "Nothing inspirational, I'm afraid. Outnumbered, the Realm is failing miserably, my darling. Nevertheless," he added quickly, "your parents rally-on."

"And Nick?"

A rosy blush colored his cheeks, his eyes sparking a hellacious mix of bedevilment and infatuation. I resisted a grin.

"Oh, he is fabulous, isn't he! Quite the specimen, I dare say. A very formidable opponent from what I gather," he rambled on; a trancelike film further diluting silvery pupils. "A hard man to pin down and all that," he finished with a shiver. "But, alas, I cannot speak from experience."

Grinding my teeth, I grabbed his shoulders and shook him; his dangly earrings swinging as they picked up momentum.

"Is Nick all right?"

"Yes, yes. Doing quite well, from what I understand. Now, unhand me, lass," Fane said and straightened his hoodie.

"You said the Realm is outnumbered, but wasn't that an expectation?"

"The count continues to grow. The Harvesters are

recruiting unsuspecting victims at an alarming rate as each day passes."

I swallowed past an expanding lump and said more to myself, "What if we can't defeat them?"

"Dear girl, if that should happen, the planet is doomed."

CHAPTER 34

Obsessing over my parents' safety—as well as that of Nick and Tristan—while leading the search for several missing children, left little time to think about Ethan, selecting a divorce lawyer, or finding a suitable place to live.

Dragging the last of the boxes Ethan had left strewn about the curb, some pitched haphazardly into the street, I closed the door to number eight at the Royal Motel. Whoever had chosen its name possessed either a wicked sense of humor or an abundance of misplaced optimism; there was certainly nothing aristocratic about it, most of all the tacky neon crown perched atop the *Vacancy* sign. Even it seemed ready to topple.

Digging through the boxes, I eventually located the nasal spray, which I hoped might put an end to a protracted sneezing fit. Because I suspected the moldy carpet was the culprit—which looked like something foolishly rescued from an old movie theatre, contacting a rental agent became my top priority.

Successfully recruiting a five-star agent, I ended the call just as Social Services returned one I'd placed earlier.

Following a ten-minute argument in which I pleaded Jeanette Dawson's welfare, the Director assured me she would see Jeanette approved for either an around-the-clock nursing assistant or, more likely, admission into a state-owned nursing facility. Satisfied Jeanette soon no longer a danger to herself or anyone else, I leaped from a grimy wooden chair, realizing I was late meeting Fane for the daily update.

I wasn't the only one who was late. I had nearly given up waiting when I noticed him prancing into a quaint little café two blocks from the precinct. Squinting irritation, I waved him toward my table in the back. Swishing a burgundy velvet cape with cream-colored satin lining, I heard him utter *humph!* as he appraised me through two sets of false eyelashes.

Suddenly self-conscious, I patted and finger-combed, until satisfied I had molded my windblown hair into more organized chaos.

"Don't even start," I said as he took a seat across from mine.

He shrugged impishly and arched a contrived, heavily penciled brow.

"I thought perhaps the circus was in town, a brute had dispatched a clown, and you found yourself relegated to deploring undercover work."

Through winged, soggy nostrils, I retorted. "Forgive me, but I can't imagine taking fashion advice from you. What's with the hair? It's purple."

"Fastidious Fuchsia," he corrected, obviously wounded. "You know, Celeste, Rod could work absolute miracles with that dreadful color. What is it—swamp-water blonde? I dare say the man is positively genius. I suspect he'd quite enjoy a challenge."

I folded my arms smugly across my breasts, partially to impart dominance, mostly to hide a splash of ketchup.

"The term is dishwasher blonde. Just tell me what you've got."

Fane rolled his eyes and flung some seriously beaded hair extensions over his ridiculously padded shoulders.

"With Yesenia once again on the run and out of France, those renegades have suffered mammoth casualties! Hooray for our side! There's just no telling where the little wench has gone, but do not dismay; find her and find her we shall, undoubtedly under a rock or a burning bush."

I pinched the growing valley between my eyes. It was often difficult to interpret his comments as metaphorical or literal.

"Where are my parents? Where is Nick?"

"Laconic little thing, are you not?" He sucked in a breath, his skin washing intermittently gray to green to peach. I blew my nose while delivering a brutal scowl. "I assume you wish me to get on with it! To summarize, those vagabonds found neither peace nor seclusion in Italy. Quite the contrary. Smite, smite, and more smite, as it were, the Realm delivering thousands of those wretched, soulless creatures into the bowels of hell. I convey all, by the by, with not an ounce of exaggeration!"

I tapped my forehead against the table, convinced I now had a temporary crease. Raking my face with gnarled fingers, I said, "Good God, you call that a summary? Can't you just say, *Everything's going as planned*, or *they're winning the freaking war!*"

Fane glowered in response, twisting a rope of hair.

"Heaven forbid! What an appallingly boring and ghastly discourse that would be!"

"Where are my parents now? Italy?"

"Spain, I should think."

"You don't know?"

The tip of his nose saluted the faux-tin ceiling. "I hesitate to elaborate, given your aversion to communication."

"Come on, Fane! I don't have time for your childish games."

Buffing a fingernail against his cape, he said, "Si, Spain."

"And then they'll return to Kansas City?"

"Posthaste," Fane snapped, crossing his arms defiantly.

I leaned across the table, insisting on eye contact.

"This isn't a joke! Those goddamn demons are taking little kids . . . babies! And there's not a damn thing I can do about it."

Fane seemed to be mulling something over. I threw my arms to the side in a what-gives gesture.

Reluctantly, he said, "I have discovered a monumental lair. Within it lay a faction of those blood thieves, numbering twenty or more."

I lurched forward, this time lowering my voice.

"Is that where they're hiding the children?"

Fane shook his head. "I remain unconvinced. Nevertheless," he added, jabbing a finger, ceiling-bound, "the wee tykes are undoubtedly proximate."

"Let's go find out." I popped from my chair, and Fane grabbed my wrist.

"Oh, no! Dear girl, you are quite incapable."

CHAPTER 35

"*P*ut aside your preposterous delusions of gallantry!" Fane warned again. "I was cautioned, with fervid ambiguity, mind you, that your destruction guarantees my own."

"I can't just sit by—"

"Oh, well then, yes, by all means, let's! Let's allow those blood-sucking dupes to welcome you into their despicable fold! So that you too can roam this miserable earth for eternity slaying innocents, all the while, I am nothing but a cherished memory!"

"There has to be a way," I pushed through gritted teeth.

"Heed my counsel, you poor mad mortal. There is but one alternative."

"I don't believe that. There's always more than one solution to any problem."

"Problem?" Fane laughed. "Is that really how one refers to a demonic phenomenon?"

"What about fire? I know it's not foolproof—"

"Foolproof," Fane echoed. "What an idiotic term, though I most definitely applaud your deduction, as fire is decidedly not foolproof."

"Isn't it worth considering? Apparently, it's worked in some instances."

"The success is limited to the power of the opposition. Allow me to define by example: Should you fire your weapon at two very distinctly different targets, will they suffer the same consequence?"

"Will one person survive while the other won't?"

Fane nodded animatedly. "For argument's sake, let's conclude that target number one is virile—a most healthy specimen, while target number two is quite scrawny and insalubrious."

I scratched my head, attempting to remember the definition of *insalubrious.*

"All right," I said, blowing out an exasperated breath, "if the second target is scrawny and unhealthy, it's quite possible he wouldn't survive, depending on the location of the bullet and the severity of his injuries."

"Precisely, but I think we can agree his a presumably diverse contrast to our first fabricated fellow's fate."

"And I'll be up against twenty or more number ones?"

"Not necessarily, my winsome mortal."

I exhaled bottled-up frustration and assumed my eyes had turned homicidal, because Fane pushed away from the table and pressed a palm urgently in my direction.

"Mercy! Such countenance is most unbecoming! How am I, one not possessing powers of clairvoyance, to educate another regarding participants in a future event?"

"You said, not necessarily!"

Fane flashed a sly grin. "Perhaps I should have elaborated."

Once decoding the onslaught of unnecessary words— buried deep within Fane's infinite explanation—I ignored him completely.

My mind was on other things now, sorting through feasible strategies, like flamethrowers, garlic, and holy water.

"I see this as an opportunity, one that can't wait for the others' return. We're going in tonight. Gather the members of the Realm who have remained behind and meet me at the motel, 9 p.m. That *is* when they're most active?"

Fane nodded unenthusiastically. "Were it but possible for me to destroy my very self and spare my master the nuisance," he muttered, following a theatrical sigh. "I shan't be late."

FANE ARRIVED a few minutes before nine o'clock, three warriors the Toroks had left behind shadowing him.

"I feel it is my duty to dissuade you, m'lady," stated a warrior I had never met before.

"Not a chance," I said, grabbing one flamethrower off the inadequate and grimy vanity counter just outside a bathroom the size of a compact broom closet. I dipped my head at Fane, then at the three remaining weapons. Flamethrower in tow, Fane flanked me at the door. I glanced over my shoulder, only to discover the others had already vanished.

Fane stepped onto the sidewalk and slanted his eyes up the street then down. "I seem to be at a disadvantage. Wherever is your wretched mode of transportation?"

"You're it," I said and strapped the weapon securely against my body.

Fane emitted an insulting yelp and tugged the largest vampire in my direction.

"Your chariot awaits, my buxom friend," he told me, grinning. "If I could offer but a few words of advice: This is no time for diffidence. Accost this fine fellow, snare him but good around the middle. Although Veillantif is a most valiant warrior, many have branded him both clumsy and daft, most accurately, I dare say."

Veillantif hoisted me off the ground effortlessly. I detested heights and estimated the vampire's height in excess of seven feet. I gulped a deep breath, afterwards squeezing both eyes shut. Nearly colliding with a bat on our ascent, my eyes flew open, and a strangled scream caught in my throat. Out of the corner of my eye, I saw a small private plane, approaching rapidly. To counteract the lethal impact, Veillantif plunged roughly fifty feet, and my heart thudded against my chest, my eyes seeing stars that weren't even there.

When we touched ground, just beyond the city's industrial section, Bianca awaited, her long hair slithering about her as if a den of disturbed vipers out for revenge.

"Have you devised sufficient strategy?" she demanded, hawkish eyes darting toward Fane, tentatively observing her from his position behind Veillantif.

I stepped forward, flamethrower in hand.

"Ha! Who but a child would enlist a toy in such a battle? Perhaps you've forgotten your promise to me, Celestine."

"It couldn't wait," I said. "Fane discovered—"

She pushed a translucent palm in my direction, the veins in her hand like strands of black pulsating rope.

"Do you think me not aware! Have you determined the number of your enemy?"

I considered she already knew the answer and was only baiting me.

"Twenty or more."

She threw her head back, her laughter roaring into the night. "When we drove the Harvesters out of Europe, where do you suppose they sought refuge?"

I remained quiet, wanting to tell her how relieved I was that she was here, but too proud to say the words.

She folded her hands in front of her, reminding me of Nick's elementary school teachers preparing to unleash an organized lecture, his classmates sitting quietly as their lively eyes revealed anticipation.

"Celestine, nothing can prepare you for the task at hand.

Admittedly, there are moments I think our adversaries indomitable. So, please, allow me one less worry."

I opened my mouth in protest, just as she drew my attention to the dark figures blemishing an otherwise starry sky. Moments later, Razvan, Nick, Tristan, and a band of warriors glided toward the earth. My father, stern and rigid, expressed his disapproval with a threatening glare, while Nick appeared entertained and typically contemptuous. Judging from Tristan's expression, he shared my father's opinion.

"Yes," Bianca said, reading my thoughts, "as usual, your father and I are in complete agreement, Celestine. You will return home. On second thought, Veillantif will dispatch you to safety."

I shook my head and felt my jaw stiffen. "I won't go."

Her eyes—glossy and black, save for a spinning red pupil that left me nauseous—blinked back at me. "This is not up for debate! You will only hinder our efforts."

For the first time in my life, rather than walk over to me like a human being, Razvan materialized at my feet, landing a fearsome scowl.

"Much preparation is at hand. You must obey your mother," he said, his words booming into the darkness, persuading a frightened fox to distance itself from its makeshift burrow.

Turning his back to me, he led Bianca by the elbow.

"Tristan has professed a solution," I heard him tell her.

CHAPTER 36

"'ll only follow," I yelled after them. "At which point, I'll be alone."

Their shoulders slumped almost simultaneously, and they whipped their heads around, their skin impossibly pale, their eyes expressing both agitation and dubious resolve. Communicating without so much as a word, as they often did, my father then pulled Tristan aside. Straining to hear the conversation, I took a few steps in their direction. I got the impression both my father and my mother shared the mistaken opinion only Tristan could change my mind.

Following a brief interaction, I heard Tristan say, "As she said, she will only follow. Perhaps it's best we keep her close."

Standing alongside Razvan one moment, in front of me the next, without uttering a word, Tristan scooped me up and took to the sky, leading the others.

When we arrived outside the dismal, crumbling factory, hundreds loyal to the Realm converged on Razvan, seemingly eager to carry out his plan.

"We all know what is at stake, our option but one. Our attack will be twofold; poisonous, swift, and absolute. I shall lead the first charge, my son the second."

Razvan's intense glare settled suddenly on a rail-thin vampire, whose incisors frothed a nauseating continuous flow, his long lizard-like tongue intermittently flicking it away, as his putrid yellowed eyes devoured me inch by inch.

"Look away, Silas," my father bellowed, "lest I pluck out those menacing offenders."

In response, the vampire sucked his teeth, a slurping noise affecting the deadly quiet. Renegade strands of stringy, thick mucus plopped onto the cracked cement.

Realizing, only then, I'd been holding my breath, I released a swelling lungful of air, which prompted the majority of the crowd to sniff the air and follow that with a communal sorrowful sigh. Satisfied he had contained the threat, Razvan soared inside, perching upon a steel truss.

"To ensure victory in the horrendous battle that lies ahead, my brethren, I have selected the most gallant to lead the charge. No one possesses a greater ability. I give you Tristan of Tomisovara. Join me, my son," he said, cupping his fingers, and Tristan stepped forward. Clipped animated conversations sprang up around me. A surge of astonishment followed Tristan as he floated through the crowd and took up position alongside my father. "To my son, Nicholas, I implore you not regard this as a form of disparagement, for you too are a formidable warrior. It is but time Tristan allotted the recognition he so deserves. Hear me, Defenders of the Realm! And by so doing, you shall execute Tristan's orders as if my own." Razvan turned to face Tristan. "Now, my son, the time has come to disclose your remedy for our perplexing dilemma."

Tristan gave me a strange, fleeting glance, hung his head, and fell to his knees.

"Forgive me," he said, and a prolonged gasp, including my own, sprang up from the crowd.

Razvan's eyes met Bianca's. Surprised, they both twitched a brow, and I could see my father's anger build. "What manner of man prefaces a strategy with a grievous confession! We have not gathered here to suffer pious penitence! Forsake such sniveling countenance and stand tall!" Tristan remained on his knees. "Speak your mind! I will not ask again."

Tristan rose slowly, his hands folded in front of him. "I have waited nearly four centuries for the Omniscients to discover my knowledge of this most surreptitious and precarious secret and, thereby, bequeath my demise." He shifted his weight and appeared to consider what he should say next.

"Proceed!" my father roared, and a few windows exploded.

"Would I but have the opportunity to harbor this confidence for eternity. For you see, long ago, I discovered the potion to annul immortality."

The vampires collectively hooted a symphony of disbelief.

More windows shattered, Razvan's eyes now starburst and oozing blood. "Ha! Nothing but a derisive archaic rumor, Tristan!"

"Do you not know of me, my father! Am I not one devoid of mistruths, one who embraces veracity, above all? I speak true, as I have personally proffered this potion and found it efficacious."

I thought of Nick's immortality, and rage tore through me like an unforgiving wildfire. I felt betrayed. Not only because Tristan could have spared Nick from roaming the earth for eternity; if he loved me as he said he did, he'd held within his power all this time the ability to make love to me without abruptly disappearing, give me children, grow old with me. Blinking past furious tears and favoring a homicidal urge, I glanced longingly at the exit. It took every shred of self-control to remain there, to share the same space with him.

"If this is true, give me the name of the recipient of this counterfeit concoction," my father said, obviously immersed in Tristan's disclosure.

Tristan averted his eyes, placing his hand over his heart.

"Crixus, for one, the brother of my beloved wife."

Razvan paced the floor and appeared to consider. He arched a brow and engaged his audience.

"It seems Tristan's revelation substantiates a most persistent rumor." Flicking his hand, he said, "Who am I to debate such logic? Most who knew him would agree Crixus but a demon, no one more deserving of this just reward." He laughed suddenly, and a few of the others joined in. Amid a return to stony silence, Razvan paced the floor and scrubbed his chin. When he spoke, he said to Tristan, "And you believe this our solution?"

Tristan delivered a pronounced nod.

"However, it will take time, as it is not readily at hand."

Razvan's eyes evidenced his disappointment.

"What comprises such a potion?"

"The herb vernicadis, which grows abundantly in our beloved Romania, be it only at the highest point of Brana Aeriana."

"And how did you first learn of this?"

Tristan sighed and appeared reluctant to answer.

"When a witch, determined to make me pay for my romantic indiscretions, laced my wine."

Explosive laughter shook what few windows remained, and Razvan demanded the others quiet while I dug fingernails into my thighs and gnawed the insides of both cheeks.

"I beg you describe the effect in considerable detail."

"Within minutes, I grew weak, my immortal capabilities wholly abolished. As I lay dying as if mortal, my lover came to my rescue. I witnessed a battle like no other, but the witch's powers were no match for Helena. Once the battle ended, Helena refunded my immortality."

"Such a potion would be a temptation for many," Razvan said, sharing a forlorn look with Bianca. "I would be remiss not to confess your harboring such a discovery is most disappointing, Tristan!"

Bianca laced her fingers through Razvan's. "It would seem time is on your side, Tristan, as we do not have the luxury to chastise further."

Razvan bowed his head in agreement, then squared off with Tristan. "Divulge your plan, in its entirety, which will succor our success. State it without delay or trepidation!"

"As you wish. The method will be difficult as I fear the mortals will resist ingestion."

"What is this talk of the innocents?"

"It is the most proficient course. Once the Harvesters drink from their tainted hosts—"

Razvan waved him off. "Yes, yes. I am aware of the dynamics. How can you be certain of the mortals' safety?"

Tristan stalled, his eyes darting my way but only transiently. He lowered his voice, but I heard every word.

"In the past, I have taken several mortal lovers, who remained mortal once ingesting the potion . . . despite my, er, enthusiasm."

His words reignited my fury. I wanted to shove the potion down his beautiful throat just so I could strangle him afterward. Bianca caught my eye. She appeared equally enraged. I let out a sarcastic laugh; I certainly didn't envy the sneaky son of a bitch.

"Enough said," Razvan bellowed, failing to conceal a subtle grin which I found more than just a little annoying given the circumstances. "This herb, vernicadis, what quantity will be necessary, and how many need be assigned to ensure its transport?"

"Only a very small amount is required, a miniscule drop. Two, perhaps, three could easily transport all we shall need."

My pager sounded, its ear-piercing beep nearly as unnerving as the code flitting across the screen: *All off-duty law enforcement to report, STAT.*

Bianca grabbed my wrist. "I beg you, do not intervene."

She tipped her head toward Tristan. "You are much too distraught. Leave this to us."

"I have no choice. Aren't you the one who taught me responsibility?" I lingered for a moment as she brushed the back of her hand against my cheek.

The darkness in her eyes softened to a glowing amber, and I thought I saw a tear—similar to a small ruby—escape.

"Mom, why are you so upset? If what Tristan says is true about the antidote, I've got nothing to lose." My thoughts raced from my mother Samantha and father Russ to Bianca and Razvan—the commanders of the Realm—who had fought against rival immortals for centuries, and I snugged her close, committing the unusual scent of her hair, as comforting as it was mystifying, to memory.

Reluctantly, I attempted to break away, but she held me tight. "We shall advise you as to our course, first chance, my darling. Godspeed."

THE STATION WAS TOTAL MAYHEM. Amber alerts were hitting the airwaves, a new one each half-hour. Every available detective interviewed frantic parents, the line growing steadily; tens of preschoolers within twenty miles of the precinct were missing, their teachers found exsanguinated.

Detective Quaid acknowledged me with a scowl as I entered the room. Side by side, we prepared for the painful ordeal, pulling vital information from distraught parents.

"According to the chief, the commissioner has notified the FBI," Quaid told me, once we'd concluded the interviews, as he scoured his desk drawer for a pen that worked.

I winced at this time-wasting effort and resisted a comment. I didn't understand why he preferred to record the reports in longhand when administration ultimately required he enter the information into the system, at some point. But then, there were quite a number of things about Quaid I couldn't begin to comprehend, and I'm not sure I wanted to.

"We could use the help," I said for lack of anything better. *The commissioner can call for the CIA and Special Forces for all the good it will do*, I thought, tempted to say it aloud. I was afraid—for the children, for my family, for myself. I envisioned a world in which immortals ruled the earth; the entire human race reduced to unimaginable demonic creatures, and it took everything I had to focus on the job and will my hands from shaking.

"I imagine the FBI has its hands full," Detective Juanita Ramirez chimed in. "You can bet your ass their Director will assign the majority of the agents to cases on the east coast."

Nearly shift change, I watched as a band of officers arrived for roll call, talking among themselves as they made their way down the ill-conceived, shabby corridor—with its inferior lighting, dead-end, and blind corners—toward the squad room.

Seconds later, Quaid answered his desk phone, a terrified expression suddenly obscuring his usually bland demeanor.

"Grab your gear!" he called to me over his shoulder. Unlocking the bottom drawer to his desk, he pinched a box of ammunition between thick, stubby fingers.

"Where are we going?" I said, grabbing my jacket and loping after him. Taking ragged breaths, I managed to keep up.

"Lincoln Elementary . . . the school's under siege."

When we arrived, we discovered the facility surrounded by cop cars, a few fire trucks, and SWAT. As Ramirez had predicted, the FBI was a no-show.

"The school's in lockdown," we heard Sergeant Dickerson tell Chief Patterson.

The chief puffed out his chest, bringing to mind a dominant alpha-male kangaroo.

"In case you're not aware, that's protocol in this type of a scenario," he said as if he, himself, had formulated the nationally adopted security measure.

"I'm aware of that, Chief, but no one's answering the phone."

"So, no clue as to what's happening inside?" Patterson asked, his fear suddenly palpable.

"I've got four snipers on that roof," Sergeant Dickerson told him, pointing west to an adjacent building, "four over there," he continued, pivoting toward a building just east, "two to the north—directly parallel, and not one of them has seen a goddamn thing!"

"What about the basement?"

"Milk-glass windows, Chief," the sergeant barked back. "We can't see shit."

Patterson signaled for SWAT. Battering Ram in tow, six tactical officers rushed the main entrance and waited for his order.

"Shut off those damn sirens!" he bellowed through a megaphone.

A moment later—eyes wide, mouths agape, we all heard shrill screeches coming from inside.

CHAPTER 37

"Go! Go! Go!" Patterson ordered, squeezing his walkie-talkie mercilessly, as he gestured manically toward the main entrance. The enigmatic noise from inside nearly deafening, an ominous silence suddenly fell over the grounds.

Quaid and I joined the sea of blue rushing to the building, our confidence modestly bolstered by the rooftop sniper's presence. Splitting into tactical formation, Quaid and I joined the search on the first floor. By the time we reached the end of the hall, we'd discovered each classroom abandoned.

Quaid scanned the darkened hallway. "We need to find the entrance to the basement."

I'd noted a door, perched midway down the corridor, leading who-knows-where; I'd assumed it a janitor's closet. I raced ahead, expecting to find it locked. Ecstatic when it wasn't, I swept the door to the wall and darted through. I knew, from his clunky footsteps, Quaid wasn't far behind.

I heard him as he alerted the rest of the team, afterward barking something that sounded like a warning that I wait for backup. I ignored him and bolted down the stairs—two, sometimes three steps at a time—and landed at a full run.

Someone called my name just as a secondary door banged closed behind me, separating me from Quaid.

"We must delay them," Tristan said, suddenly blocking my path, gripping my forearm.

"Don't fucking touch me," I said, yanking my arm away.

"Now is not the time to settle our differences, Celeste," he said, his lips poised to offer something else when Bianca wafted through his muscular physique effortlessly, her extraordinary features masked by remnants of rage.

"The children are safe; however, we require more time, Celestine. We must inoculate all of them before the others arrive," she said, tipping her head toward the noise coming from the law enforcement strategizing beyond the secured door.

"So soon?"

"It would seem the lab is truly our most beneficial enterprise. We were able to find a successful medium, and we will soon succeed in inoculating millions. My apologies, darling, for not advising you. I am certain you realize that time was of the essence!"

"Millions? Those are children," I said pointing beyond her to a room I believed held them. "They're helpless. They have no say. Older people—older kids, for that matter—may not be as compliant."

"Of course, we have entertained that prospect, Celestine!" She laid her head to one side, a sly grin playing across blood-red lips. "One must always have friends in high places."

I puffed my cheeks. "I'm afraid to ask."

"The CDC Director is one such friend. He is one of us and has been most helpful. Razvan has already instructed him on how the masses best be approached." I started to add my opinion and she pressed a forefinger to my lips. "Once the Director convinces the American people of the dangers of a new and deadly virus spread by the harmless housefly, they will most certainly charge the hospitals in search of a preventative!"

"You do realize there are people who refuse to have their children vaccinated to prevent childhood diseases? And you think you can convince them to protect their kids against some unknown, unproven disease?"

"James Vanslyke can be most persuasive."

"The Speaker of the House . . . he's already taken office?" I asked Bianca just as my father materialized.

"But an hour ago, we annihilated President Niore— Drakus." Razvan's head fell back, and his mouth exploded with cynical laughter. "He was always the arrogant fool! His sophisticated surveillance and elite security detail was no match against the Realm."

Behind me, judging from the *thud-thud-thud,* SWAT had enlisted the battering ram to attempt access through the six-inch-thick steel fire door. Bianca flicked her wrist, cocked her head in my direction, then toward the door.

"Do alert your little emperor, or whomever he fancies himself, and assure him the children are safe. Her body became instantly rigid, her gaze fixed on the room which I suspected held the children. And I knew, beyond a shadow of a doubt, she was engaging her telepathic powers to determine the progress of the inoculation process. Snapping out of her self-imposed trance, she kissed my forehead, before she and Tristan simply volatilized.

The battering continued its assault on the door. Metal pounding metal, the deafening clank-clank-clank echoed throughout the basement. Grunting and sweating, putting all my weight behind it, I pried the fire door ajar, breaking off a few fingernails in the process. I had prepared myself for the onslaught of questions.

Quaid was first in line outside the door, his face flushed with rage, his forehead dripping sweat. "What the hell happened? Why did you close the friggin' door?"

Palms up, eyes wide, I attempted to convince Quaid I had no clue as to why the door closed. "I've been doing my best to open it," I said, drawing attention to my broken nails. "I have no idea why it slammed shut behind me."

A few of the officers chuckled. The tactical unit didn't seem the least bit amused.

"You expect me to believe a heavy steel door shut on its own!"

"Maybe the floor's not level, Quaid. I'm a detective, not a freaking engineer." At that, the majority of the tactical unit softly chorused a round of laughter.

Quaid scowled, the veins in his forehead—resembling neon cords—pounding dusky skin. He pushed me aside, landing a glare, a glint of skepticism flashing across gray-blue eyes.

"So, where are the kids?"

I jerked a thumb over my shoulder, my heart's accelerated rhythm drumming in my ears. I sprinted ahead, almost on Quaid's heels, and waited alongside him for the rest of the Tactical Unit to take up their position.

I squeezed my eyes closed and choked past a deep inhalation, fearful of what lay beyond the door. While I knew all of the children remained alive—Bianca would have told me if this wasn't the case—I assumed the Harvesters had most likely murdered the adults. I wondered how best to explain the devastation we were about to witness.

My eyes sprang open immediately when the door croaked a loud objection. Pairs of officers, wary and hunched low, surrounded me. Chief Patterson grabbed my arm and cocked his head toward the long line of law enforcement prepared to engage. I resisted a sigh of relief and obeyed, avoiding eye contact with the others as I shuffled toward the back of the line.

The barrage of clandestine hand signals that followed was impressive, but a wasted effort. The sweeping of the room, choreographed as well or better than a Broadway musical, was also pointless; the Harvesters had long departed either by choice or formidable force.

I heard Patterson speak first from my place at the end of the line.

"What the hell?" he said, apparently to no one in particular. "Take a headcount," he commanded of Dickerson. "You, you, and you, come with me," he ordered those among us with the most experience. "We need to find out what's happened to the goddamn teachers!"

CHAPTER 38

*W*ithin a few hours, a televised Special Report communicated James Vanslyke's message, nationwide. Bianca was right; he was damn convincing. The impromptu press conference was a success, and all within twenty-four hours. Men, women, and children flocked to hospitals, clinics, and urgent care centers, begging for the vaccine. No one suspected anything, including the Harvesters.

I resigned to the fact I needed Bianca's help. She not only wouldn't answer her cell phone, but she also chose to ignore every telepathic message I attempted, and I pushed aside a wave of hopelessness. Reports regarding abductions within the U.S. were presently nonexistent, so I assumed the Realm had expanded its reach outside the country. However, we'd yet to find the children initially missing. Quaid, the other detectives, and I had hit a brick wall. We'd exhausted our search, which included every nook and cranny within the city and the surrounding outskirts, and came up empty.

I sulked toward the canteen. Taking strangled gulps of my morning coffee, I reflected on my father's mood as Tristan described the herb's power. I remained convinced I'd caught a split-second glimmer in his eyes. And that look he shared with

Bianca . . . was it a look of intent? With a solution to immortality at their fingertips, would they consider their own destruction? Resting my chin on my palm, I abandoned a long sigh while considering the possibility. Although I've never felt it my right to judge anyone (as if it were possible for any run-of-the-mill person to contemplate such a supernatural phenomenon), I couldn't imagine why anyone would prefer death over immortality, particularly given the fact both Razvan and Bianca were in excellent physical condition. Maybe they'd just grown tired of battling insurgents. The subject in its entirety brought more questions to mind, and I knew if I didn't sort it out in my head, I'd compromise the attention my caseload deserved.

Ultimately, I decided that, first, if my parents had wanted to end their lives, they would have succeeded long ago, and, second, that perhaps for them, paradoxically, this was their only shot at eternal life.

The taskforce was bustling as it focused on the remaining missing children and investigated the whereabouts of the missing teachers. Fane had "dropped in" briefly while I was using the restroom—of course—and informed me the Harvesters were holding the teachers as blood donors. Provided the irreverent vampires didn't destroy them in the meantime, they'd receive a dose of the potion once the Realm secured their rescue. Of course, this was information I couldn't possibly share with my superiors, and my heart ached as I witnessed the squad spin their wheels, some suggesting the beloved teachers were involved in an underground kidnapping ring that, for one reason or another, went sideways.

I inserted a dollar and listened as the gears inside the vending machine whined and rattled a denial. I was just about to kick it when a handful of chocolate bars of various kinds spewed from the tray like coins in a slot machine. Sensing a presence, I craned my neck and looked over my shoulder.

"Celeste," Tristan said, "I feel I owe you an explanation."

"You don't owe me shit," I said, prepared to walk away. "You need to get out of here before someone sees y—" Before I'd even finished the sentence, I found myself staring at the trees which bordered the rear of the building, Tristan beside me. "I've got nothing to say to you, and there sure as hell isn't anything you have to say that I want to hear."

"Grant me a few words," he said, his eyes pleading.

"All right," I said, parking my hands on my hips. "Let's start with Nick."

"The potion was not at my disposal the night Nick died."

I cocked my head, my eyes penetrating his like poisoned darts. "What about after that? A month, a year? How about now?"

"Countless times I have anguished over my decision to deny Nick the potion. It is difficult to put into words—"

"Try!"

Tristan pressed his palms in my direction. "The relationship between the Maker and the Fledgling is . . . complicated." He twisted his lips between his thumb and forefinger, his beautiful forehead blemished by lines. "When I gave him the Adaption, he became a son to me . . . I gave him endless life, Celeste. How could I take it away?"

"You," I said, poking his chest, "took away my brother. And what about us? If you were mortal, it sure as hell would level the playing field." *We could make passionate love without fearing your love could mean my life's end! We could raise a family! Grow old together!*

He turned away, but not before I saw blood spill from his eyes and track his cheeks.

"I am a coward, Celeste," he managed through ragged breaths. "Death frightens me more than all the unspeakable terror I have faced. Because after all that I have done, all that I have become, I am not convinced of God's forgiveness. I am not willing to blindly accept his promise of eternal life as others are."

I gulped a breath, his confession crushing my soul.

He turned to face me, the usual vibrant energy gone. "I love you, Celeste. If I must prove it by renouncing immortality, then I shall."

Staving off tears, I shook my head. He offered his hand, and I fell into his arms.

~

ONCE I'D PULLED myself together, I returned to the heart of the command center, buzzing with state-of-the-art surveillance equipment. Every member of law enforcement personnel continued to work around-the-clock, save for two-hour overlapping breaks—comprised of a less than satisfying meal, often only a protein bar or drink—followed by a nap on one of the numerous army cots that now lined the wall of a large back room. From the somber expressions and swollen and bluish half-moon crescents under nearly everyone's eyes, it was obvious that the urgency of the circumstance, and the long days were taking their toll.

~

BY MID-MORNING, of day-four since the first abduction, an informant gave us the break we needed. Vanslyke personally contacted NASA, after which a drone verified thirty-five heat signatures on the top floor of an abandoned hotel. The tactical team organized within minutes, and a convoy of twenty patrol cars, seven unmarked Dodge Chargers, and ten black government-issued SUVs began a fevered pursuit. Quaid and I were in the first Chevy Tahoe, along with Detectives Ramirez, Donahue, Lindley, Franklin, and Briscoe.

As we neared the hotel, I searched building tops, trees, alleyways, even the sky, hoping against all hope to discover the Realm present and ready to assist. I checked my weapon again and suffocated a pathetic laugh; if the Harvesters *were* up there with these children, any number of guns was useless.

"Take up the rear, Detectives Ramirez and Crenshaw," Chief Patterson barked. "That's an order!"

My scalp tingled while my face grew hot. A glance in Juanita Ramirez's direction convinced me I wasn't alone in my resentment over such a ridiculous, sexist command.

As I stood there debating an angry response, Patterson jerked a thumb toward the end of the formation. "I said the rear, Detectives."

"The hell if I will," Ramirez whispered after we'd fallen back. She waited until the chief disappeared inside, then stealthy made her way up the line.

A beat later, I suddenly found myself in an alley, alongside Tristan, dizzy and confused.

"You shan't be relying on traditional weaponry," he said, as my head continued to swim. He pressed something that resembled a small paint gun in my hand and stuffed another within my trouser pocket. "I have loaded each projectile with six vials," he said, jamming a hand against a hip when he noticed my grin. "Such jocularity is most untimely, Celeste!"

"You're right. I'm sorry. That is an injector," I said, nodding toward the metal tube. "The vial is the projectile."

He arched an eyebrow and moved closer; so close, my heart picked up its pace. "Each vial contains the vaccine, which will render a vampire mortal. The effect is quite swift. Once instilled, your primitive weaponry will serve its purpose. Do you suffer conclusions?"

My brows puckered, and I scrubbed my forehead. "If you mean do I have any questions . . . No."

Fear showed in his eyes, in the almost indiscernible hesitancy to his speech.

"I must go now. My thoughts, my heart, my strength are with you always." He pulled me close and held me there, so tightly against his body, there wasn't room for either of us to take a breath. "Return to me, Celestine," he whispered in my ear, his soft, warm breath awakening every part of me, "for a world in which you no longer exist is a world intolerable." Then he was gone.

Chills continued to rack my spine, and I wrapped my arms about myself, pinching flesh here and there, desperate to focus on the matter at hand. My heart jackhammering in my chest, rather than deny my fear of what lay ahead, I embraced it and manipulated the position of the jet injector Tristan had pressed into my hand until I was as comfortable with it as I was with any handgun. As I hurried to catch up to the others, I thought it fortunate the task force hadn't insisted on a night-time attack. If they only knew how much a daytime assault increased our advantage. Maybe Vanslyke had insisted on daylight hours for the attack. As I entered the building, I could hear the babies' cries, a depressing mix of terror and hunger.

My eyes and throat burned from a combination of mold, dust, and intense focus. My heartbeat echoed in my ears and mimicked the *thump-thump-thump* of machinery somewhere overhead.

From the top of the long winding staircase, Patterson was in the midst of shouting an order but stopped suddenly, the last syllable hanging in the air like the distinct ring of a suspended bell. Surrounded by a fleet of decorated officers— some standing stock-still while others remained immobilized in a macabre mid-run stance, the chief stood motionless. His jaw lay open in mid-sentence while his arm hung paralyzed in a kind of gathering motion. I searched the perimeter for Bianca, convinced she had employed Silentium.

When I didn't see her, I took the stairs two at a time, side-stepping those rotted or slick with mold, urine, and fecal matter. Nearly to the top, I caught a shadow out of the corner of my left eye, but not in time. The thing flew at me, its lips curled back to expose pointed incisors, which brought to mind bull-necked resilient icicles, as it emitted not a growl nor a high-pitched screech but rather a demonic combination. A scream caught in my throat, and as I backed away, the Harvester—brandishing a menacing grin—glided forward, as if I was a willing participate in a bizarre tango.

Feeling the rickety stair railing press against my lower back, it protested with a forewarning *crack*, and I tumbled backwards, clawing the air onehanded as I freefell. The Harvester swept me up, midair, its piss-yellow eyes victorious, as razor-sharp fangs, oozing century-old secretions and a malodorous odor, lingered—greedy and foreboding—near my jugular vein.

Holding tight to the injector, once certain I had it pressed against his heart, I depressed the plunger and heard a hiss as the vial released a high-pressure stream. Producing an ear-splitting cry, the vampire pitched and writhed, before letting me go, and I plummeted five to six feet onto the lobby floor. When it landed with a thud alongside me, I scrambled to my feet just as its eyes blinked open as if from a deep sleep. Its gaze swept over my detective shield and the rest of my gear.

Then, it went for my gun.

CHAPTER 39

*T*he gunshot alerted the Harvesters to my location. Taking refuge in a dark corner under the staircase, I heard a thunderous sniff, more like a pig's grunt, and knew one was nearby.

I noticed his brilliant, incandescent blue eyes first as they showered fiery sparks which crackled and popped upon contacting the floor. As he drew closer, taking his time as any victor preparing to reap the spoils, I sank further into the corner, both fascinated and frightened by his imposing size. Loose, wrinkled skin, to include a balding head, expanded and contracted, and I sensed this was a well-honed scare tactic rather than an unexplained phenomenon. My mouth was wide open to let out a silent scream. I resisted closing my eyes and, instead, waited for him to close in, then jammed the injector into his slack fleshy cheek. This time, I didn't wait for the metamorphosis, drew my Glock, and fired two rounds, center mass.

Tiptoeing from my hiding place, I stayed low, peering between the stair risers until I'd once again reached the first step. A child, no older than three or four, came out of nowhere and rocketed toward me. Upon me now and preparing to sink in tiny incisors, I placed the injector beneath her ribs and hesitated.

"Do not be fooled, Celestine," I heard Bianca say. "It only appears a child to you. Some possess such preternatural power." A tear escaping one eye, I released the projectile. The body lying at my feet shapeshifted into a dwarfish middle-aged man. I put a bullet between his eyes.

Time had become both irrelevant and indistinguishable. If I had to guess, I'd say only sixty, possibly ninety seconds had elapsed before a swarm of thirsty vampires surrounded me; wicked grins exposed terrifying teeth. Every available exit was blocked, and I panicked. This time I didn't have the luxury of counterattacking each one individually. And because I wasn't able to inject them all simultaneously, I prepared for the inevitable. They would either kill me or, worse, ensure my Godforsaken immortality. Unwilling to go down without a fight, using my right hand, I aimed the injector at one advancing more rapidly than the others, as I trained the Glock on the remaining eleven. With a violent thrash, while clacking dripping incisors within an inch of my throat, the vampiress gripped my wrist, nearly breaking it, and I dropped the injector. I heard it clank, then skid across the floor.

She lifted me off my feet, effortlessly, raising me ten feet in the air, just as I prepared to fire the Glock in a last-ditch effort. The bullet bounced off her chest and penetrated my Kevlar vest. Feeling as though I'd been struck hard with a hammer, I released a pathetic groan. Unwilling to give up, I punched and kicked; resorting to biting after unsuccessfully landing blows.

Sinking my teeth into her wrist, and tasting something similar to rotted meat, my stomach lurched violently. Throwing her head back, she laughed as I gagged and vomited thick bile, afterwards propelling her head forward, the movement as swift as it was dramatic, testing my throat's soft flesh with pointy fangs as sharp and intimidating as any bayonet.

I raised the Glock again, this time placing it squarely against the side of her head, adjusting my position as best I could to combat a possible ricochet. I pulled the trigger, the concussion ringing my ears, and the bullet exploded what little glass remained of the hotel lobby's vandalized window front. Other than a small hole in her head, already in the stages of healing, she remained unscathed. A sinister smile further eroded her unpleasant features as I attempted to wrestle free.

The others had grown impatient and drifted closer, growling at one another like a pack of hungry wolves. I closed my eyes, surrendering to a fate I guess I'd always assumed mine.

Opening my eyes to an unearthly passionate chorus of high-pitched shrill cries, I saw one hurling itself in my direction and felt my eyes protrude from their sockets. I recognized Nick as he'd appeared in the basement long ago. Lips curled back and fangs exposed, he amputated my captor's arm with one vicious bite. She dropped me instantly, dashing overhead to seek refuge. Slack-jawed, my eyes followed her, as Nick battled the others, Tristan appearing suddenly at his side.

Racing across the lobby, my feet twice losing their grip on slimy, slick flooring, I grabbed hold of the jet injector and charged the stairs. Clamping her opposite hand to her side as if a phantom limb hung from her shoulder, the vampire wobbled in the air as though a damaged aircraft prepared to crash. With a determined jump, my intent to snag one of her feet and propel her down onto the landing, she delivered a violent kick to my nose, and I fell back.

I attempted the strategy again, but this time I enlisted a small wooden box. Still in reasonably good condition, despite hunter green paint flaking off here and there, I assumed it once belonged to a shoe shiner. Positioned shrewdly at the top of the long winding staircase no longer grand—the intent to waylay unsuspecting guests—I imagined the platform supporting the renowned soles of Harry S. Truman and various visiting aristocrats in its day. Satisfied it would support my weight, I lunged for her again, and she crumpled to the ground, emitting a half-groan, half-growl.

I vaulted atop her, pinning her down, a noxious smell similar to decaying garbage stinging my nostrils. Squirming to free herself, rocking us both this way then that, I nearly lost my grip on the jet injector. She seemed to tire, and I seized the opportunity, jabbing the injector tip through a soiled layer of brittle, yellowed lace, finding purchase just below her collarbone. She howled a bone-chilling shriek, and I fired the Glock just as she transitioned to a mortal state. I stood over her body and resisted a smug smile, knowing the vile bitch would never again be a threat to anyone.

Hesitating on the landing, I glanced over my shoulder, knowing what I would see could never be unseen; Tristan as an irreverent demonic plague, my brother mercilessly slaughtering entities, not so divergent from himself or the man I loved.

My eyes settling on him, Tristan whipped his head in my direction, ungodly fangs dripping a thick, black liquid, eyes no longer loving or sensual but angry and forbidding. I looked away, in Nick's direction, before Tristan could see the repulsion I felt certain flickered across my eyes. Nick's head snapped back toward his spine, observing me greedily—in that awkward and impossible position—as though I was either prey or an enemy he needed to destroy promptly. Tristan emitted an alpha growl, and Nick's neck swiveled three hundred sixty degrees, bringing to mind a ghoulish weathervane in the throes of a wicked cyclone. Expelling a guttural growl, which shook the building, Nick soared in Tristan's direction, his lips drawn back to expose intimidating incisors. Convinced, if the two came to blows, they would destroy one another, I inhaled, my heart thudding against my chest.

Ear-splitting screeches once again erupted, and Nick— nearly to Tristan by this point—abandoned his course.

Shapeshifting into something resembling an enormous prehistoric falcon, he apprehended two Harvesters simultaneously and flattened them beneath deadly talons then ripped off their heads in one swift sickening movement.

His head whipped in my direction just as a stabbing pain between my shoulder blades prompted a carnal scream. The ache was intense, and I nearly blacked out. I attempted to break free, but whatever had a hold of me carried me through the air, content to perch upon a mammoth chandelier, its silver-dollar-sized, dust-laden crystals tinkling in response. My feet dangled two stories above the ground floor, and I considered my chance of survival should my captor let go. My intuition convinced me it might be best if I stopped kicking.

From this ideal vantage point, I bore witness to everything transpiring below. Creatures—the kind born of terrifying nightmares—combated one another. Translucent amphibian-like creatures would suddenly become something else entirely and I could hardly distinguish the Realm from the Harvesters. One morphed into a medieval knight. It wasn't until he raised the visor attached to his helmet that I recognized Lazarus. Another suddenly appeared as a glistening gargoyle, and it was only due to my time spent in the Circle that I knew this to be either Stelian or Paulo, just as I remained convinced the chimera and the griffin battling less horrifying entities were Ariel and Lucas, respectively.

The intensity increased, and body parts flew in all directions as though birds caught within a jetliner's engine, before culminating into nothing more than piles of smoldering ash.

A bone-chilling shriek suddenly rattled the few remaining windows, and a heart-stopping specter resembling the mythical creature, the Mothman, soared in my direction. Morphing into something reminiscent of a three-headed, winged dragon, it sprayed fountains of fire past a terrifying growl. My captor released me instantly, and I plummeted toward the ground floor, the sound of metal melding with metal assaulting my ears. Preparing myself for impact, another winged Mothman swooped me up before I hit the ground. I recognized the familiar scent, a mix of mint and licorice, just as my father settled me on the floor and vanished.

I glanced overhead, certain now that the dragon was Bianca, and my gaze settled on the melted hardware, which not so long ago had served to secure the gigantic chandelier, its glass components liquefied and now little more than lime- stone and potash. The dragon dove and soared overhead in pursuit of my captor, which by this time had taken on the appearance of a prehistoric bird with a shell comprised of stainless steel.

Bianca once again dispersed the equivalent of volcanic lava, and the bird suddenly exploded, showering the room with sharp reflective particles. Yesenia appeared from within the shimmering downpour and disappeared just as quickly amid her thunderous laughter. Razvan and Bianca vanished, and I assumed, this time, they intended to destroy her.

I caught movement out of the corner of my eye and saw a small child, her tiny feet landing solidly upon the splintered rail at the top of the stairs. I jerked myself upright and bolted toward the staircase.

When I reached the top, my feet sliding in her direction, injector poised and ready to fire, she opened her mouth and liberated a mournful sob, and I knew I couldn't go through with it. My conflict didn't result from fear I'd make a horrible mistake, as when I'd hesitated earlier. I knew what she was, the danger she surely represented. I simply couldn't bring myself to destroy something so child-like, so seemingly innocent, so beautiful. That, and my instincts, convinced me her allegiance lay with the Realm. I dropped my arm to my side, and she smiled, her teeth white and normal-appearing, coffee-colored eyes—opened wide and lacking sin—revealing a sort of calm serenity, as well as a theoretical knowledge far beyond her years.

A prolonged clink-clink-clink sounded, like hail contacting pavement, and my eyes flew toward the lower level just as Tristan and Nick evaporated amid a shower of crystalline ice pellets and a foggy shroud. Their conquests lay scattered, now resembling nothing more than mounds of molten ash. The Harvesters I had killed remained where I left them. Satisfied the squad would discover only human traffickers who had met their deserved end and, hopefully, relegate any ash they might notice to anomalous debris, I steered myself in the direction of children wailing.

Members of law enforcement suddenly came to life, Chief Patterson was in the midst of finishing his earlier command and the squad responding. I sprinted after them down the musty bleak corridor just as something grabbed hold of my hand. I instantly pulled away, and the child reached for me, her arms opened wide.

"I can't take you with me," I said and continued down the hallway.

She ran after me, latching onto me, wrapping both arms around my thigh, and whimpered something, which sounded like, "Please, m'lady, you must."

Gently prying her hands away, I exhaled a sobering sigh and studied the molded tin ceiling, wondering how I might explain this child with hair dressed in ringlets, Victorian clothing to include tattered pantaloons—entirely rotted bare in spots—and a now scruffy, mildewed, laboriously ruffled and bejeweled dress. After studying her eyes and satisfied her benevolent smile sincere, I swooped her up, resting her on a hip opposite my holster.

"What's your name?"

"Raina," she whispered in my ear, her breath warm, the scent reminding me of crisp air on the heels of a spring shower.

"In there," she said, jabbing a delicate forefinger at the door once painted a soothing and promising robin's-egg blue.

"Hurry!" she whispered, followed by a discomforting giggle. "They are always so very thirsty for the blood."

I set her on her feet, and with her hand in mine, we entered the dismal space as shrill blasts from outside announced the arrival of several ambulances. No one seemed to notice our sudden presence; everyone was intent on comforting the children, although most of them were in the process of acquiring IVs and appeared catatonic. A young boy —rail-thin and motionless—was receiving CPR by an EMT.

Chief Patterson noticed us then, and with his eyes locked on Raina, he abandoned a conversation and stormed toward me, undoubtedly prepared to ask a question I couldn't honestly answer.

The wind suddenly picked up outside, ushering crusty leaves through various thoroughfares, some intended, some suffering either the effects of time or the idle hands of rebellious youth. The sky darkened beyond the cobwebbed, bullet-holed, grimy windows, and the air hung heavy and deoxygenated. As I struggled to inhale a breath, my ears began to ring, while my skin prickled, cold and clammy, and before I slipped into a state of unawareness, it occurred to me that the Realm must have required additional Silentium, deciding it best they clean up the aftermath.

When I came to, everything was as it had been. Except, Raina was missing.

CHAPTER 40

*R*euniting the children with their parents and taking their statements took most of the night. The kids remembered nothing of their encounter with the Harvesters —which I attributed to Bianca's ability to purge memories. Assured the Realm had intervened before the Harvesters could compromise the children, I could finally inhale an unrestricted breath.

Although Bianca had assured me that Raina remained safe and content within the Torok Mansion, I found myself thinking of her again. I was drawn to her and she to me, almost as if the universe had intended for us to meet.

Within a loft in the abandoned warehouse, I exhaled a satisfied moan as Tristan simultaneously vanished, my orgasm bittersweet as I had never witnessed his. Although I'd agreed it hardly seemed a fair compromise, I'd offered—and on more than this occasion—to either take the potion or gamble immortality. He'd adamantly refused either.

When he returned, I nestled close, my fingers lazily exploring and occasionally entwining a few hairs on his chest. "What now? Did we destroy them all? Or scare them away, at the very least?"

He blew out a breath, his exquisite abdominal muscles tightening in response.

"To say, they no longer exist, Celeste, is to say the rain shall never come again. There will always be more. Would you decree every criminal reformed upon release?" I shook my head, my hair falling softly across his chest. "There you have it. As is the way with mortals, oftentimes evil prevails, no matter the deterrent."

I sighed and rolled over onto my back.

He rolled toward me, his eyes probing my soul.

"Do not despair, my love."

"I was thinking about the girl."

"Ah. Raina," he said simply and rolled over, propping his arm beneath his head.

"So that's really her name?"

"Indeed, Raina Brown; seized by the Harvesters in the 1800s when the ship *Grace*—carrying emigrants from Australia —caught fire."

"And her parents?"

"I cannot say. Perhaps, by this time, Bianca has the answers you seek."

"What will happen to her?"

"It would seem the bewitching tyke has rendered a spell over you," he said with a wink, once propping himself upon an elbow. "If only I possessed such powers, perhaps you might embrace much-needed slumber."

"I'm just worried about her, is all."

"Perhaps you should worry about me, your valiant warrior. For the sun is dawning, and I find myself hungrily awaiting repose."

I laughed and rolled into him. "So, translated, you need to get some sleep?"

"I would be forever in your debt," he said, brushing his lips across my shoulder.

"I'm too wound-up to sleep," I said, stroking his cheek.

"What happens when I'm old, my body shrivels up like a prune, and my hair turns gray?"

"I shall present you a suitable companion."

Feigning a scowl, I playfully pushed him away. "You'll dump me?"

"Such words, I shall never utter!" He wrestled me close and grinned. "I was merely saying that when that time is upon us, I shall happily shapeshift into a comparably loathsome, withered, and detestable creature."

I threw my head back and laughed, then laid my head on his shoulder. "What can you tell me about Bianca?"

Tristan groaned dramatically.

"Did she really know Cleopatra? Will you tell me that much?"

"If she states it was so, it was so. Who are we to assume otherwise? Furthermore, why do you think me alive in 69 B.C.?" he asked, with a sideways smirk. "How old do you think I am?"

I squinted, resisting a grin. "I always assumed you'd learned a few things from Spartacus."

Tristan cocked his head and looked me in the eye.

"The Thracian gladiator?"

"That's the one," I said, smiling up at him.

"I should think it more the other way around."

"What about Yesenia?"

Tristan clutched his chest as if I'd physically wounded him. "Ah, Yesenia, the vile vixen. She pursued me for ages until finally, one particularly lonely night, I allowed distasteful capture."

I remembered the time I'd witnessed them together in the kitchen and puffed a cheek. "I don't want to hear any of that; I meant, what's happened to her?"

"Alas, I cannot say. The hunt continues."

"I trust your womanizing days are behind you," I purred, snuggling closer.

"My womanizing days?" Tristan said, feigning ignorance and insult. "Whatever do you mean?"

"Bianca told me about your adaptation, for one."

"Ah, yes, my dalliance with Servilia Caepionis. I would think it Fane who told you. The imp would sooner turn to stone than retain such delectable information."

"Don't even try to pull Fane into this. To hear Bianca tell it, Servilia wasn't your only dalliance that night."

"'Tis true. Believe it or not, I am blushing."

I pinned him against the pillow, my hair brushing his face.

"I don't believe it." I studied his beautiful eyes and ran my fingers across his lips, allowing them to linger there, before caressing his face. "Bianca said she isn't your mother. Will you tell me about her?"

"Alas, my dear mother did not survive my birth."

"So, Bianca raised you?"

Tristan shook his head, a slight smile testing his lips, the glint in his eyes hinting adoration.

"Much time had passed when she came into my father's life and awakened him as if from a state of cursed oblivion. He soon was no longer the father destiny had bequeathed me, but rather a father of my choosing."

"Will you tell me about your wife?" His breathing increased, and I felt his body tense. "What was her name?"

"Alexandra," he whispered, a fleeting smile transforming terse lips.

"How did you meet?"

"In England, amidst a Saint George Day celebration." He chuckled softly. "A merchant had swindled her of a silver sixpence, and I felt certain she would pluck out his eyes!"

"When was that?"

"Fifteen-fifty-seven," he replied dreamily.

"What did she look like?"

He cleared his throat and was quiet for a long time. Then he propped himself on one elbow. "Much like you," he whispered, his practiced fingers skimming the soft, receptive skin between my breasts.

"What happened to her?"

He flipped onto his back and stared at the ceiling.

"Why do you torture me so?"

"I'm sorry," I said, tentatively stroking his chest.

"The Black Death," he murmured moments later.

"The Bubonic Plaque?"

"Yes, she and our son."

Blood seeped from the corner of his eye, and he reached up and brushed it away.

CHAPTER 41

One Month Later

*B*ianca had made the suggestion the morning after we'd battled the Harvesters before her return to New Jersey. Now, it seemed all my earlier concerns were unnecessary. True, Raina was a vampire, and one not given the Adaptation by any member of the East Coast Coalition, but rather long ago by Fulvia of the Realm's West Coast Alliance. Recently fighting the Harvesters side by side with Bianca and the others throughout Europe, Fulvia—mistress of the West Coast Coalition—was destroyed by a particularly ruthless vampire with superior skills. Although to hear Bianca tell it, Fulvia was a formidable opponent whose presence most often persuaded her adversaries to flee rather than confront her. A reliable witness's account suggests that Yesenia aided Fulvia's destroyer, which only reinforced Bianca's compulsion to annihilate her at the earliest opportunity. Following a very brief but thoroughly introspective debate, Bianca felt she had no choice but to take charge of Raina.

Bianca pleaded her case during a lengthy discussion, in which she outlined a very persuasive argument: *Your father and I have discussed this in much detail. Though one of us, the child simply cannot accompany us throughout the world, as we battle our enemies. As she became immortal at the age of five, she will forever remain a child. That being the case, it is surely in her best interest to live life as if a mortal. Because you have made your decision regarding a life spent with Tristan, and he shall never give you a child of your own, this would appear a Godsend, Celeste.*

I wasn't convinced and told her as much.

Tristan dotes on the child. Have you not bore witness? If you shan't consider your happiness, consider his. She'd looked away from me then, but her expression revealed crippling sadness. *One day you will leave him behind, a day far in the future, God willing. Do not leave him to wander the earth alone, my darling.*

"Mama, I shall be late for school," Raina said, interrupting my thoughts as she bounded down the stairs within our loft, her Pokémon backpack slipping from one shoulder.

"*I'm going to be late* for school," I corrected, readjusting the backpack and pinching her cheek. She looked at me, her wide eyes confused, as I zipped her pink hoodie, drawing the hood snuggly over her glossy dark hair. "Never mind. Tonight, I want to hear all about your big day!"

She slipped her hand in mine, just as she'd done the day we met, and I hiccoughed a sob as we approached the school entrance. I was able to convince the principal that Raina was a child with special needs, including extreme photosensitivity. I tugged an extensive list of instructions from my blazer pocket as Raina skipped ahead once setting her eyes on a group of kindergartners lining up in the hallway. She turned, before the line continued its idyllic march toward the assigned room and blew me a kiss. I inhaled a deep breath and wiped the tears from my face.

Once delivering my maternal mandate to the office, although the principal assured me he'd given the staff rigorous instruction, I returned to my car, wondering what would happen next year for Raina couldn't remain in kindergarten forever. Only two options existed as I saw it; a yearly move to another school district—counterfeiting Raina's records once again—or homeschooling with frequent visits to the park or zoo where Raina could interact with other five-year-olds.

∽

THE NEXT FEW months flew by. Raina had made an endless stream of friends, and I had hosted an exhausting number of Disney-inspired slumber parties, which kept my mind off Tristan, who was often away battling the Harvesters.

The Realm continued its search for Yesenia, rumored somewhere off the Straits of Gibraltar. Bianca and the Omniscients trained a vengeful and consistent eye.

Humming, I left the precinct on foot and started toward our cozy, charming apartment. A slight breeze was in the air, clouds raced overhead, and a transient raindrop or two plopped onto my Royals baseball cap, which often served as raingear. Nearly to the corner of 10th Street and Grand Avenue, a half-mile or so from home, my knees buckled, my face suddenly smashing against a graffiti-laden sidewalk. I brushed my tongue over my teeth, convinced the impact had knocked a few loose. My head throbbed, and from the intense burning sensation pulsing through my forearm, I assumed my abrupt landing had met shards of broken glass. Pulled off the ground, with a ferociousness no human could possibly possess, I assumed my assailant was immortal.

I froze when I'd heard Yesenia's familiar cackle of joy. Then my survival instincts kicked in, and I buried my elbow squarely between Yesenia's eyes, which didn't slow her down in the least. Immediately after, I found myself hurtling through space. By the time I reached her intended destination, Yesenia was already there and batted me back the direction I had come. I was hardly a worthy opponent, and she soon tired of the game. Yanking me from the patched crumbling concrete, she showcased a set of lethal, slippery fangs. I kicked and punched, my screams filling an abandoned lot.

Bianca materialized and unleashed a primal howl. Morphing into a terrifying reptilian-like creature, her long hair snapped the air like a frenzied crocodile, and her glowering eyes promised a painful end. A dense fog rose up around her, and she soared in Yesenia's direction. Rather than ready a defense, Yesenia sank dagger-like incisors into my throbbing jugular vein. Bianca snapped off a tree branch and pitched it toward the sky. I watched as a sword appeared instead, its hilt glowing green then red, its long blade razor-sharp and glistening in the sunset. Yesenia withdrew her fangs, arched her back, and growled as though she were a dog guarding a bone. Bianca swung the blade and loped off her head. Yesenia emitted a torturous gasp and, though her head was no longer attached to her body, words promising revenge continued to spew from her mouth. I lost consciousness, aware that this was the last mortal memory I would ever have.

EPILOGUE

*M*y immortal eyes blinked open, and I saw the sun's surface, a barren and crackled expanse. Within the dark, linear stria, bright specks identified the magnetic fields. But it took a moment for my eyes to provide feedback to my brain, random mathematical symbols skittering across sparking waves like a complex algorithm, the sensation similar to the plucking of a violin.

I heard classical music—Beethoven's *Moonlight Sonata*, Vivaldi's *L'estate*, Mozart's *The Marriage of Figaro*, and Dvořák's *Symphony No. 9*—playing in a disorganized frenzied unison. I heard insects as they scurried about in a chaotic survival mode beneath the ground, and I covered my ears to no effect.

I diverted my focus to the sky; one more vivid than any I'd ever remembered. To define it merely blue seemed a travesty. Sea-green streaks randomly splashed throughout various hues of powder and electric blue as though an indolent artist's afterthought.

There were flowers all around me, boasting colors so vibrant my breath seemed to catch in my heart. Bathing my nostrils with the heady scents of assorted roses, alyssum, petunias, and lilacs, I pushed off the ground, my hands contacting lush grass, feeling more velvet to the touch. I studied it, the color so implausibly green that for a moment, I'd forgotten the color classification entirely.

A siren shrilled in the distance, and I listened again for the underlying sound of bells pealing.

"That's not possible," I said aloud, realizing the bells I heard originated from the Unity Village Tower, twenty-some miles away; the bells hadn't tolled for years but I'd never heard them at this distance.

The acrid smell grew stronger, stinging my nostrils, previously lying dormant beneath the near-hypnotic floral scents. I popped upright—anticipating a slow rise at best—and hovered slack-jawed, inches above the ground. My gaze settled on the glowing ashen mound, just to my right, and a solitary spark flickered, then sputtered into nothingness.

"Yesenia shall never again bring you harm," Bianca said, enveloping me in her arms.

"I . . . I can't—" I began, unable to think beyond the cacophony of sounds competing with one another.

Bianca twittered a doleful laugh and brushed the back of her hand across my cheek.

"In time, you shall adjust, Celestine."

As our hands clasped together, Raina and Tristan appeared. Raina tugged Bianca and me toward earth, my feet landing with a thud as I struggled to maintain my balance. She smiled up at me, lacing her tiny, delicate fingers through mine, her beautiful brown eyes gleaming and revealing the depth of joy most—whether mortal or immortal—never experience. Then she gestured for Tristan to join us.

In her lyrical and angelic tone that always made me think of a gentle rain as it nourishes leaves in a garden, she said, "Now, we shall always be together."

FOR FURTHER DISCUSSION

1. What was the most compelling scene/part of the story to you? What drew you in?
2. Who was your favorite character? Why?
3. Which account of historical figures mentioned did you find the most interesting, and why?
4. How did you feel about Ethan and Celeste's relationship?
5. Did you want Tristan and Celeste to be together or did you agree that they shouldn't be in a romantic relationship?
6. Which of the characters could you relate to best? Why?
7. If you could go inside the Circle what memory would you want to see?
8. If you were a vampire, what power would you want to have?
9. If Hollywood came knocking, who would you like to see portray the main characters: Celeste, Nicholas, Tristan, Bianca, Razvan, Yesenia and Fane.

10. How did you feel about Celeste's fate at the end of the novel? Did you see this coming or was it a surprise to you?

REAL WORLD INSPIRATION

As an author that loves historical fiction as well as mystery and suspense, D. B. Woodling thought it seemed only natural to meld the two genres together. As a fan of Stephen King novels, the author chose paranormal as the main ingredient with a pinch of horror thrown in.

The first part of the novel is set in New Jersey and contains references to the Cape May-Lewes Ferry, Asbury Park, Ocean Avenue, and Pier Point. As a frequent visitor to the Garden State, it seemed only natural to Woodling to make Celeste and Nick's home in this part of the east coast.

The second part of the novel takes place in Kansas City; Woodling's birthplace and the birthplace of jazz, renowned for its exceptional barbeque. The novel pays homage to several notable sites: the Blue Room, the Country Club Plaza, the Nelson-Atkins Museum of Art, and Worlds of Fun. She also included descriptive and humorous passages of legendary celebrities, such as Walt Disney, Ernest Hemingway, Cleopatra, Julius Caesar, Albert Einstein, Thomas Jefferson, Martha Washington, Marie Antoinette, King Edward II, King Henry VIII, Anne Boleyn, King Ferdinand, Queen Isabella, and more!

One of her favorite characters she created for this novel is Fane, a sixteenth-century animated and flamboyant vampire. He is as entertaining as he is lovable.

Because a reader reads to escape, Woodling thought it was important to take the audience on an adventure far removed from a nation of political and racial unrest and a world battling a terrifying pandemic.

ACKNOWLEDGMENTS

I suppose I should begin by thanking my husband, the man who tiptoes by my desk, pretending he doesn't notice when I'm pulling my hair out by the roots while writing a complicated scene. Or when I'm hurling four-letter obscenities at inanimate objects as I wrack my brain while searching for the perfect word.

I also want to thank my children for bringing my life joy and dimension and for all those batshit crazy memories to draw upon, which, hopefully, make me a better writer.

Last, but certainly not least, I want to thank CamCat Publishing, more specifically, my editorial team, Bridget McFadden and Helga Schier, for their gentle nudges and encouragement, that extra little push toward the road to perfection.

ABOUT THE AUTHOR

D. B. Woodling is an author that refuses to limit her writing to one particular niche. As a writer for nearly two decades, she has dabbled in the genres of historical fiction, young adult fiction, and paranormal fiction, although she has a penchant for mystery thrillers.

Woodling's creative process is a bit unconventional. She admits to having a few props nearby when writing, including a cowboy hat, pom-poms, and a wad of Double Bubble parked inside her cheek as headphones blast the latest hit from Ariana Grande. She added a wooden stake and a garlic clove during the creation of *The Immortal Twin*.

Prior to embarking on a career as a writer, D. B. Woodling was a celebrated entertainer in the Midwest. Woodling confesses to having a healthy obsession for the East and West Coasts, dolphins, and whales. She currently resides in Missouri with her husband, one dog, three cats, and two horses.

In 2016, following the death of her beloved Labrador Retriever, Woodling established Annie's Gift, a cause benefiting No-Kill Animal Shelters and select veterinarian clinics throughout the United States. She donates a large portion of her royalties to Annie's Gift.

MORE FROM CAMCAT BOOKS

IF YOU ENJOYED THE IMMORTAL TWIN . . .

. . . try *The Brighter the Stars* by Bryan Prosek—

*In the midst of mounting intergalactic hostilities, a young legion soldier
sets out with his best friend to escort the love of his life to an
ambassadorship on the other side of the galaxy and say goodbye to her for
good, only to be pulled away from his responsibilities by the
chance to avenge the death of a beloved uncle.*

THE BRIGHTER THE STARS

AN EXCERPT

Jake quickly raised his sepder for a block. It was a weak blow, and he stopped it easily. The next swing would probably be low, and then one more high swing. His opponent was so predictable. Holding his sepder with only one hand, Jake dropped it low. Another block. Jake ducked, and as anticipated, his opponent's next swing went over his head. Jake lowered his sepder to his side. He wasn't a bit fatigued. He could do this all day. He needed a better challenge. Sure, his opponent was an officer with much more battle experience than him, but he could take the guy anytime he wanted. His opponent came up unexpectedly with a backhanded swing, and Jake instinctively jumped backwards. That was close. Time to go on the offensive. Jake countered with four swings: right, left, high, low, moving the officer backwards.

"Pretty good, Private," the officer said. "You know what you're doing. The commander warned me about getting into the ring with you. But now let's see what you really have."

The officer came at Jake with his sepder high, striking at Jake's head. *Clang, clang, clang, clang.* Jake blocked each blow but was driven backwards on his heels. The officer then did a complicated down-and-up move with his sepder. It was difficult to block, but Jake did so. He wasn't happy about it, though. He was completely on the defensive.

"That's what I thought," the officer said. "You can handle the standard stuff, but get a little tricky with you, and you're all mine."

Jake could feel his heart race faster. I'm taking this guy out, he thought. Jake faked a low swing, then turned a one-eighty to block the officer's counter. A tricky move, but the officer didn't counter as Jake anticipated. Instead, he kicked Jake in the chest. Jake didn't see it coming. The blow knocked him backwards into a roll. He'd been outmaneuvered.

Jake hopped up. "That's it!" He'd had enough of the officer's tricks and arrogance. He would show the guy what he could really do.

"What's the matter?" the officer said with a grin. "Can't handle an old man?"

Jake saw Romalor's grin on the officer. Eight years couldn't erase Romalor's face from his mind. He could feel the muscles in his face tighten instinctively as his eyes focused on the man's midsection. That was the kill zone. He really wanted to kill this guy. No, he couldn't kill him, but he also couldn't lose to him, not the way the guy was grinning and taunting him. He was going to finish this once and for all. Jake raised his sepder high, holding it in both hands, and began swinging as he moved forward into the officer. First to the left, then to the right. Swing left, swing right, faster, faster, swing harder, harder. The officer blocked each blow while continuing to back up, just as Jake planned. That was more like it. Jake quickly pulled his sepder above his head and put all his strength into a blow coming in high on his opponent. The officer blocked, but was knocked backwards by the force of the blow. With a roll-over move that Jake had never seen before, the officer came up under Jake and, with a backwards thrust of his sepder, knocked Jake's sepder out of his hands. He stepped into Jake with his sepder pointed at Jake's chest.

Jake stood frozen. He felt his chest heaving as he gasped for air. How did the officer do that move? How could I have lost to him? He's twice my age.

"Never come high and hard, Private," the officer said. "Anyone who knows what he's doing will turn it around on you." He lowered his sepder and held out his hand.

Jake shook it. "Thank you, sir."

"Nice fight, Private," said a deep voice from behind Jake. "Until the end."

Jake turned around. Captain Alfons Gorski approached them. He was a very large, heavy-set man in his mid-fifties. Jake had always thought that Gorski had clearly eaten his share of kielbasa and kishka, two of Gorski's favorite foods from his native region, formerly Poland.

"Sir." Jake saluted as Gorski approached them.

"I'm going to hit the showers," the officer said. Jake and Gorski stood alone at the side of the ring.

The familiar smell of sweat permeated the room. Jake liked it. He liked training. And with sepder training, physical fitness, and one-on-one, hand-to-hand and sepder fights in the ring, the training room was a sweaty place.

"Jake, I've been around this gym for longer than I care to remember," Gorski said. "And I've watched and trained more cadets, privates, and even officers than you can count. You're one of the best I've ever seen. That is, when you can control yourself. You would have won that fight if you hadn't let him get to you. You let the taunting get to you, and then you fight with anger, not with intelligence. At that point, you've already lost. Jake, in real battles, if you keep letting your enemies get to you, you're going to get yourself killed one day."

"Sir," Jake replied, "I just do what I need to do to win." He knew Gorski was probably right, but what else could he do? That's who he was. The anger gave him strength, and motivation. But for what? For Romalor. That's what.

"No, Jake," Gorski said. "You do what your opponents

want you to do. They want you to get angry. They use that against you. Think about it."

Jake nodded, trying to look appreciative and respectful. Part of him knew that Gorski was right, but he wanted the anger. He needed the anger. "Thank you, sir."

Jake and Cal made their way across and down the street to the new Sector Four command center, construction on which had begun shortly after that night eight years ago. Jake looked down the street. It had changed so much in the past eight years. The buildings were still designed in the traditional style, white dome-shaped structures. However, there were so many new buildings, and the streets were bustling. People and hover cars were everywhere. Sector Four headquarters had truly become a city in and of itself. Jake instinctively ducked his head and winced from the roar as a spacecraft took off over their heads. He could tell a spacecraft from an aircraft just from the sound. He had learned that from his Uncle Ben. A spacecraft made more of a deep roar, as it was heavier and more powerful. The weight and power were needed to enter and leave the atmosphere of planets. Aircraft didn't need that ability just to travel around Earth.

They entered the building, went through the now-standard security clearance checks, and made their way directly to Commander Frank Cantor's office. Cal knocked on the closed door.

"It's open," came a rough voice from inside.

Jake and Cal walked in. No surprise: Frank was seated behind his desk with an unlit cigar in his mouth, chewing on it as he always did. And the picture wouldn't be complete without Frank's trademark cowboy hat hanging on top of the coat rack in the corner. How many of those hats did he have, and where did they all come from? Who still made such things? They looked like the military-style hats worn by the cavalry in the old United States western movies of the twentieth century that he and Frank used to watch all the time.

"You wanted to see us, Commander?" Jake asked.

"Yes, yes, have a seat," Frank said, gesturing toward the chairs without looking up from the work on his desk. "And close the door."

Jake glanced at the chairs, and was surprised to see Diane sitting there. "Diane, hi. I didn't know that you were going to be here." Oh, that was real smooth, he thought as he shut the door. Couldn't he come up with something a little nicer? But then, did it really matter? After all, they were there on business. But of course it mattered. It mattered to him. He had that warm, somewhat nervous feeling again, like he always did around Diane, like a silly schoolboy.

Jake and Cal sat on either side of Diane.

"Do you two know who the Imperial Majesty is?" Frank asked.

Cal replied, "Yes, that's the title that Vernius gave to its leader about eight years ago."

Jake jumped in. "They didn't think the title of Vernition Queen or King was politically correct anymore."

"Correct on both counts," Frank said. "And I suppose you know that they recently elected the new Imperial Majesty. She took office a couple of months ago."

"Yes, sir," Cal said. Jake and Cal both nodded.

Frank continued, "And when they elect a new Imperial Majesty, he or she picks a new ambassador from Earth, from our selected prospects."

"Yes, sir," Jake said, "but may I ask, what's all this have to do with us?"

"I have a new assignment for you two cowboys," Frank said. "You are to escort Earth's new ambassador to Vernius. What's more, you hit the trail at daybreak, so you'll need to pack up your saddlebags tonight. I don't have to tell you how important Earth's relationship with Vernius is. They're our closest ally. You'll take a small Legion transport. It'll have a couple of guns just in case, but it should be a smooth ride, seeing that everyone is at peace in that region. If I give you any more firepower, you could alarm the settlers in the area."

Jake didn't necessarily like the idea of going that far from Earth with nothing more than a transport, but he trusted Frank's judgment one hundred percent. After all, as commander, Frank was the number one ranking Legion soldier in Sector Four. Some people thought Frank inherited the position as one of the last officers standing after the attack, but Jake knew better. He hated it when he heard someone say that. Jake remembered Frank as a captain in Sector Four prior to the attack. He remembered how much Uncle Ben liked Frank and how hard Frank seemed to work. After the attack, with most of the Sector Four officers killed, Frank was promoted to the new Sector Four commander and given the unenviable task of trying to put Sector Four headquarters back together. He was the youngest Legion soldier ever to achieve the rank of commander. Jake laughed to himself. At almost fifty, Frank hadn't slowed down a bit and could probably whip just about any soldier in the sector in a fist fight. "Sounds good, Commander." Jake looked at Diane. "But why is Diane here?"

"You're looking at the new Vernition ambassador," Frank replied. "On her last visit, the Imperial Majesty interviewed everyone we put in front of her until she met Diane. She stopped right then. Diane was the one."

It took a minute for it to register with Jake. Then it hit him. Vernition ambassador. That's generally a long-term assignment. Very long term. He looked at Frank. "But is it safe, sir? Are you sure she should go?" As soon as the words left his mouth, he realized that wasn't a smart comment.

Diane looked at Jake with a raised eyebrow. "Really, Jake?"

"You're right," Jake replied. "That was out of line."

"Jake, this is what I've been working for," Diane said. "I want this. This is the opportunity of a lifetime."

Frank interjected before she could go on, "And I just said how important an ally Vernius is. If they want Diane and Diane wants to go, then we'll give them Diane."

Jake's day had just gone from bad to worse. He had to find some hope in this. He looked at Diane. "How long is the assignment?" He already knew the answer.

Diane started to answer, but Frank interrupted her. "Indefinitely. You know that the Vernition queen, I mean Imperial Majesty, is elected for life, unless she decides to retire. As long as she wants Diane and Diane wants to serve, then the position is Diane's."

Jake was speechless. He didn't know what to say. There would be little chance for him to see Diane. He would likely never have an assignment on Vernius. There was little need for Legion soldiers on such a peaceful planet. And an ambassador had little, if any, leeway or time to return home. Maybe Cal was right. He needed to have more fun. Cal used to always prod him to ask Diane out. Cal was always trying to set them up. Cal would say how he noticed how Jake looked and acted around Diane. Cal told him that Diane did the same thing around Jake. That they were a perfect match. But it always seemed that he, and probably Diane too, never had the time. Lately, Cal had pretty much given up trying, except for an occasional comment here and there. Jake stood up, extended his hand to Diane, and forced a smile. "Congratulations, Ambassador."

Diane rose, took his hand, and smiled back. "Thank you, Jake."

Jake stood there for a moment holding her hand. Her touch was soft, and her dark brown eyes still penetrated right through to his heart.

Cal hopped up, put an arm around each of them and smiled. "My big sister. An ambassador!"

CamCat
Books

Visit Us Online for More Books to Live In:
camcatbooks.com

Follow Us:

CamCatBooks   @CamCatBooks   @CamCatBooks

Printed in the USA
CPSIA information can be obtained
at www.ICGtesting.com
LVHW091638121024
793139LV00006B/84/J